CW00506449

Under the Moss

Steven Mitchell

SRL Publishing Ltd

SRL Publishing Ltd
London
www.srlpublishing.co.uk

First published worldwide by SRL Publishing in 2022

ISBN: 9781915073037

1 3 5 7 9 10 8 6 4 2

A CIP catalogue record for this book is available from the
British Library

SRL Publishing is a Climate Positive publisher, removing more
carbon emissions than it emits.

For Laura, Peter, and Lola.

1

I knew I'd lost my girlfriend to moss the night she secretly crept round our moonlit garden.

Waking to footsteps crossing the kitchen and the creak of the back door, I noticed Sophie wasn't lying beside me, and rubbing my tired eyes, I rose from bed.

Through a narrow gap between our bedroom curtains, I watched Sophie take a rusted spade from the shed and stab it into the lush carpet of moss growing beneath the oak tree. She drove the spade in hard with her foot, rocked it back & forth, and pulled it out. Side-stepping to the right, she stabbed again, repeating the action until, after perhaps five minutes, she'd marked a large rectangle in the moss. With the back of her hand, Sophie wiped sweat from her brow, then slid the spade beneath the moss rectangle, jerking it up and down, loosening the moss from its fragile hold on the soil. When finished, she dropped the spade, and hands on hips, surveyed her work.

Sophie shook off her trainers, hoisted her t-shirt over her head, and peeled off her jeans, heaping them in a pile behind her. Then, wearing just her bra and knickers, her eyes darted towards the house, and I jumped back from the window.

After a moment, convinced I was hidden by the curtains, I dared to look again.

Sophie unhooked her bra and threw it on top of her

jeans and t-shirt. Then pulled down her knickers and stepped out of them, leaving them where they lay. Her naked skin shone luminous, like marble.

Kneeling down, she lifted a corner of the moss and slipped beneath it as if it were a blanket. Turning flat on her back, head poking out at the far end, she gathered the moss blanket close to her body and caressed the moss lying on her breasts, her stomach, her thighs, as she pulsed with delight beneath.

I watched, mesmerised for an hour, until an orange glow rose with the sun, and she slipped back out, gathering her clothes, and returning to the house.

As Sophie crept back to bed smelling of musty earth, I stayed still and silent. She snuggled inside the duvet, and I listened as her breathing became the steady rhythm of sleep.

When I woke in full daylight, Sophie was already out of bed, her space on the sheets smeared with mud, and dusted with fine crumbs of soil. I went to shower, and when I returned, she'd stripped the bedcovers to wash them.

Sophie launched herself into my life six months ago on a bright Saturday afternoon in May.

Returning home from the library through the park, a book tucked beneath my arm, and sunshine bathing my face, Sophie skipped towards me like a little girl. She was smiley, tanned and glowing, wearing a short summer dress revealing slim legs. Blocking my path, she grabbed my arms, pinning them firmly to my side. Alarmed, I dropped my book and shook her loose.

'I just need to check my make-up,' she pleaded with doe-eyes, pointing to the sunglasses I wore. 'Please?' Her voice was as soft and sweet as candyfloss. She smiled innocently, and I relaxed.

Again, she held my arms, gently this time, and standing on tiptoes, moved close, so her breasts pressed warmly against my chest. She smelt of sun-cream and perfume.

As she inspected her reflection in my sunglasses, I stared into her wide eyes, lost in her iris's whirls of brown—dark through to cream, like milk diffusing through coffee.

'You make a good mirror,' she said.

Sophie tilted and turned her head, examining each possible viewpoint of her face, before releasing one of my arms to smooth away a strand of chestnut hair from her forehead. My arm hung loose, heavy and awkward by my side.

'I'm looking good,' she said. 'Thank you.' She let go of my other arm, bent down to pick up my book and handed it to me.

'Is it good?' she asked, studying the cover.

My mouth dried up. So many possibilities flitted through my brain, I couldn't choose what to say.

Sophie leaned forward and kissed my cheek—my mouth falling open in shock. Stepping back, she looked as surprised as me. Then, as quickly as she'd appeared, she dashed away without a word.

I stood stunned, stroking my cheek where her lips had touched, marvelling at the electric feel of the kiss. A tingle ran through my limbs, making me warm and light and powerful, able to hover and turn somersaults. Pretty strangers had never suddenly kissed me. But had I been the victim of some cruel joke or a bet? Was she was returning to a friend, hidden in the bushes, to giggle at her antics?

'Hey,' she shouted behind me.

I turned, and she sauntered back towards me, hips swaying, eyes down, coy.

'You're a good-looking boy. Would you like to meet tomorrow? Coffee?'

My smile was so wide, I thought my face would split. A few slurred and jumbled words spilled from my mouth, and Sophie nodded and smiled until I'd suggested we meet at the park café nearby at 10am. She agreed.

We parted in opposite directions, looking back over our shoulders until out of view, and I went home, smitten. I hadn't even asked her name.

Every minute of the evening became an infinite strand of spaghetti, every hour an ever-inflating balloon. It was disorientating, nauseating. Was this stomach-churning joy love at first sight?

I was so excited, I couldn't eat. Ignoring my grumbling stomach, I emptied my wardrobe and drawers on to my bed—throwing clothes to the floor as too scruffy, too smart, too faded, too bright, too baggy, too tight. I viewed every option in the mirror, never more conscious of my looks: the length of my arms, the girth of my neck, the width of my shoulders, and the sheen on my forehead, the gape of my nostrils, the dryness of my hair.

I ironed a shirt and wiped my trainers with a damp cloth, before trimming my eyebrows, and cutting my chipped and bitten nails so close to the skin my fingertips were sore. My hair, in need of a trim, stuck out at funny angles behind my ears, but it was too late for a haircut now.

In bed, wide awake and trembling with excitement, I rehearsed how I'd greet her, what I'd tell her about myself, what questions I'd ask, how I'd smile and laugh.

As soon as my eyes opened that morning, excitement turned to fear. My hands fumbled with my shirt buttons, and foamy toothpaste dribbled down my front as I brushed my teeth. Hurriedly, I chose another shirt and burned my hand as I ironed it, spending ten minutes running my scolded fingers beneath the cold tap. Cornflakes dropped from my spoon to the floor as I tried to eat, and my sore and shaking hands struggled to lock the door as I left the house.

I'd never had a first date, not a proper one. There'd been a girl once, almost ten years ago at University, but it was a strange relationship and didn't last. I'd not had any luck since. Not that I'd tried. So, when Sophie entered the café, unmistakable even beneath the wide straw hat hiding much of her face, my already nervous body leapt in temperature, cheeks flushing, the back of my neck prickling with perspiration.

I raised my hand and waved. But when she spotted me, she looked at me oddly as you would a stranger, turning her eyes away. Was she changing her mind? Would she bolt for the door?

'Sorry,' she said, eventually coming over, screeching a chair back on the wooden floor and sitting opposite. 'I didn't recognise you without your big sunglasses.'

In relief, I laughed so loudly Sophie jumped.

I apologised, and she reached across to rest her hand on mine.

'I'm nervous too,' she said.

I stared at our hands. It'd been so long since someone touched me, my heart slowed and my breathing stopped, the bustle of the café disappearing, until someone knocked my elbow as they headed to another table and I snapped out of my trance.

Beneath her hat, Sophie looked more beautiful than I'd remembered from the day before. Her nose was a little red where she'd caught the sun, and her straight, ivory teeth gleamed between moist lips.

Suddenly, I jerked my hand from under Sophie's—
I'd forgotten to offer her a drink.

'Coffee?' I asked.

Startled at my abruptness, she didn't reply, and
instead looked at her limp and lonely hand on the table.

'Would you like a drink?' I tried again awkwardly,
sorry I'd ruined the moment.

'A latté,' she said, and I went to order at the counter.

As I queued, she looked at me from beneath her hat
with the same odd expression, seeming to question if it
was really me she'd agreed to meet—like she'd expected
me to look different. I smiled back at her. Other than an
absence of sunglasses, my appearance was much the
same as the day before. Perhaps in a different light, she'd
realised how ordinary I looked? Not the tall, broad
shouldered, and square-jawed man attractive women like
Sophie usually dated.

When I returned with her coffee, milky foam running
down the side of the cup, she said, 'You look so different
without the glasses. Your eyes aren't how I imagined
them.'

Once I'd sat down, she stared into my eyes as if
looking for something down a deep well. I tried to hold
her gaze but blinked uncomfortably.

'They're so big and blue,' she said, breaking her stare.
'Like, enormous.'

'Thanks,' I said, unsure whether enormous eyes were
considered good. No one had commented on my eyes
before.

Sophie reached across the table, and I didn't resist as
her slim fingers slipped into my hair and ruffled it, each
follicle excited by her touch.

'Sorry,' she said, sitting back, sipping her coffee, and
admiring her styling. 'You remind me of someone. But he
had messier hair.'

'Who was he?' I asked, running my palm across my hair, flattening it down slightly.

Sophie looked out the window.

'Just someone I used to know.' There was a wistfulness in her voice. 'So, tell me about yourself,' she said, turning back to me. 'I don't even know your name.'

Sophie's pink tongue appeared and slowly licked milk from her top lip. It was so sensual and erotic, a tiny thread of saliva dropped from my mouth.

'I'm B, B—,' I stuttered, flushed with embarrassment. 'I'm Ben Hayward.'

'Hi Ben,' she giggled, tucking some loose hair under her hat. 'I'm Sophie Marshall.'

By the time we'd finished our coffees, I'd relaxed a little. Sophie laughed at my jokes, and I lost my stutter. And with the sun shining through gaps in the heavy clouds, we left the café to walk around the park. We linked arms and Sophie nestled tightly against my side, as if she didn't want to lose me to the wind.

As we chatted, we discovered we shared the same taste in music, the same books. We loved visiting the zoo. Our favourite animals were bears—cute and scary at the same time. Eighties' films were the best. We refused to swim in the sea because we'd seen Jaws too young and too many times. We loved drinking tea, but ordered coffee in cafés, because £2.50 for a tea bag, hot water, and a splash of milk was a sign of everything wrong in the world. We hated pickles, and marmalade, and the jelly in pork pies. We liked people-watching on weekends, and lingering outside laundrettes, breathing in the fragrant scent of clean washing. We didn't like board games.

I hadn't realised someone so beautiful could be so normal.

I was thirty, Sophie was twenty-eight. We didn't have brothers or sisters. I was an accountant for a construction firm, and Sophie worked in a stationery shop in town. Sophie was from Plymouth, and I was from Cambridge.

'What's Plymouth like?' I asked.

She paused, then shrugged. 'Boring,' she said.

We'd both moved away from friends and family. I'd moved here for work, and Sophie once knew a friend here and liked it so much she stayed. It was a beautiful little market town, not too far from London, and Sophie loved the feel of it—the uneven cobbled roads, crooked buildings topped with ornate chimneys and rusting weathervanes, mature trees lining broad avenues.

'But it's hard to find friends in a new place, isn't it?' she said. 'I don't really know anyone here anymore. Just people at the shop.'

I'd also found it hard to meet friends. This conversation was the longest I'd experienced with someone not related to me since moving here.

We walked laps of the park. In silent moments, Sophie looked up at me, eyes sparkling, and I wanted to kiss her, to hold her and tell her how amazing she was. I didn't want the date to end, but unlike the beautiful day before, the wind billowed in our coats, threatening to steal Sophie's hat, and her tightening grip on me told me she was cold.

'Do you want another coffee?' I asked.

'Are you inviting me back to your place?'

'No,' I said, surprised she thought me so forward. 'I meant we could go back to the café.'

'That's a shame,' she said. 'Because if you invited me back to your place, I'd say yes.'

While I grew nervous on the way home, Sophie almost danced, pulling me along as if she knew the way. It was hard to read the signals—did she expect sex? It'd been so long—I'd only disappoint.

I lived alone in a Victorian terraced house on a quiet, leafy street. After renting a spare room for years from a man who played computer games non-stop in his living room, only moving to collect takeaway deliveries from the front door, my parents helped me to buy this house. It had small rooms with high ceilings and a garden enclosed by tall, ivy-smothered walls.

When I'd moved in a year ago, I cleansed the house: vacuuming, washing, scrubbing, brushing, and giving the ceilings and walls a coat of bright, white paint. But I couldn't afford to replace the orange kitchen and avocado bathroom suite, or the beige threadbare carpets, and ugly textured wallpaper. They remained as haunting traces of the previous occupants, an elderly couple who'd not decorated, or maybe even cleaned, since the 1970s.

'You'll only read about it in the papers,' said the estate agent, as I'd looked round for the first time. 'So, I might as well tell you. They both had cancer and euthanised one another. It's sweet, really.' He didn't know what room they'd died in.

Dust hung thick in the air, lit by sunbeams through large windows, and a musty aroma, like something dead and desiccating inside the walls, permeated the house, no matter how long I kept a draft blowing through the rooms.

Before we entered through the front door, I asked Sophie to excuse the look of the house—it was a work in progress.

'I don't care,' she said. 'You should see my place.'

As I closed the front door behind us, Sophie threw her hat to the floor, pulled my face down to hers, and we kissed. Her lips were full and warm and soft. She tasted like cherry lip-salve. My lips were dry, my post-coffee breath strong and sour. I'd not kissed anyone for years, and this moist, soft, delicate kiss was the best I'd experienced.

Suddenly, she stopped kissing.

'Give me the tour of the house,' she said. 'Starting upstairs.'

I led her up by her hand.

'This is my bedroom,' I said, opening the door to my unmade bed covered in clothes, a toothpaste splattered shirt on the floor, a half-drunk mug of tea on my bedside table.

Ignoring the mess, Sophie pulled me to the bed and sat me down. Straddling my lap, she kissed me fiercely, and pushed my chest, so I fell backwards to the springy mattress. She wiggled where she could feel my erection.

'Have you got condoms?' she whispered.

After we'd dated for a month, Sophie announced she was moving in with me.

'That's okay, isn't it?' she asked.

It was okay. It was fast, but I had no doubts. Sophie was the greatest thing that had happened to me. We'd seen each other every day, and Sophie stayed over most nights—it made sense she moved in. My happiness was warm and exhilarating—almost a dream, but with heightened senses. Everything looked, sounded, tasted, smelt, and felt better with her around, and it was as if I'd known her forever. I wanted to spend every possible moment together, totally in love. And I was pretty sure she loved me. Who'd be first to say, 'I love you'?

We emptied her studio flat—a dingy room above a hairdresser's she'd been too ashamed to let me see until leaving it. Sophie had already placed her few belongings into three heavy cardboard boxes and a single suitcase that, with some shoving and swearing, all fitted into the back of my small car. Sophie handed her keys back to her long-faced, unshaven landlord who'd come to inspect the place. He eyed me suspiciously as he checked for damages, opening cupboard doors, drawers, and the fridge. Sophie had told me he'd once caught her in just her knickers, having walked into the flat on the premise of reading the electricity meter. He winked at Sophie as we left.

By the end of the day, we'd unpacked her things— her books on *our* bookshelf, her clothes in *our* wardrobe, her toothbrush alongside mine in *our* bathroom. And just when I thought we'd finished, I noticed a box unopened on the floor.

'What's in here?' I asked, lifting the lid. Inside, my face greeted me from a large, glossy photograph.

'Don't look in there!' Sophie cried.

She rushed over and slammed the lid shut, almost crushing my hand.

Surprised, I backed away.

'It's only a photo of me,' I said. 'When did you take it?'

'That time in the park.' She sounded unsure—it was almost a question.

'I don't remember you taking it. Let me see.' I reached for the box.

'No!' She slapped my hand away and pushed the box under her side of the bed with her foot. 'The box is private. I trust you not to look. Okay?'

I nodded in shock. I'd not seen her react like that before.

Sophie stared at me seriously, letting her words sink in, before smiling, taking my limp hand, red where she'd slapped it, and gave it a gentle kiss.

I wouldn't look in the box. But what was so secret?

Towards the end of the week, it felt like we'd lived together for ages. It was natural, comfortable, right. The dust and mustiness which had permeated the house vanished, as if Sophie's arrival had conjured an incredible freshness from somewhere. I forgave her the discarded plates around the house, the piles of dishes by the sink she left me to wash up, the dirty clothes on the bedroom floor which, at weekends, I'd scoop up, put in the washing machine, hang them on the line to dry, and offer to iron and fold them. After having lived alone for a while, I enjoyed having someone else to tidy up after.

Sophie and I spent a lot of time in bed, exploring each other's bodies with our fingers and tongues, tasting the saltiness of our skin, the sweetness of our saliva, stroking the soft down on our cheeks, and running our hands through the fine strands of each other's hair. My fingers traced the outline of a tattoo that ran down the top of her right arm. The colours, probably once bright, had faded to dull green, orange, and blue.

'Why a fish?' I asked.

'It's a reminder,' she said.

'Of what?'

'I'll tell you one day. But only if you're good.'

We had sex in every room of the house, receiving burns on our knees and elbows from the living room carpet, bruises from the sharp corners of the kitchen cupboards. We tried every sexual position we could think of, as flexible as snakes, and looked for more on the Internet. Our bodies fitted together perfectly, like two halves now whole—everything we tried brought sexual ecstasy. The smell of sweat and sex perfumed the house.

After sex, lying next to each other, panting, our sweaty bodies sticking to each other, I'd tell Sophie all the things I liked about her body: her small, neat nose, the curve of her hips, the tiny lump in her collarbone from when she'd broken it falling out of bed as a toddler. And I'd ask her what she liked about mine.

'I like all of you,' she said. 'Every single piece.'

And when not having sex, we'd curl up quietly together on the sofa, like sleepy kittens, to watch television.

It was a brilliant time. I'd rush home from the office each evening, having spent the entire day thinking about Sophie. I'd daydream of her in meetings, or suddenly become aroused while staring at spreadsheets, memories of the previous evening's sex replaying in my thoughts— my penis pushing painfully against my trousers, forcing me to stay covered by my desk until it softened.

We spent all our free time together, just Ben and Sophie, building our own perfect little world with everyone else shut out—entirely self-sufficient. We never went on dates anywhere, not to the cinema, out to dinner or on walks—we didn't need to, happily cocooned in the cosiness of our house—but at some point, we had to let the world in.

'It's probably time we met each other's parents,' I said one night as we lay on the sofa together.

'Why?' asked Sophie, startled eyes turning to face me.

'We've been living together for two months. It's weird you haven't met my parents.'

'No, thank you.' She looked away and stretched to pick up a glossy magazine from the floor and started leafing through it. 'I don't think they'd like me.'

'Of course they'd like you. Why do you think that?'

'Just from what you've told me about them.'

'They'll love you. They really want to meet you. Every time I talk to them, they ask me about you.'

'And what have you told them about me?' she asked with suspicion.

'Not much,' I said. 'Just that you're great.'

'Yes, I am,' she said, leaning over to kiss me on the forehead before returning to her magazine.

I was silent for a moment.

'How about we visit your parents?' I really wanted to meet her parents, to know the people who'd created my wonderful girlfriend, and learn about the upbringing she kept so quiet about. I imagined them telling me funny stories about her as a little girl and digging out cringy photographs—bad haircuts and frilly, pink dresses.

She pretended not to hear me, flicking to another page of her magazine.

Maybe she hadn't even told her parents about us. Perhaps she was embarrassed by me?

'Please? It's normal to meet each other's parents,' I said.

She closed her magazine and put it down. 'It might be normal, but I like it being just you and me. We'll meet them one day, okay? Just not now. I want to enjoy *us* for a bit longer.'

Driving home from work a few evenings later, squeaky windscreen wipers clearing rain as eagerly as I planned to greet Sophie after what had been a trying day, I passed the local cemetery and spotted Sophie through the railings. Intrigued, I parked round the corner and walked back beneath my umbrella to see if it was definitely her. Sure enough, there she was, sitting cross-legged before a gravestone, a bouquet of yellow flowers gripped in her hands, and her wet hair draped, limp and slick, over her face.

I fought the urge to shout and offer her a lift home, and instead watched discretely through the railings, using the umbrella as cover. What was she doing here? Whose gravestone was it?

Sophie propped the flowers against the gravestone and busily picked up fallen leaves, creating a pile to the side. She tugged at something attached to the gravestone and paused a moment, seeming to shiver. She placed something on her palm and held it close to her eye before sniffing it and placing it carefully in her coat pocket.

Sophie looked up at the sky—the raindrops were swelling. And as she stood and waved goodbye to the gravestone, I ran back to my car, splashing through deep puddles, soaking the bottom of my trousers, and drove home with wet feet.

Sophie returned to the house shortly after, pale, shivering, rain dripping from the end of her nose.

'I'm going to run a warm bath,' she said, socks squelching up the stairs. 'Will you bring me a cup of tea?'

'You should have called me for a lift.'

'I had something to do on the way.'

'What?'

'Nothing much.'

I didn't want it to seem like I'd been spying, so I didn't question further.

She had her bath, and I changed out of my wet clothes.

When Sophie came downstairs later, body wrapped in a towel and hair slicked back smelling of coconut shampoo, she took a seat at the kitchen table and watched me prepare dinner. I chopped onions as I told her about my morning. Then peeled potatoes as I described my long afternoon of Finance team meetings. I put a pan of water on to boil and heated oil in a frying pan while telling her of my boss's idiot comments about our Year-End figures, and as I fried onions and six meaty sausages, I laughed about a colleague spilling her coffee over a director—how his face turned fire-engine red, and I thought she'd be fired on the spot. Sophie listened quietly, nodding occasionally, without asking questions.

'So, how was your day?' I asked, placing a plate of bangers and mash in front of her, hoping she'd tell me about the cemetery.

'It was all right.'

'Just all right?'

'Yeah, nothing special.'

I desperately wanted to know whose grave it was but couldn't bring myself to ask her—she'd mention it at some point.

We ate dinner quietly, with Sophie gazing at me.

I looked down at my plate, uncomfortable with the intensity with which she was looking at me, like she was about to toss her food aside and devour me instead.

'Lift your face,' she said. 'I want to see you properly.'

'Why?'

'Because you're nice to look at.'

I laughed, and she reached out to stroke the back of my hand.

'It's comforting to look at you,' she said.

'Why do you need comforting?'

She looked away at the floor.

'No reason,' she said. 'I'm just in one of those moods.'

After dinner, we watched TV. Sophie seemed distracted, eyes only half on the screen as she picked dirt from beneath her fingernails.

Later, in bed, curiosity about Sophie's cemetery visit made me restless. I flipped from lying on my front to my back like a flailing fish, catching glimpses of the time in the illuminated bedside clock: 1.03am, 2.15am, 2.39am, 3.09am. I'd normally read to drop off to sleep, but I'd wake Sophie by turning on a light. I stared at Sophie's sleeping silhouette, watching her chest rise and fall with her steady breath, wondering why she was secretly visiting a dead person. Was it a family member? Friend? Boyfriend? Why was I so bothered by not knowing?

When it became light, I dressed quietly, and as Sophie slept, I sneaked out of the house and drove to the cemetery.

A low mist blanketed the ground as I hurried through the graves, dew on the mown grass wetting my still soggy shoes. The silence was eerie—no dawn chorus of birds, no rustling of leaves in the wind—just the sound of my feet on the ground. Wary I may have woken Sophie on departing, I had to be quick.

By looking at the railings bordering the cemetery, I pinpointed where I'd watched Sophie, and soon found the grave I was looking for.

A bunch of wilting daffodils, petals browning at the edges, stood against the polished granite gravestone. Tufts of long grass grew up round the base and moss crept up the sides. The epitaph, engraved and gilded gold, told me this was the resting place of Eugene Gray. He'd died just nine months ago, aged twenty-seven. *Beloved son and brother. Rest in peace.*

I rested my hand on top of the cold gravestone.

'Who are you?' I asked. 'Who are you to Sophie?'

I stood there, considering the possibilities: friend, boyfriend, husband, brother, stepbrother, half-brother, cousin, uncle, colleague? I'd hoped the gravestone would give me more clues.

The grating caw of a crow in a nearby tree startled me out of my thoughts, and I headed back to the car.

On the way home, I stopped at a corner shop to buy milk. And on my return, I held it up for Sophie to see, my excuse for having left the house, before putting it in the fridge next to an almost full bottle of milk already there. She was sitting at the kitchen table, studying something in her hands, turning it over and around, inspecting it from every angle.

'What have you got there?' I asked.

'A bit of moss.' She held it up for me to see.

One side was a lush, dark green, the other pale,

almost yellow.

'Where's it from?'

'Off someone's grave.'

So that's what she'd pocketed yesterday.

'In the cemetery?'

'Where else?'

'Why were you in the cemetery?' I asked, voice full of expectation she'd now tell me about the grave.

'I was looking for moss,' she said defensively. 'Why else would I be there?' Sophie placed the moss on the table in front of her and stroked it like a miniature pet. 'I love how soft it is.' She picked it up, rubbed it across her cheek, and shivered like she had in the graveyard, giggling with pleasure.

'Are you okay?' I said.

'It tickles.'

I raised my eyebrows.

'So, why the sudden fascination with moss?' I asked, willing her to tell me about Eugene.

'There's just something about it—something pure and alive. And moss is such a nice word, don't you think?'

'I guess so.'

'Moss. Moss. Moss. Moss. Moss,' she repeated. 'Moss.'

2

I woke with a jolt. After a moment, I turned my head on the pillow to see if I'd woken Sophie, but she slept peacefully beside me, curled on her side, hair covering her face. My pillow was damp beneath my cheek, my hair soaked with sweat. I'd been dreaming.

In the dream, Sophie, dressed in a white gown, sat across my waist, pinning me to the living room carpet, piling cushions upon me—countless soft, heavy, velvet cushions of green and brown that magically continued to appear in her hands. Surrounded by a shimmering golden mist, Sophie laughed soundlessly, smiling like a wide-mouthed clown. I screamed a silent scream, and my flailing hands passed through her as if she were a ghost. Sophie placed a final cushion over my eyes, my dream turned black, and I woke.

I took deep breaths of stale bedroom air until calm, then rose slowly, the bedframe groaning as I swung my legs from the bed and stood on shaky legs. My bedside clock read 3.30am. I paused for my wobbling knees to still, then in the dark, careful not to trip on piles of Sophie's discarded clothes, felt my way downstairs.

Soft moonlight lit the kitchen. I filled a glass of water and drank it down, gasping with the coldness of it. I took a seat at the kitchen table and slid my laptop towards me. Turning it on, the screen's harsh light stung my eyes, and I shielded them until they'd adjusted. Then, fingers paused over the keyboard, I considered what I was about to do—the guilt of sneaking around sat unpleasantly in my stomach—I shouldn't have to do this.

I'd slept fitfully since seeing Sophie in the cemetery a few days before, troubled by images of her shivering and lonely at Eugene's grave. Why hadn't she told me why she was there? Twice, I'd opened my mouth to say I'd seen her, and each time I faltered and said something else. Maybe she'd tell me about Eugene at some point— we'd not known each other long—there were things I hadn't told her about myself yet. But I typed **Eugene Gray death** into an Internet search engine and watched the results appear.

I scanned through dozens of obituaries from across the world: Ottawa, Melbourne, Leeds, Atlanta, Swansea, Alicante, among others; victims of cancer, heart attacks, accidents, and old age.

I read eulogies written by friends and family. The dead Eugene Gray's were generous, loving and loved. It made me wonder what they would write about me. Suffocated by cushions, taken too soon?

None of the dead Eugene Gray's died in the year etched on the gravestone. None died in this town. There were no obvious connections to Sophie.

I rubbed my sore eyes and suppressed a deep yawn. Frustrated by my unsuccessful search, I closed the laptop and crept back to bed.

Sophie had spread across my side of the mattress, and I rolled her gently to slide myself under the duvet. She stirred.

'Where have you been?' she asked sleepily.

'I just needed some water.'

'Okay, sweet dreams,' she said.

When I went down for breakfast, Sophie was crying at

the kitchen table in her dressing gown. She dabbed her eyes with a sodden tissue, then used it to blow her nose loudly, like the call of some wild animal. I glanced at my laptop lying open in front of her. Had I left the webpage open I'd been looking at? Had she seen Eugene Gray, New York, jazz drummer? Or was it Eugene Gray, a solicitor from Leicester? Guilt seized me, and I braced for confrontation. But instead, she held up a small plastic bag for me to see. Inside was the piece of moss from Eugene's grave she'd shown me the previous evening. It had turned brown.

'Look,' she said. 'I've killed it.' She sniffed and blew her nose again. I winced at the noise. 'The moss was alive in there, breathing, and I've suffocated it.'

'It's only a bit of moss,' I said, relieved, and trying to calm her. 'It's just a plant.' I put my hand on her shoulder.

'It's not just a fucking plant,' she screamed, throwing my hand off and thundering upstairs to the bathroom, slamming the door.

Surprised at her reaction, I left her for a few minutes before asking if she was okay. Her muffled sobbing carried through the door.

'Just leave me a minute,' she said.

An hour later, Sophie found me stretched out on the sofa, the radio playing piano music on low volume. I'd been worrying about her, waiting for her to calm down. Her reaction had been wild, but I think I understood why she was upset. When Grandma died, Mum kept just one thing of hers: a silver owl broach. With finely engraved feathers and heart-shaped face, it lay in a drawer, gleaming within a velvet-lined, tortoiseshell trinket box, except when Mum brought it out each year for Grandma's birthday, when she polished it, pinned it to her top, and stared down at it throughout the day as it conjured happy memories. The moss could be Sophie's owl—a connection to Eugene Gray. A weak connection—only a wild plant found on his gravestone—but maybe she had nothing else?

'I'm sorry for earlier,' said Sophie. 'I was being silly. I shouldn't have shouted at you.'

Hair was plastered to her tear-damp cheek, and her bloodshot eyes sank into puffy skin. She smiled sadly, and I sat up to kiss her on the forehead.

'That's okay,' I said. 'No harm done.'

I'd been wondering whether I should tell her about what I'd learnt from Ava.

Until I met Ava, I used to get upset a lot, and she really helped.

I was introduced to her in my last year of university. Ava was a frizzy-haired, middle-aged lady fond of floral leggings and tie-dyed headbands who spoke in slow, hushed tones that often grated while trying to soothe. Her living room was a confusion of salt lamps and crystals hidden among a jungle of verdant pot plants. I'd never been able to talk to anyone as easily as I could talk to Ava.

She introduced me to her 'positivity pockets'—a way to cope when I became stressed. I laughed when she first mentioned them. But after initial reservations, the positivity pockets seemed to work. When someone pushed past me on to the bus home from Ava's, rather than seething at the unfairness, I placed the anger in a mental pocket. When I received a poor grade on some coursework, rather than beat myself up, I pocketed the disappointment, leaving only the knowledge of how to do better next time.

I wasn't good at pocketing at first—it took practice. But soon I'd do it with little thought. If I got upset or annoyed, it would be for a moment. My pulse would quicken, my muscles would tense, and I'd breathe deeply, and pocket the feelings until my calmer self could deal with them. I no longer stewed on negative thoughts. Instead, they sat inert in my positivity pockets until they'd lost their potency, and I could safely retrieve and dispose of them. My pockets were relatively empty at the moment—Sophie's secrecy about Eugene took up a little space, but her screaming over a dead piece of moss was a bit of fluff.

'But don't keep too much in your pockets,' Ava warned, 'or your trousers will split.' She laughed, slapping her knee three times before becoming serious. 'If they get too full, tell someone, okay?'

Before I'd met Ava, everything had become too much. I'd been unwell—seriously ill. And at some point, I'd tell Sophie about it. But as she'd cried in the bathroom and I'd listened to music, I realised we both had secrets we didn't want to share yet.

I moved my feet as Sophie sat down on the end of the sofa.

'I've done some research,' she said. 'Moss can stay dry for decades and survive. I revived it with some water. Now it looks fine, see?'

There were beads of water in the plastic bag, the moss looking soggy at the bottom.

'That's great,' I said.

'Anyway, I'm feeling better now.' She squeezed herself in so she lay behind me and gave me a hug. 'Do you want to come to the shop? I need to go to work to buy something. You could meet my friend. Not a friend, really—a colleague. You want to meet people I know— now's your chance.'

Sophie and I walked hand-in-hand to the stationery shop where she worked. She was cheerful, and we swung our arms playfully and bounced hips together. Every couple of minutes she smiled up at me from beneath her big straw hat and I smiled down at her, and we kissed without missing a step.

Since we'd started going out, Sophie had warned me off visiting her at work.

'Please don't come,' she'd said. 'It'll be weird.'

I understood. Taking Sophie to my office would have been equally strange. But I was pleased she was taking me now. I was excited to see the place.

As we passed the cemetery, Sophie's arms stopped swinging as she peered briefly through the railings, before gripping my hand tighter and quickening her pace.

To distract from the awkwardness, I told her about my cushion dream.

'What do you think it means?' I asked.

'It means you're scared of cushions,' she laughed, as a high-pitched bell rang on entering Sophie's shop. 'Dreams don't mean anything.'

Tall shelving loomed over narrow aisles of worn grey carpet and hazy sunlight illuminated slowly drifting dust. The shop's aroma was sweet, musty, and chemical, and the noise from the busy road outside was muffled, bringing a sense of tranquillity.

'Don't you love the smell of new paper?' asked Sophie as she led me down one of the aisles.

'Look, you can try out all the different pens,' she said, uncapping and handing me a chunky felt-tip marker with a wide, flat nib from a display of tester pens. I wrote *I love Sophie* in large red letters on a pad of paper scrawled with the jumble of multi-coloured lines, spirals and waves of previous pen-testers.

'You're such an idiot,' she laughed, slapping me on the back.

It was the first time I'd told her I loved her.

Sophie tore off the sheet of paper, scrunched it into a tight ball, and walked breezily to the front of the shop. I stood there, stunned. Why didn't she say it back?

I followed her towards a lady stood behind the counter.

'This is my colleague, Emily,' said Sophie, taking off her hat and laying it on the counter.

Emily was a freckled, red-cheeked young woman with a bird's nest of blonde hair and feathery eyebrows. Large earrings shaped like daisies hung from her small ears, and she wore a pale-yellow jumper that looked home knitted.

'Pleased to meet you, Ben,' said Emily loudly, almost shouting, and shook my hand. She had a warm, firm grip which scrunched my fingers together and lingered longer than necessary. 'I was wondering what kind of person would take on our Sophie.' To Sophie she winked and said, 'He seems a good'un.'

'He'll do,' said Sophie, nudging me in the side with her elbow.

Sophie returned my frown with a wide smile.

'I've come to show Ben around,' she said, handing Emily the scrunched-up paper, which she dropped into something by her feet.

'It's a lovely shop,' I said.

Sophie nodded. 'We like it, don't we, Emily?'

'I wouldn't work anywhere else.'

Just then, the shop bell rang, and a young man stumbled into the shop with who I assumed to be his mother close behind.

'Hi Alan,' said Sophie.

He lowered his head of floppy hair and scratched at the back of his neck.

'Say hello, Alan,' said his mother.

'Hi, So- So- Sophie,' he stuttered.

Violent acne covered his chin, and a greasy whisper of a moustache lay on his top lip. He wore a bright red waterproof jacket and walking boots, both covered in mud.

'Have you come in for your order?' asked Sophie.

His fringe shook as he nodded.

'Wait there and I'll get it for you.'

'No, I'll get it,' said Emily. 'You're not working today.'

'It's no bother for my favourite customer.' Sophie winked at Alan, who turned his head, blushing and giggling. His mum smiled. Sophie disappeared through a door to find the order. Alan saw me looking at him, and he pretended to examine a display of calculators.

'I'm going to look around,' I told Emily.

I walked the aisles of silver fountain pens and heavy gauge paper, easels and paintbrushes, crayons and coloured pencils. I ran my fingertips across the coarse grain of a white canvas.

I compared the calmness of the shop with the bleeps, whirrs, and chatter of my busy office; Sophie's relaxed walk to work to my ooze through rush hour traffic to the other side of town; her friend Emily to my colleagues, who, though nice enough, constantly sniped and moaned about our dull jobs and how our idiot boss was an idiot.

As I scanned the rows of oil paints, fascinated by the names of colours: Cobalt Chromite Green, Terre Verte, Windsor Emerald, Emily sidled up to me. She leant in close.

'You need to be good to her,' she whispered. Her warm breath tickled my ear. She smelt of tuna sandwiches. 'That girl's been through a lot. She's fragile.'

I sidestepped to gain a little distance.

'Why?' I said, matching her quietness.

Emily just smiled, like I already knew. Perhaps she

26

knew about Eugene? But before I could ask, Sophie's voice interrupted us from the front of the shop.

'Here's your order, Alan,' she said.

I followed behind Emily as she went back to her position by the till.

'Thank you,' said Alan, brushing his fringe from his eyes and peering into the carrier bag Sophie had given him. His mum handed him her purse, and he took out a crumpled five-pound note.

'Is this the right amount?' he asked, thrusting it towards Sophie.

'That's perfect.' Sophie took the note and handed it to Emily, who straightened out its creases and put it in the till.

'Let's be going,' said Alan's mum.

He glared at her.

'We can't stay here all day,' she said.

'It's always good to see you, Alan,' said Sophie. 'See you soon.'

'Bye, Alan,' said Emily.

'Bye,' he mumbled, glancing at me under his hair before tripping out of the shop with a sharp ring of the bell.

'Who was that?' I asked Sophie.

'Alan? He's just a customer.'

'He fancies you,' I teased.

'He doesn't.'

'It's obvious.'

'Are you jealous?'

'Of him? No.' He was just a silly teenager.

'Why not? What's wrong with him?' Sophie shot me an icy look before picking up a black leather notebook from a shelf behind her. Emily tutted at me. I shouldn't have made fun of Alan.

'I'm going to buy this,' said Sophie. 'Do you want

anything?' Shamefaced, I shook my head.

Emily scanned the barcode of the notebook through the till with a beep.

'Are you going to start writing poems again, Sophie?' asked Emily.

Sophie lowered her head and blushed as Alan had done. 'No, it's just for notes.'

'I didn't know you wrote poetry,' I said.

'She's very good.'

'I don't do it anymore.'

'Well, you should,' said Emily, putting the notebook in a paper bag. 'They were always so beautiful.'

Sophie paid for the notebook and received the change.

'I'll see you on Monday,' said Sophie, grabbing the bag and pulling me out of the shop by my hand.

Outside, and a little way down the street, Sophie said, 'Are you happy now you've met my friend? Does that prove I'm not embarrassed to be seen with you?'

'I never said you were embarrassed of me.'

'That's what you thought.'

I couldn't deny it. There had to be some reason she hadn't wanted to introduce me to anyone.

Sophie halted.

'My hat,' she said, holding her hands to her head, panicking. As I waited, she ran back to the shop and returned wearing it pulled low on her head as always, as if she was trying to hide herself.

'Emily seems nice,' I said, as we walked home.

'Emily's great. She's got a big mouth, though.'

'Because she mentioned the poems?'

'Forget she said anything. They were never any good. They were sentimental nonsense.'

'Can I read some?' I asked.

'I don't like people reading them.'

'Emily's read them.'

'That was before.'

'Before what?'

'Just, before.' Sophie looked at the ground and mumbled. 'I don't show them anymore.'

'Please?' I asked sweetly.

'No.'

Maybe the box she'd hidden under the bed was full of poems? Poems about Eugene? Perhaps she'd write some about me one day.

'So, what's the notebook for?' I asked.

'You'll think it's geeky.'

'I won't.' Someone as cool and beautiful as Sophie could never be geeky. Quirky, maybe.

'It's for making notes when I find new mosses.' She looked at me for a reaction, and I nodded. 'I've been looking around, and moss is everywhere. It's so fascinating how it lives in places nothing else does, isn't it? We destroy the environment, replace plants and trees with concrete, and yet moss doesn't give in—it returns to tell us nature can't be conquered. It gives hope that even in the most cold, barren places life can return.'

On Monday evening, I returned home from work and followed a musty aroma, like damp earth, to the kitchen.

Lying on the table were a dozen pieces of moss ranging in size from a fingernail to a hand's width. They were a mixed pallet of greens: some dark and dull; some bright and bold; textures from dense velvet to fern-like fronds. Moist soil and tiny fragments of stone lay among the moss. Sophie was nowhere to be seen.

I gingerly prodded the pieces of moss, fingertips exploring their texture.

'Do you like my moss?' asked Sophie, appearing behind me, making me jump. She held a chunky Polaroid camera covered in dust.

'What's it doing here?'

'I'm starting a project.' Sophie picked up a lime green moss, brought it to her nose, and inhaled deeply. 'This was by the back fence in the garden. Have you ever noticed it? It was sitting there in the shade.' I'd barely been in the garden since moving in. It had grown wild and weed-choked, the long grass and tangled hedges intimidating by the effort needed to clear them.

Sophie returned the moss to the table.

'Do you like the idea of a moss garden?' she asked.

I remembered a time I waited at the dentist's for a filling, browsing through photographs of Japanese Zen gardens in a magazine, marvelling at the gardens' neat moss and raked gravel, cloud bushes and pagodas—their beauty and tranquillity soothing my fear of the scraping and drilling to come.

'Like a Japanese garden?' I asked.

She nodded.

The garden did need a make-over, but Sophie's moss fascination was escalating quickly—she'd been collecting a few bits of moss, and now she wanted a garden full of it. How had a single piece of moss from a grave sparked so much interest? Could the garden be a shrine to Eugene—a mossy memorial?

'It'd be a lot of work,' I cautioned.

'I know. But I want to do it. It'll keep my mind off things.'

'What things?'

'Just things,' she said, lowering her eyes.

Would she ever talk to me about Eugene?

Sophie waved the Polaroid camera at me. 'Can you believe they still make cartridges for this thing?'

She pointed the camera in my face and clicked the shutter. The camera whirred.

'Hey!' I cried.

'You don't always have to look so grumpy,' she said.

The photograph slid slowly from the camera. She yanked it from the camera's grip and shook it.

'You're not supposed to wave it about,' I said.

'But that's the fun bit. It helps it dry.'

'I'm just telling you what they say you shouldn't do.'

'Don't be so boring all the time.'

She held the photo so I could see it. As it dried, the image of my face formed—grey skin and sagging eyes. It'd been a tiring day at work.

'It's a terrible photo,' I said, reaching to take it from her. She held it away at arm's length.

'That's what you look like.'

'Throw it away.'

Sophie studied it.

'It's a keeper,' she said, pushing it into her jeans' back pocket.

She took a piece of moss, placed it away from the others, bent over it with the camera, and took a photograph. And as the photo slid out of the camera, she positioned another piece of moss.

I went upstairs to get changed out of my work clothes and take a shower.

When I came down, a neat line of photographs had replaced the pieces of moss. The kitchen door to the garden was open, and I could hear Sophie clattering in the shed.

I picked up one of the photographs. The Polaroid camera took a surprisingly good picture, capturing every detail of the moss, all the nuances of colour, shade and texture, like a work of art.

'They're good, aren't they?' said Sophie, appearing at the back door.

I agreed.

31

'I'm going to do a bit of gardening, now,' she said. 'Do you want to make dinner?'

Sophie went back to the garden, and through the window I saw her go inside the shed—a rotten, weather-beaten thing, leaning to the left, with a single cracked window, and a door that had to be yanked open and kicked shut. It was full of rusted tools left by the former occupants and blanketed in spiders' webs. She emerged with some blunt-looking sheers and a spade before carrying them to the far end of the garden.

I still held a photograph in my hand and was about to put it down when I noticed faint impressions of writing through the image. I turned it over. She'd written on the back in pencil:

Windsor Emerald
enjoying ice-cream van chimes
on an Elm, Keele Park.

While preparing dinner, I watched Sophie under the amber evening sun as she hacked at grass and weeds with the sheers until she'd tamed a sizeable patch. With the spade, Sophie then dug out a square of grass from the shady spot beneath the oak tree. She put the turf to one side, then stamped upon the bare earth to flatten it, circling several times until satisfied. Sophie took her pieces of moss from her pocket and placed them together on the ground, rearranging them until it pleased her, then pressed them firmly into the soil. She filled a tarnished metal watering can from the garden tap and used it to shower the moss. Pausing to survey her work, she nodded approval to herself, then put the sheers, spade and watering can back in the shed, and returned to the kitchen.

As the sun disappeared behind the garden fence,

Sophie wrapped her hands round my waist from behind and rested her head on my shoulder.

'You're great,' she said.

'Why?'

'Because you're here.'

Over the next week, I watched as Sophie turned our run-down garden, given to weeds, into a neat Japanese moss garden. She gardened in all weathers—nothing stopping her. I offered help and she refused.

'It's better if I do it alone,' she said. 'It's important I do this myself.'

Using pictures from gardening magazines and the internet for reference, Sophie planted and potted; cut and cleared; heaved and hoed. Weeds, leaves, and branches lay in tangled heaps. She dismantled an old rockery in the garden's corner, overgrown with ivy, constructed from great lumps of limestone and sharp slate slabs, and with a lot of hauling of rocks and shovelling of soil, refashioned it into something resembling a beautiful ancient ruin.

And as I watched her, I continued to worry about her reasons for creating the garden. If grief was something to do with it, then I could see this was making her happy—I should be supportive. But I was jealous—jealous of Eugene Gray stealing attention from me. A jealously I wanted to pocket away until it shrank to nothing—but I struggled to do so.

On Saturday morning, Sophie, with soil-stained clothes and hands, led me to the garden.

'Have you finished?' I asked.

'Let me give you the tour.'

I followed as she pointed out the moss growing upon rocks and logs, in damp hollows and shady crevices, marvelling at her passion, and wondering where all this moss came from.

'So, what do you think?' she said.

I looked around the garden, taking it all in. I was standing in the middle of a neat, lush, tranquil paradise.

'It's beautiful,' I said.

'You really think so?'

'It's amazing.'

Sophie threw her arms around me and held me tight. She was crying.

'Why are you crying?'

'I'm just so pleased with it,' she said. But behind her smile, her eyes, dewy and red, were sad.

3

'We should go for a night out,' I suggested on Saturday morning as Sophie stared into the bedroom mirror, playing with her hair. She piled it on top of her head, then let it fall. 'To celebrate finishing your garden.'

'I don't really fancy it,' she said.

Sophie had spent any spare daylight hours in the garden, honing it to perfection, and when dark, we'd lounged in front of the television, Sophie complaining of exhaustion, her head resting in my lap as she picked earth from beneath her fingernails. We sat like that until we dragged our weary bodies to bed, where Sophie fell asleep immediately, and I read until my eyes grew heavy. We'd not had sex since she'd started the garden. I hadn't complained, but it was less than 3 months since we'd met. My lust was a surging river of energy with nowhere to go, making me twitch and blink. I tried to pocket away the sexual thoughts whirring around my mind, but I couldn't contain them. I was ashamed to have masturbated in a toilet cubicle at work. It was just the one time and the release of tension was such a rush I shook for minutes afterwards.

In our brief time together, we'd never been out for a drink, a meal, to the cinema, or anything like that. We hadn't dated in public since our first date in the coffee shop. At first, it had been because of all the sex, and then it was because Sophie spent so much time in the garden.

If I could get Sophie out of the house, do something different, maybe a romantic meal, anything that wasn't gardening or looking for moss, then maybe we could recapture the passion we had when we first met.

'I might do something with my hair soon,' Sophie said.

'Like what?'

'I don't know. Just something.'

'We could go to a restaurant,' I said, persisting we go out somewhere.

She looked out the window.

'But it's raining. It's not going to stop raining all weekend.'

It was a weak excuse, and her sheepish look told me she knew it.

'Please,' I said with pleading eyes. 'It'll be fun.'

The doorbell rang. Sophie didn't react, continuing to play with her hair.

'I'll go,' I said. 'Just have a think about it.'

I ran down the stairs and opened the door to a postman struggling to hold an enormous cardboard box. He thrust it at me with a sigh of relief. It was so heavy, I almost dropped it, and immediately lowered it to the floor. The box was wrapped in red tape, FRAGILE written all over it, arrows pointing THIS WAY UP, and addressed to Sophie. Recovering from his exertion with laboured breaths, the postman asked me to sign for the box before walking back to his van, cursing.

'It's a parcel for you,' I called to Sophie, closing the door.

She skipped downstairs to the hallway.

'I wasn't expecting it until next week,' she said, clapping excitedly. 'Can you bring it through into the kitchen?'

I dragged the box to the kitchen, and on my second

attempt, managed to lift it onto the kitchen table.

'It weighs a tonne,' I said, wiping my brow with the back of my hand.

With a knife, Sophie sliced open the tape sealing the box, lifted the lid, and dozens of small, white, polystyrene balls protecting the parcel's contents burst over the table and floor. She pushed the balls aside, scattering them to all corners of the kitchen, sank her hands deep into the box, and heaved out a large, heavy object wrapped securely in tape and bubble-wrap. She asked for help and we lifted it out together. It clunked when placed on the table. With the knife, she cut open the tape, pulling away the bubble-wrap to reveal a foot high, grey, and solidly built microscope—like one I'd used in school biology lessons to examine strands of hair plucked painfully from my head, or the plump cells of leaves collected from the playground.

How much had she spent on this?

'I'll be able to see moss in all its beautiful detail,' said Sophie, as she set up the microscope on the kitchen table so it could make use of the natural light from the window.

I couldn't believe how seriously she was getting into moss. This was taking it to yet another level.

After she'd adjusted mirrors and lens, Sophie went to the garden and returned with a tiny piece of moss. She placed it on a glass slide, a pack of which had come in the box, and looked at it under the microscope, turning a wheel to finely focus the lens. She stared at the moss for a long time, frowning with concentration.

'Look at this,' she said, stepping back, allowing me to look into the lens. 'It's amazing.'

In a bright circle were long, irregular rectangular cells so densely packed with little pear-green ovals it looked as if the cell walls would burst.

'It's handsome, isn't it?' she said.

Handsome?

Sophie eased me aside and with a freshly sharpened pencil began sketching what she saw under the lens into her notebook. I watched, mesmerised as her hand moved across the page, capturing the shapes in fine detail.

After a couple of minutes, she held her notebook up for me to see. She seemed delighted with what she'd done.

'You're good at that,' I said.

'You really think so?'

'I couldn't do it. It's very accurate.'

'It's amazing how detailed life can be, isn't it? We don't normally see any of this stuff. You always see moss around, it's everywhere, but once you stop and look at it you realise how incredible it is.'

Throughout the day, Sophie fetched other samples of moss, viewing each under the microscope and sketching them, as I busied myself with housework. Since Sophie had moved in, it amazed me how quickly the house became a mess with an extra person in it.

In between cleaning tasks, including corralling the polystyrene balls from around the kitchen and mopping away mud trailed in from the garden, I persisted in asking Sophie to come out with me until she relented.

'If it'll shut you up, I'll come,' she said, glancing up from her microscope.

I knew she'd enjoy herself once she was out.

Later, Sophie showed me the eight pictures of moss she'd drawn in her notebook, all strikingly different in appearance, all brilliant. And as I praised them, I noticed a faint red ring around her right eye from looking into the microscope all day.

'The first moss is my favourite,' she said, placing its drawing on the table and stroking her finger across it.

'He's different from the rest.'

Fat rain drops spotted the pavement as Sophie and I walked into town for a drink before dinner. And as the rain grew heavier and threatened a soaking, we hurried into a nearby pub.

The Witch & Hammer was a crooked Tudor building slumping-in on itself, stained with soot, and gutters weeping. Neither of us had been there before.

On entering, we ducked under a low ceiling embedded with thick, dark wooden beams. An open fire spat & crackled, casting an orange glow and flickering light onto brass ornaments nailed around the exposed-brick chimney. The aroma of sour beer spilt over decades, maybe centuries, in the cracks of the pub's floorboards, mixed with the fragrant wood smoke. Grimy windows, set in paint-flaking frames, were steamed up with the warmth.

'Cosy,' said Sophie over her shoulder as we headed to the bar. She'd swept her hair over her face in a style she'd not worn before, completely covering the eye now bruised from looking through the microscope for so long, and she wore heavy make-up—thick mascara, dark eyeshadow, and crimson lipstick. It was a kind of 80s New Romantic look. She wore a black cardigan over a black dress, and cherry Doc Marten boots. She looked incredibly cool, but I may not have recognised her passing her in the street. In contrast, I was underdressed in jeans and a plaid shirt beneath a waterproof jacket.

The pub was quiet for a Saturday evening. Two white-haired men, shrunken with age, sat in a gloomy corner, hunched and silent, their wooden stools creaking as they turned to look at us. A wiry, bald man, densely tattooed up both arms and across his neck, fed coins into a fruit machine lit like a funfair.

A cascade of coins rattled down the machine signalling a win and the tattooed man slapped the side of the machine in triumph. Distracted, I stumbled on a low step and smacked my forehead on a beam. The impact seemed to shake the entire building.

I swore, staggered backwards, and clutched my hand to my head. Pain rolled in a wave from the front of my skull to the rear, then rolled back again. When I removed my hand, my palm was smeared red. With my finger, I traced a warm trickle of blood weeping from a cut within a wrinkle on my forehead. It was sticky.

The old men watched silently, blankly. The tattooed man gathered his winnings into his pocket.

'Watch your head,' said a tired-looking barman with a mullet, Hawaiian shirt, and a gold donut-shaped earring pulling down his earlobe. He was leaning, arms folded, against the bar, like he was ready to lie down his head and sleep.

Sophie asked if I was okay.

'Nothing a drink won't fix,' I said, laughing it off. But my head throbbed with pain and a subtle, shrill ring sounded from deep within my skull.

'Let me see,' said Sophie. She held me by the shoulders, inspected, and stood back with a concerned look. 'How many fingers am I holding up?'

The poor light and the way her fingers blurred made it difficult to count.

'Three?'

'Close,' she said. 'Are you sure you're all right?'

This was our first night out, and a knock on the head wouldn't spoil it.

I said I was fine and rested against the bar, looking at the drinks on offer. Neon paper stars, stuck around the wall, advertised pork scratchings, salted peanuts, and crisps. A poster over the barman's shoulder announced a darts tournament against a rival pub, and a string of red tinsel, a remnant of Christmas past, hung limp above shelves of spirit bottles.

I stared at the bottles, halos of glowing light surrounding each one. The light pulsed, ebbed, and flowed. It was mesmerising, beautiful. Where did the light come from? Within the bottle? They were angels, luminous angels.

'Ben!' Sophie shouted, clapping her hands in front of my face. 'I asked what you wanted to drink.'

I hadn't heard her.

'You totally spaced-out,' said Sophie.

I looked at the spirit bottles again. Their halos had vanished, now notable by their faded labels, dust, and greasy fingerprints.

The barman stared at us, drumming his fingers on the bar.

'Maybe you shouldn't have anything to drink? We should go home,' said Sophie.

'I'll have a lager,' I said.

Best not to mention the angelic bottles. Sophie would only worry.

We took our drinks to a table far from the fruit machine. I walked behind Sophie so she wouldn't see me listing from side to side, as if walking on deck in rough seas, and when we reached the table, I held the back of my chair to steady myself before sitting down.

I wiped the back of my hand across my forehead to check for fresh blood. The cut was healing. But where was the nearest place to buy painkillers?

'So, what should we talk about?' said Sophie, resting her elbows on the table and propping her chin on her hands, looking bored already.

I swigged my drink. It was tasteless, watery.

'I don't know. What do couples normally talk about?'

Were my words slurred?

'They usually talk about other couples and how they're better than other couples,' she said.

'Do you know any couples?'

'No.'

'Neither do I.'

If this was how our conversations would be for the rest of the night, it'd get pretty boring. I realised how little Sophie and I actually talked. We spent loads of time together, but we rarely had long chats about anything.

'Okay, so if you knew an imaginary couple, what would you say about them?' I asked.

She paused in thought.

'I might say that they don't look right together. She's too tall for him. He's too old for her. Something like that.'

'Do you think we look good together?'

'We're a very cute couple, Ben.' She leant over and ruffled my hair.

'You're cuter than me,' I said.

'Obviously,' she laughed.

I jokingly pulled a face to appear wounded. But it was true.

'You're pretty cute yourself,' she said, pinching my cheek.

As I drank, I imagined our future together. We'd get engaged, then married, buy a dog, maybe a cat, maybe both, call them something ridiculous like Mr Fluffy or Hercules, then have a baby or two, and grow old together. We'd have a perfect, little, suburban life.

'Right, drink up,' said Sophie, snapping me out of my daydream. 'Do you want another?'

'Do you have any paracetamol on you?' I asked, but she had already gone.

Soon, Sophie placed two more drinks and a couple of

food menus on the table.

'I think we should eat here,' she said. 'The rain's not stopping.'

'But I've booked a restaurant.'

I'd reserved a table at an Indian place people in the office raved about.

'They won't care.'

'But what if they don't let me book next time?' I didn't want to be on some restaurant blacklist.

'They won't remember you.'

'They might.'

'Use a fake name.'

Sophie started reading her menu as I considered the fake names I could use for future bookings: Toby Smith, John Matthews, David Woods; and stopped when I realised I imagined only boring names for myself. Why wasn't I Johnny Sparks or Kurtis Danger?

I picked up the laminated menu, written in Comic Sans, a list of cheap fried foods, and a black & white illustration of a plump roast chicken.

'Do you think the food here's okay?' I whispered.

'I'm sure it won't kill us,' she replied bluntly.

My cut itched and throbbed as I studied the menu. Nothing tasty was leaping out at me.

'Should I get this sown-up?' I asked.

Sophie put down her menu, lent in for a closer look, and shook her head.

'I think I'll have the burger,' she said decisively. 'A double, with extra bacon. And chips.'

'Wow, you must be hungry.'

'When I eat out, I want to feel stuffed. So stuffed my stomach swells and pushes through my dress. I want to be in actual pain because I've eaten so much and can't fit any more in. What are you having?'

'I'll have the same.'

'You go order then.'

I felt dizzy as I stood and headed to the bar, my legs loose and unpredictable beneath me, like they'd take-off in a direction I didn't want to go.

Interrupting the barman as he read a newspaper, I asked if I could order food.

'Table number?' he asked, staring at my forehead.

'I don't know,' I said. 'That one there.' I pointed to where Sophie sat. Sophie waved at us.

'You need the table number before you can order.'

He said it like I was an idiot. I glared at him. He glared back.

Unsteadily, I walked back to the table to find the number—stick-like numerals deeply scratched into the wood. Sophie smirked.

'Eleven,' I said, returning to the bar, then ordering our food and handing the barman the money.

He repeated my order back to me in a slow monotone before handing me the change.

'Have you got any napkins?' I asked, pointing to my wounded head. I'd use them to clean my cut.

'Napkins, cutlery, and sauces, over there.' He nodded towards a trolley by the fruit machine where the tattooed man searched for more coins in his turned-out trouser pockets. I staggered over and took what I needed.

'The barman's friendly,' I whispered to Sophie when I returned, glad to sit down.

The barman cleared phlegm from his throat and coughed.

'I think he heard you,' Sophie whispered back, grinning. 'I hope he spits in your food and not mine.'

We sat and drank.

'It's nice to be out, isn't it?' I said. 'We haven't been out for an evening since we met.'

'And why's that bad?' she frowned.

'It's not, it's just that—'

'Are you getting fed up with me already?'

'No.'

'Are you tired of all the sex we're having? All the cuddling and kissing? The cosy nights in? Are you?'

I didn't want to say the sex had dried up recently, but it was good to hear she didn't seem to have gone off it completely.

'That's not what I meant,' I said.

Sophie smiled.

'Good.'

Two women entered the pub and scanned around for somewhere to sit down. Despite all the tables being empty, they chose the one right next to ours.

Sophie raised her eyebrows at me.

One of the women, hair dyed bright red, took off her coat to reveal a scarlet dress, unflattering lumps and bumps straining at the material, dark sweat patches under the arms. Her chair legs bowed as she sat down. Her thinner friend, orange-skinned, with short, white hedgehog-spiked hair, wearing white jeans and a floaty top, sat opposite her. They picked up menus and studied them in silence.

Sophie and I matched their quietness, wary they'd hear anything we'd say. Instead, I tried to guess what Sophie was thinking. Her blinking eyes, slight smile, and tilted head told me the pair next to us fascinated her.

After a while, a door swung open at the back of the pub, bashing against a wall, and a middle-aged waitress with blonde, greasy hair and a tiny skirt appeared carrying our food.

'Burger with extra bacon?' she asked.

Sophie raised her hand, and the waitress placed her food squarely in front of her.

'Here you go, darling,' she said with a wink. 'Careful,

the plate's hot.'

She turned to me.

'The other burger?' she asked.

I nodded, and she dropped the plate in front of me so heavily I thought it'd crack.

She smiled at Sophie. 'Enjoy.'

The waitress scowled at me as she went.

'What's her problem?' I said.

Sophie shrugged.

Our burgers were flat and limp, with egg yolk coloured cheese and raw onions poking from beneath browning lettuce.

'Looks great,' said Sophie. She gripped her burger with both hands, and half of it disappeared into her mouth. Globs of grease and melted cheese smeared onto her chin. She grinned. 'Amazing burger,' she said between chews.

I began eating, but couldn't taste the chips. I seemed to have lost my sense of taste and smell.

The women at the table next to us looked at us eating.

Sophie put down her burger and said to the red-haired woman, 'Does it bother you that you're so fat?'

The woman's jaw dropped in surprise.

'Sophie!' I sprayed chewed bits of chip over the table. 'You can't say that.'

Sophie continued, 'You must feel unhealthy, right? Can you feel the fat clogging your arteries?'

'Stop,' I said. 'What's the matter with you?' My forehead throbbed and my ears began to ring—the noise quickly growing louder and sharper, like someone turning up a volume dial.

'Someone needs to tell her for her own good.' She looked at her friend. 'A friend, a good friend would tell her she's killing herself.'

Sophie stared wide-eyed at the red-haired woman, who looked sadly at Sophie, and then to me.

'I know I'm fat,' said the woman. 'I've always been fat. I don't know any different. I'm okay with it.'

Sophie picked up a chip and bit off an end. 'Have you ever had a boyfriend?'

'Sophie!'

A shooting pain crossed my eyes, and rainbow-coloured circles floated in front of me. My head felt heavy, my stomach uneasy.

'There's someone,' she said, looking at her spiky-haired friend for support.

'You're making it up,' said Sophie.

The red-haired woman, surprisingly agile, jumped to her feet, knocking her chair backwards.

'I'm not!'

Through my kaleidoscope vision I could see everyone watching us: the tattooed man, the barman, the waitress, the old men.

The woman's eyes narrowed; her nostrils flared. She leaned over the table, shaking fist clenched inches from Sophie's face, a mountain confronting a mouse. I was a coiled spring, ready to jump between them.

Calmly, Sophie said, 'If your boyfriend's real, I bet he's as fat and unattractive as you.'

I leapt up to prevent the woman punching Sophie, and my head sloshed forward as if full of water. My eyelids shut instinctively to prevent liquid from spilling out. My knees buckled and I fell into my chair. Pain pierced my temples like knives. The ringing in my ears became a passing train. Among the din, I heard the faintest of voices say, 'And your hair's awful too,' before vomit welled in my throat and I passed out.

Head upon the table, I came to with Sophie finishing her

burger in front of me.

'Welcome back,' she said.

As the fat dripped from the last of her burger to the plate in creamy, pink-tinged raindrops, I sat up and wondered what had happened? The pain in my head had disappeared. I felt much better.

I looked around the room. The red-haired woman and her friend had gone, their chairs neatly tucked under their table. The old men were perched on their stools. The tattooed man fed coins into the fruit machine. The barman and waitress stood at opposite ends of the bar, half-heartedly polishing glasses, waiting for customers.

Sophie wiped her mouth with a paper napkin and licked around her lips.

I picked up my pint and rinsed away the acidic film of vomit lining my mouth. There was no evidence to show I'd been sick.

'I fainted,' I said, touching the cut on my forehead. It itched, but otherwise my head was clear and painless.

'You fell asleep.'

I thought about that for a moment.

'People don't fall asleep that suddenly.'

'Some do,' she said. 'I had a school friend with narcolepsy. She'd fall asleep anywhere—on her desk, on the bus, even halfway through a netball game. It was horrible, really. Our classmates would smear stuff on her face while she was asleep: mud, make-up, food. One time, they drew a penis on her forehead with a marker pen. She didn't understand why people were laughing at her until I took her to the toilets to wash it off. I thought maybe you had a similar thing—like when you get stressed you fall asleep. You were peaceful and breathing, so I left you. The important thing is you're okay.'

I'd never suddenly passed out before. It must have been the knock on my head, but I felt much better having slept.

'Did that woman hit you?' I asked.

Sophie leaned back in her chair, folded her arms, and shook her head.

'Why would she?'

'You were fighting.'

'I was giving her advice.'

Sophie was normally so lovely, cool and calm—I'd never imagined she could behave like that. Did she change into a monster once alcohol passed her lips? She didn't seem drunk.

'Look, I've probably saved her life. She'll be thinking about what I said and now she'll do something about it.'

Did Sophie believe what she was saying? The poor woman could go home and comfort-eat herself into a coma.

'I've changed her. If you see her again, she'll have lost weight. I'll bet money on it.'

'But you didn't have to be so mean.'

'I don't want to talk about it anymore,' she said, looking towards where they'd sat—a slither of remorse in her voice. 'It's still raining. Shall we get another beer?'

'I shouldn't. I've been unconscious.'

'You've been pestering to come out all day, and now we're here you're not backing out that easily.' she said. 'I'll get you a glass of water too.'

Sophie went to the bar and bought more drinks.

I'd not realised she enjoyed drinking so much. We didn't drink at home and I barely drank alcohol at all. Not because I didn't enjoy it. I did. But I'd once had an unpleasant experience. Something scary.

In my last year of university, about seven years before, I'd become ill at a house party. I'd sunk a few vodka and lemonades, but was fine until a pretty girl dressed in black passed me a joint between her slender fingers.

We'd sat, drunk and tired, on a loosely sprung sofa, the sagging cushions hugging us close together, smoking the joint down to the end, and tapping the flaking ash into an empty beer bottle, when suddenly my body jolted, the bottle dropped to the wooden floor shattering glass over our trainers, and it seemed like control of my body had been handed to an invisible force. I saw my limbs jerking and twitching as if controlled by a joystick, and the pretty girl vanished to another room.

I leapt from the sofa and the joystick guided me, stumbling and swerving out of the house and through the blurred streets, until I reached the town's riverbank.

'Give my face back!' I chanted at a group of swans gliding like ghosts on the water. They all resembled me, their beaks were my nose; their eyes were big and blue, they had my eyebrows, and their laughs sounded like my laugh. I remember the cold of the river, the heft and drag of my clothes, flailing, splashing, handfuls of greasy feathers, a flash of beak, blurred gargoyle faces of a crowd shouting, kicking, and spitting as I was pulled up the bank and lain in the long grass of the embankment to be restrained by a firm grip and a deep, calm voice. I struggled and swore, but I'm thankful the Police saw I was ill and took me to the right people.

Dazed, I woke in a strange bed, hard pillows, sheets instead of my duvet, the smell of disinfectant, duck-egg blue walls, fluorescent tubes on the ceiling, and Dad sitting beside me in a plastic chair. Except it wasn't Dad—it was a crow, wings folded in its lap, with Dad's face.

'You're all right, Benny,' it squawked.

I leapt from bed and backed up against the wall.

'What's the matter?' asked the crow, standing and stepping towards me on spindly black legs.

I barged past the crow, knocking it to the floor, and ran into the corridor screaming for someone to save me. But there were no people there—only birds: robins, geese, seagulls, eagles, blue tits, sparrows, storks, pelicans, pigeons.

Locking myself in a toilet, I curled up, trembling, as birds on the other side of the door asked me to come out, until a softly spoken woman convinced me she'd chased away the birds, and I gingerly opened the door. At first, there was no one there, but then a swan rushed at me, and before I could close the door, four or five winged attackers pinned me to the floor. I thrashed around until exhausted, and I must have fallen asleep. And when my eyes opened, the birds had gone. Dad was there, his left cheek black and yellow with bruising, and an arm plastered and suspended by a shoulder sling.

'What happened to you?' I asked.

A short stay in hospital, a tetanus shot, small pink tablets, friendly chats with doctors and nurses, and I was well enough to leave. Psychosis, they called it. It may never happen again. Exam stress and a touch of depression following a relationship break-up the previous year were probably the underlying cause, triggered by heavy drinking and cannabis. Stay off the drugs, watch the alcohol intake, and I'd be fine.

The blue bruises on my arms and torso healed quickly where the swans had beaten me with their wings, and only two tiny white scars remained where they'd pecked me on the cheek. But the terror of the experience never left me. I didn't know myself anymore—I didn't trust myself. I was this strange new person who could go crazy at any moment. I'd never feel normal again. What did normal even feel like? And the worst thing about the entire episode was the shame of having hurt Dad.

I stayed with my parents for a few months, moving

into my old room, redecorated since I'd left for university as a guest bedroom—my teenage posters and photographs removed to create an empty magnolia shell with no memories. It was just like me—I'd been painted over and needed to decorate from scratch. Mum and Dad were brilliant—non-judgemental and caring—giving me space and plying me with good food, smiles, and encouragement. Dad's arm healed well and he never complained about it. But when I suddenly reached for the pepper pot at dinner one night, Dad winced, as if I was going to hit him—as if he was scared of me.

I went for long walks, trying to make sense of what'd happened, and whether I'd know the warning signs of it happening again. If I knew it was coming, what would I do? Following any path or trail I came across just to see where it led me, I occasionally stopped to take deep cleansing breaths of fresh air and admire my surroundings: woods, meadows and hills. I avoided going near rivers and lakes, and was suspicious of birdsong, but enjoyed the rustling of leaves, and the surprise of where the paths took me. I'd walk for miles, sipping water from a bottle and sucking on butter mints Mum had stuffed in my pockets.

'Your Grandad was a mountain climber,' she'd occasionally remind me. 'He got buried for four nights under an avalanche thinking he'd not be found until the spring thaw. And he had nothing to eat except a few butter mints. They saved his life.'

The sweet creaminess of butter mints dissolving in my mouth reminded me I was lucky to be alive—I could have drowned in that river.

Being in my hometown, I feared running into old school friends. I didn't want them to know what'd happened to me, and thought they'd be able to see how messed up I was, like my illness was physical, and they'd seize upon my weakness as they'd have done in the school playground. I avoided streets where they lived, only bumping into Elliot, who I'd sat beside in Maths, as he waited at a bus stop. Luckily, his bus arrived before he'd said anything more than hello. Sometimes, I'd think of getting back in touch with old friends, but it'd been too long—I wasn't the same person they knew.

Every week, Dad drove me to Ava's. At first, she had to tease things out of me like an interrogation. I wasn't good at talking about my feelings, but with her special warmth and patience I opened up and she taught me about her positivity pockets. And when my sessions with Ava ended, we hugged, and I left quickly before crying.

After four months, I needed to return to some kind of normality—I'd never be fixed unless I did.

I completed my exams and easily landed a job before I got the results. My parents were pleased, but worried about me moving away for work.

'It's not far and I'll visit all the time,' I said.

On the morning I left, my compact car stuffed with my few belongings, my parents hugged me goodbye as Mum cried freely.

'Remember, we're here if you need us,' Dad whispered in my ear. 'But stay off the drink and drugs.' I promised I would.

Evening became night, and growing bored with our surroundings, Sophie and I finished our drinks and left the Witch & Hammer to seek other pubs. The barman waved us farewell with a curt, 'Bye, folks.'

The rain that had fallen all day had freshened the air, glossed pavements, and formed puddles in their cracks and hollows. Streetlights beamed orange, and I turned from the glare of car headlights.

The town was busy with the Saturday night crowd.

Restaurants were full, and people queued in doorways hoping for spare tables. Taxis dropped-off partygoers in their best evening wear, checking their hair in the taxi windows as they drove away, and we stepped aside to allow a group of middle-aged women to pass, giggling, swerving puddles, tottering on high-heels that threatened to topple them.

Warm air smothered us as we entered the next pub. We shouldered our way to the crowded bar and took our drinks to an empty spot near the toilets, standing with our backs tight to the wall to allow people to pass.

'It's loud in here,' I shouted to Sophie.

'I can't hear you, it's loud in here,' she said, laughing.

We watched the scene, sipping our drinks. Everyone having a good time, shouting into each other's ears, a boisterous cacophony of conflicting voices cancelling each other out.

I went to the toilet, and when I returned, Sophie was chatting with a woman.

'I love your hair,' shouted the drunk woman, breasts looming over her tight pink top, lumpy mascara smudged towards her temples. Sophie waved the woman's arm away as it tried to stroke Sophie's hair. 'It's so shiny.'

'Thanks,' said Sophie.

'And you're exquisite.'

'Sorry, I'm taken.' Sophie nodded towards me standing quietly beside her.

'He wouldn't mind if I gave you a quick kiss.' She winked at me. 'I enjoy kissing girls.'

'Perhaps another time,' said Sophie.

The woman pulled a sad expression, and Sophie leapt as the woman pinched her bottom and ducked away into the crowd.

'Let's get out of here,' said Sophie, downing her drink. 'It's so loud I can't think in here. Let's find somewhere quieter.'

On leaving the pub, chilly rain wetted my face, washing away some of my tiredness. Considering I'd fallen unconscious earlier, I felt good.

The streets were quieter. The few people we saw hurried, heads lowered from the rain with hunched backs, disappearing into bars or mini cabs.

'Do you get chatted up a lot?' I asked jokingly, as we walked quickly, swerving puddles.

'Not really.'

'Has a girl has chatted you up before?'

'Maybe.'

'Have you kissed a girl before?' I found the idea arousing, though the reality would likely be sickening jealousy.

Sophie stopped and glared at me.

'Why do you want to know?' she asked.

'I'm just curious.'

'We all have a past,' she sighed. 'I don't ask you about yours, do I? I just think about the future. Can you drop it now?'

'What happened to your head?' asked the drunken bleached blonde woman in the next pub. She ran her index finger, nail painted glittering silver, across my cut. It tickled. Sophie had gone to the bar as I'd found us a table to sit at.

'He was cage fighting,' said Sophie, returning with our drinks, eyeing the woman coldly. Would Sophie cause another scene? 'This man is the European gay cage fighting champion.'

'He don't look like a cage fighter,' said the woman, retreating.

'Element of surprise. Works every time,' Sophie called after her.

The woman returned to her table of friends. They looked me up and down and shook their heads, laughing—no, not a cage fighter.

'Slut,' Sophie murmured. I reached out and held her hand, hoping to distract her from the woman and prevent another fight.

This pub, the Eagle, was more relaxed. We didn't have to scream to make each other heard. The tables were more spread out, and the clientele's hair was greying.

Sophie seemed to calm.

'Did you go out to pubs a lot with previous boyfriends?' I asked, curious how Sophie had developed the drinking tolerance of a rugby player. I was already drunker than I was comfortable with—my head cloudy.

'What previous boyfriends?' she asked, a suspicious note in her voice.

'You must have had boyfriends before?'

'Not for a while.'

'I haven't had a girlfriend since my first year at university,' I said.

Sophie raised an eyebrow.

Ever since my psychosis incident, I'd been wary of letting people get close to me—it wouldn't be fair for them to have to cope with a repeat episode. I think my parent's thought I'd turned asexual, never interested when they mentioned the single girls I'd been to school with whose parents they bumped into occasionally. And if Sophie hadn't inserted herself into my life so assuredly, then I'd probably have been alone forever.

'So how long ago was your last boyfriend?' I asked, hoping she'd tell me something about Eugene.

'Why do you want to know?' she said, taking a large gulp of her drink.

'I'm just interested.'

'Why though?'

'I want to know more about you.' I wanted to know every little thing about her: her life story, how her mind worked, her hopes, dreams and fears—everything.

'I've not had thousands of boyfriends, if that's what you're worried about?' She downed the rest of her drink and slammed her glass on the table. 'I know you men like to think you're the first and the best. Now leave it, please.'

I stopped asking questions, blaming her tetchiness on the alcohol, and offered to buy her another drink, maybe something non-alcoholic. She declined.

I sipped my drink and Sophie went quiet, drifting into herself. I wondered what she was thinking about.

Breaking the silence, I asked, 'So, what have you learnt about moss recently?'

Sophie came alive, sitting bolt upright.

'Do you really want to know?'

'Yes.'

Forgetting the link to Eugene, I was pleased she'd found something which interested her. Hobbies could be peculiar—people were into all kinds of things. And though her interest in moss initially seemed weird, it was no different to people collecting cacti, or growing giant vegetables in their allotments, or spending years perfecting rose gardens. Why not have an interest in moss? I could appreciate moss—the touch of wilderness it brought to urban landscapes, growing on driveways, roofs, pavements, walls; its sponginess underfoot, its decoration of tree trunks. I couldn't be as fascinated by moss as Sophie, but I could take an interest.

'Okay, here's a fact for you,' she said. 'Moss grows on every continent, even Antarctica. It's buried under ice and snow all winter and exposed for a few months when the ice melts in summer. They're the only plants that live in those conditions. That's clever, isn't it?'

I nodded, thinking about Grandad beneath the snow with his butter mints.

'Moss is really tough. Nothing else lives there except penguins and a few cold scientists. Moss can live virtually anywhere.'

'Could it live on the moon?'

Sophie turned away in thought.

'If it had water, perhaps, and carbon dioxide. Mosses colonise bare rock, so the moon's surface would be okay. And once there, they'd create conditions so other plants could grow. Who knows, moss could pave the way for us to live on the moon one day.'

It sounded plausible.

'And there's so many species of moss. And more undiscovered. Imagine discovering a moss no one had found before, never given it a name. That would be cool.'

'What would you call it?'

She paused and hummed.

'I'd name it after you.' She smiled.

'Ben? Ben the moss?'

'No, silly. It would have a Latin name, like *Benicus* or *Benius.*' She laughed.

'Thanks, Sophie. I'd be honoured.'

We finished the night at a narrow bar where the drinks were double the price of elsewhere and the clientele were younger and more stylish than we were. I tripped on a stray designer handbag and spilt my Mojito onto the spotless shoes of a pair of well-groomed men—smart suits, bronze tans, beards so neat they could have been drawn on with a pen. They shouted in my face, demanding compensation, jabbing me in the chest with manicured fingers, backing me against the bar like a cornered rabbit. But when Sophie came to my side, angry and fierce, they muttered under their breath, and turned away.

Shaking a little, I followed Sophie to a quiet corner.

'Dickheads,' she said.

Earlier that evening, I'd worried about Sophie's aggressiveness, and now I was thankful for it.

'We should go home,' I said, sipping my Mojito through a straw. 'I shouldn't have drunk this much.'

No warped thoughts had entered my head, and I had full control of my limbs, but I knew I was pushing the limits.

'You can't let people like that bother you,' said Sophie, nodding towards the bar. 'You're too timid.' She ruffled my hair, then relaxed back in her chair and looked at me curiously. She was so drunk her eyes were barely open. 'You know, Ben, sometimes it feels like you're not really all there, that there's only this really shallow person. There's no depth, like you're an apparition, a ghost. You need to be here, in the world.'

Why had she suddenly said that? I didn't know how to respond, and Sophie seemed happy to let her thoughts sit uncomfortably between us.

We finished the night drinking tequila shots. Two each. Sophie didn't give me a choice—it was as if she was testing me to see my limits. We sucked hard on wedges of lime, then left to hail a taxi. We'd wandered too far to walk home.

'I'm not taking him like that,' said the taxi driver through his window.

'He's fine,' slurred Sophie.

'And you look a liability and all,' he said.

4

A giant expanding ball of cotton wool was trying to escape from my skull. My tongue was dry and mouth sticky.

Stretching an arm to Sophie's side of the bed, I found I was alone. Sunlight flooded the white bed sheets through open curtains as I fought to raise my eyelids, eyelashes gummed together, while I massaged my temples.

After a deep breath, I swung my legs from bed, and stood wobbling. I spied my dressing gown hanging on the corner of the door and wrapped it tight around me like a fabric hug.

In the mirror, the cut on my forehead surprised me, forgetting for a moment how I'd received it. Surrounded by black bruising, it appeared worse than I recalled. I touched it gently and winced with pain, my eyes watering.

I held the banister to steady myself on my way downstairs.

In the living room, CD cases lay scattered on the carpet and four opened beer cans stood on the coffee table.

I used the walls to balance on my way to the kitchen. Through the kitchen window I saw Sophie, still in pyjamas, studying the damp ground beneath the oak tree. She knelt with her eyes close to the lawn. I opened the door to the garden and filled my lungs with cool air.

'Hey,' I said, my voice cracking, throat raw. I sucked my cheeks for saliva to swallow. 'What are you doing?'

Sophie stood, attempted to wipe mud from her knees, and turned to me.

'The moss is growing nicely,' she said with an enormous smile.

Sophie walked back to the kitchen, arms hugged across her chest to protect from the cold.

'How are you feeling?' She shivered and danced on tiptoes to warm up.

'Horrible,' I yawned.

'When I went to bed, you started making a racket. I had to tell you to turn the music off.'

'What music?'

'Some horrible noise. And you started raving about birds.'

'What about birds?'

'How they're always stealing things from you.'

My hand involuntarily touched my face. The membrane between sanity and madness may have been more porous than I thought.

'Yeah, it was a bit weird, actually,' she said. 'Funny, though.'

I can't have tipped into total insanity—she wouldn't have found that funny.

I apologised for being weird and offered to make tea to help Sophie warm up.

'Have you had breakfast?' I asked.

'Just painkillers.'

'Good idea. Where are they?'

Sophie pointed to a drawer, and I rummaged to find a box of ibuprofen.

I swallowed two tablets with a glass of milk, my stomach gurgling as though the milk was curdling inside me.

'I think I'm going to be—'

Milky vomit exploded into the toilet as I reached the bathroom.

Hugging the toilet bowl, thankful I'd cleaned it the day before, I then climbed back into bed, tossing a while as I massaged my aching head, until falling asleep.

I was a little more refreshed on waking. I went to find Sophie, but she wasn't in the house and didn't answer her phone when I called. Where could she be?

I made buttery toast and crunched it while slumped on the sofa watching TV. My stomach was relieved to have something solid in it. There was nothing good on, so I switched off the TV and read a book until my headache returned, the words blurred, and I lost my place on the page. *Where was Sophie?* I tried calling again. It went straight to voicemail and I left a message. I swallowed more painkillers, vowing never to drink that much again. When my headache eased, I washed dishes and ironed shirts. I kept checking my phone for calls or texts from Sophie. Surely she knew I'd worry?

I was sorting some clean washing when I heard the key turn and the front door open. Before the door shut, I'd rushed to the hallway. Sophie smiled and took off her coat.

'Where have you been?' I asked, sharply.

'You're angry,' she said.

My body was taut, like a hawk waiting to strike.

'Why didn't you say you were going out? I've been worried.'

Her trainers bounced against floor tiles as she kicked them off and she edged past me into the living room.

'I called you and left messages,' I said.

She dropped onto the sofa and looked at her phone.

'Oh yeah, sorry.'

Sophie put the phone down and picked up a

gardening magazine, flicking through its pages.

'Sophie,' I shouted, demanding she focus on me. 'I'm serious. You could have been dead somewhere.'

Sophie closed the magazine, placed it on the coffee table, and patted the sofa cushion—an invitation to sit beside her. I sat, and she cuddled up to me, stroking the cut on my head.

'I'm sorry I've upset you,' she said. 'You were asleep when I left.'

The cut was sore and spongy, and I pushed her hand away. Instead, she rubbed the back of my neck, its stiffness yielding under her fingers, and she looked at me with her wide hazel eyes and kissed me on the cheek.

'Let's go upstairs,' she said.

She kissed me on the lips.

'No,' I said, gently shaking her off. But she kissed me again and led me by the hand to the bedroom.

Sophie slowly undressed me, and I lay naked on my front as she massaged my back and shoulders using a bottle of scented oil she fetched from the bathroom. The fresh, sweet aroma of lemongrass filled the room. Knots of muscle dissolved under her fingers and I melted into the mattress.

'You're so tense,' she said.

Sophie undressed and lay on the bed with me. We had sex that left us dewy with sweat and breathless.

'I'm still angry with you,' I said, but I was so relaxed and satiated I didn't feel angry at all.

Sophie sat upright with the bed sheets held up to cover her nakedness.

'So, do you want to know where I've been all day?' she said.

I nodded, which made my head throb.

'I've joined a club,' she said.

'What kind of club?'

'The Bryology Club.' She saw my questioning look. 'It's a club for people who like moss.'

'You're making it up?'

'I'm not. It's an actual club. Members talk about the moss they've seen and there're guest speakers and workshops and field trips and social events.'

I imagined a musty room, a small group of nerds who lived with their mothers, anoraks, flasks of tea, magnifying glasses around their necks, moss identification guides rolled-up in the back pockets of their sensible all-weather trousers. Sophie didn't fit into this crowd.

'It was fun,' she said.

'Why didn't you tell me you were going to the club?'

'You were sleeping.'

'You could have woken me.'

She sighed.

'I don't have to tell you everything. And anyway, I worried you'd think it was silly.'

It would have surprised me. Bryology Club added another level of seriousness to her fascination with moss.

'If it's something you're interested in, then it's not silly,' I said.

'But?'

'But nothing.'

'There's a but.'

I paused. It annoyed me Sophie was spending more time with moss than me. Had our relationship already become so stale we'd now fill our spare time with our own activities rather than doing everything together, small things that kept us individual rather than the inseparable, glued-together creature we'd been? We'd be like Dad in his garage building model ships, and Mum absorbed in putting together thousand-piece jigsaws. Was this too much space so early in our relationship? Slight gaps now, but leading to chasms? Leading to voids? And I was annoyed at being annoyed. Sophie could do whatever she liked, and I had no right to tell her how to spend her time. I was lucky she was with me at all. But the moss was all about Eugene, wasn't it? Or had her fascination transcended that initial connection?

'I'm just glad you've found something you're interested in,' I said.

Later that evening, just as I'd finished washing the dishes, Sophie handed me a plastic carrier bag, a big smile on her face.

'I thought you deserved a present,' she said excitedly.

'What for?'

'For being a cool boyfriend.'

Why was Sophie being so nice? First the sex and now the present.

I reached into the bag and pulled out a box of aftershave—*True Rebel*. The raised gold lettering and matt black, soft-touch finish to the cardboard suggested it was expensive. I never wore aftershave.

'Open it,' she said.

I opened the box and took out an ornate glass bottle, curiously heavy for an item its size, a motorbike design cut into the glass. Sophie grabbed my jumper sleeve, pulling it up to reveal my bare wrist, took the bottle, and sprayed the aftershave on the exposed skin.

'Sniff it,' she said.

I held my wrist to my nose, and my eyes watered with the aroma of musty lemons mixed with neat alcohol.

'It's nice,' I lied, my eyes stinging.

Sophie took my wrist, pressed it against her nostrils, and inhaled deeply.

'I love this fragrance,' she said.

She sprayed some on my neck, rubbed it in, and

leaned in to sniff again, her nose tickling my neck.

'You smell amazing,' she said, pulling away. 'And I have another present. Close your eyes and hold out your hands.'

I did as instructed.

A carrier bag rustled, and after a moment Sophie draped something over my outstretched arms.

'Open your eyes,' she said.

It was a denim jacket, faded light blue, and almost white at the seams and its worn elbows.

I held it up in front of me, arms outstretched.

'I saw it in a charity shop on the way home and thought it'd suit you.'

I put on the jacket. It was a good fit. A perfect fit.

'I'm not sure it's very me,' I said. I'd never owned a denim jacket.

'Nonsense. You look cool.'

'Really?'

It was the kind of thing tough, rugged men wore—men who effortlessly grew beards overnight, worked in construction, and rode motorbikes.

Sophie ruffled my hair and turned up the collar so it stood high around my neck. She stepped back and looked at me.

'Maybe that's a step too far,' she said, reaching forward to fold the collar down. 'You're not a collar up person. Go look at yourself.'

I went upstairs and studied myself in the bedroom's full-length mirror, swivelling my hips to look at my body from different angles. Sophie watched me from behind.

'You pout when you look at yourself in the mirror,' she laughed.

'I don't.'

'You do, you just don't realise you're doing it.'

My lips pursed ever so slightly in the reflection.

'Well, do you like the jacket?' she asked.

I twisted myself one more time and peered back to the mirror over my shoulder, pouting.

'Yeah, it's nice.'

I began to take it off, one arm half out of a sleeve, when Sophie asked, 'What are you doing?'

'I'm taking it off.'

'Why?'

'Because I don't need it on. We're indoors.'

'You don't like it.'

'I do.'

'But you're taking it off immediately.'

I put my arm back into the sleeve and Sophie fastened the jacket's silver stud buttons from top to bottom.

'There you go,' she said. 'You handsome man.' With the fragrance of *True Rebel* offending my nostrils, I wore the jacket all evening as Sophie cuddled up to me as we watched TV, only removing it for bed and placing it on a hanger on the back of the bedroom door. Before Sophie joined me under the duvet, she stroked the jacket and smiled.

Suddenly waking in the night, through bleary eyes, I saw an intruder in the darkness, standing by the door watching us.

I threw the duvet off me, jumped out of bed, and stood poised, heart racing.

'Sophie!'

'What?' she said groggily.

'Get out,' I shouted at the silent figure. Its broad shoulders suggested it was a man.

He didn't flinch.

'Shush,' said Sophie, rolling over, continuing to sleep.

I stood in a tense standoff with the intruder.

Who was he?

Why wasn't he moving?

Why was he silent? No breathing, no creak of his weight on the floorboards.

Was it a ghost? I'd never believed in them, but many people did, didn't they? Could it be the ghost of the old man who'd lived here before me? Or was this Eugene Gray back from the dead, here to steal Sophie away from me?

But as my eyes adjusted to the dark, I realised, embarrassed, the invader was my new denim jacket hanging on the door.

I climbed back into bed, wondering what was wrong with me.

At the office, a headache gradually worsened over the day, and I was ready to go home and crawl into bed, but as I drove past the cemetery, I hit the brakes. The car behind blasted its horn, and I waved an apology. I had a sudden urge to talk to Eugene.

The fresh wind sweeping the cemetery soothed my head a little as I stood by the grassy mound of Eugene's grave, looking at his name etched into the gravestone. The over-hanging branches of a horse chestnut tree, heavy with dark leaves, creaked in the breeze. Decaying conker shells from last autumn lay scattered upon the ground. Moss grew around the base of the gravestone, thriving, lush and emerald-green on the soggy earth—the same moss Sophie was growing in our garden.

'Who are you, Eugene?' I asked his grave.

I'd been worrying about Sophie's relationship with Eugene more than usual today. At lunchtime, I'd watched two colleagues flirting with each other. She'd sat on his desk laughing, twirling her hair around her finger as he told an improbable story and repeatedly moistened his lips. I imagined the pair were Sophie and Eugene. Was this how they'd been together?

Perhaps Eugene had just been a friend, but I sensed he wasn't. And if Eugene had been her boyfriend, why had she got together with me so quickly after his death? Was it the same love at first sight that I'd felt? I should be glad Sophie was moving on, but surely it was too soon? She must have feelings for him still—stronger feelings for him than for me?

And had he been like me? Did we look alike? Did Sophie have a type? Sophie was so beautiful I could only imagine Eugene as some kind of Adonis of golden hair and rippling muscles. Did we have the same temperament? Did we share a sense of humour? Perhaps she liked me because I was the opposite to Eugene? Someone so far away from Eugene she'd never be reminded of him, someone impossible to compare to him.

'Why won't she tell me about you?'

At breakfast, I'd noticed Sophie looking to the distance, lost in her own world, a blank, perhaps sad expression. Was she thinking of Eugene? He'd died so young, a tragedy. I could only imagine how she might feel. All I wanted to do was help. To comfort her when she needed it, for her to trust me.

'And what's this thing with moss about?'

Was the moss connected to some special bond Sophie had with Eugene or not?

I knew I should just talk to Sophie, tell her all my worries, ask all my questions. But I wasn't good at talking. Instead, I was asking a grave, hoping for answers that would never appear. It was pathetic.

A sudden pang of pain exploded in my head. I needed to get home and take some tablets. I gave Eugene's gravestone a nudge, almost a kick goodbye, and asked one more thing before I left.

'How did you die?'

The ground trembled, and I stepped back from the grave as a violent shaking began, like an underground chamber was collapsing beneath me, a muffled roar through the earth. The whole graveyard shook, branches on the trees swaying, leaves rustling, grass swishing. My head felt as though a pneumatic drill was vibrating in it.

I ran, stumbling over the moving ground, out of the cemetery gate, to my car.

Watching from my juddering driver's seat, a man cycled past on the road as if nothing was happening. And across the road a young mother wheeled her baby in a pushchair, unaffected by the earthquake. Other people heading in my direction walked casually, as if everything was normal. Why weren't they panicking?

The pain in my head was extraordinary. I closed my eyes and rubbed my temples, and suddenly the ground stopped shaking. My headache disappeared.

I sat a moment, cold sweat in my hairline, watching people pass.

What just happened?

'Did you feel the earthquake?' I asked Sophie as soon as I arrived home.

She looked up from her microscope and eyed me strangely.

'No. When?'

'About ten minutes ago. A really powerful earthquake?'

'Not that I noticed.'

It'd been impossible not to feel it. Why was I the only one?

'Are you okay?' she asked. 'You look confused.'

'I'm fine,' I lied. The earthquake can't have been real.

How had I imagined something so vivid?

My mobile phone rang in my pocket. It was my parents.

I spoke to my parents every few days to check in and tell each other we were all still alive and well. I often had little to say, but my parents always had something to talk about—impressive for two people who didn't get out much. Dad was always the one to initiate the call. Mum was too nervous to do it, but she often joined in later. I went to the living room to answer it.

'Good to hear your voice, Benny,' he said, after our hellos.

'How are you both?' I asked.

'I'm fine. And your mum's been settled over the last couple of days.'

Mum was prone to what we called "spells"—periods of terrible anxiety, when she'd worry obsessively over the smallest things. She'd fret about whether she'd said hello to a neighbour in the right tone of voice, or panic about being late for an appointment hours before she was due. It could be a struggle to get her out of the house, she'd be so worried about being dressed correctly for rain, or terrified of running into someone she'd forgotten to send a birthday card to. An unexpected visitor to the house, like someone delivering a parcel, could send her into a spin.

'Did you do anything this weekend?' asked Dad.

'Sophie and I went out for drinks on Saturday night.'

He was silent for a moment.

'A big night, was it?'

He was worried.

'I took it easy, Dad.'

He'd drawn my attention to my headache, which had started up again.

'You be careful,' he said.

71

'It was a long time ago.'

'It doesn't mean it won't happen again. It's not worth the risk.' He paused, letting that sink in. He had to cope with Mum and her illness, and I didn't want him to have to cope with me, too. 'So, things are going well with Sophie?' he asked. 'Maybe we'll get to meet her one day?'

'Soon.'

Sophie wandered into the living room.

'In fact, I'm here with her now.'

Sophie mouthed, 'Who's that?' pointing to the phone in my hand.

'It's Dad.'

She flew from the room like a startled bird.

'Say hi to her from me,' said Dad. 'If she really exists.' He said it jokingly, but there was concern in his voice. I'd told Mum and him all these brilliant things about Sophie, yet as far as they knew she could be as imaginary as the earthquake whose tremors I still felt in my bones.

I stared at the space where Sophie had been.

'We'll come visit soon. I promise,' I said.

I heard Mum muttering in the background among the sound of drawers and cupboard doors being opened and closed.

'Is Mum okay?' I asked.

'She says she's lost something. You know how she gets. I better go and help her.'

'Okay, speak soon,' I said.

I heard him trying to calm Mum before he hung up the phone.

I went back to the kitchen to find Sophie.

'I'm sure I bought some painkillers the other day,' she said, opening a drawer and rummaging through it. 'I couldn't find them earlier. I've got a headache.'

'Sorry, I used them.'

'All of them?'

'My head's been hurting.'

'But it's been a couple of days since we went out. You can't still be hungover?'

'I'm just dehydrated.'

'You should go to the doctor. It could be serious.'

'I don't want to waste their time.'

Sophie put her palm across the cut on my head.

'Typical man, denying there's anything wrong. You could have a fractured skull.'

'I doubt it,' I said, shrugging. 'I think I'd know.'

'Are you a doctor now?'

'No, but—'

'Don't be ridiculous. Is your skull thicker than other people's skulls? Promise me you'll go.' She looked at me sternly and I nodded consent. It felt good to know that Sophie cared about me.

Later, still thinking about the earthquake, I watched the local TV news and searched for stories on the internet, but there was no mention of it.

Why had it seemed so real? I'd always feared free-falling into madness, and now it seemed like it might happen sooner than I'd imagined. My earlier psychosis, and Mum's condition, made me consider mental illness an inevitability, but I'd hoped to slip into it blissfully unaware in old age.

I was a little early arriving in town for my doctor's appointment, and as I waited outside, I tapped my foot with nerves. As well as asking the doctor to examine the cut on my forehead, I planned to confess my fears over my mental state, and this made me anxious—feeling insufficiently prepared to deal with a diagnosis.

Outside the surgery, a market stall sold cakes, pies, and crusty bread, and I spied a tempting chocolate muffin heavily laden with dark chocolate chunks. Needing the sugar to help me relax, I bought one from the stallholder, a sweaty middle-aged man with a doughnut-like body and cream bun fingers.

'I recognise you from somewhere, don't I?' he asked.

I didn't recognise him.

'I might have passed this stall before?' I guessed. I'd bought nothing, but I'd seen the stall at the market.

'No, that's not it. I recognise you from somewhere.' He stared at me, his memory struggling to place me. Suddenly, he clicked his fingers. 'Got it!' he said in triumph, but his face reddened. 'You're the guy I caught robbing the van.'

I laughed in shock. 'I've never robbed a van.'

He was serious.

'I never forget a face. It was definitely you. In Luton.'

'Can I have my muffin?' He still held my muffin in its paper bag. I'd given him the money for it.

'No, you can't have your fucking muffin, you scum. What a fucking cheek coming here and buying a muffin from the guy you tried to rob. It wouldn't surprise me if you'd stuffed a load of flapjacks in your pockets when I turned my back to get your change.' He called across to the man on a stall opposite selling children's toys. 'Here, Frank, this is the guy who tried to rob my van.'

I couldn't believe what was happening.

Frank, a mountain of a man, stopped neatening a display of board games and dolls and walked over, his money belt jostling with coins.

'It wasn't me,' I protested, holding up my hands as if surrendering to the police. 'I promise you it wasn't.'

'You're even wearing the same fucking denim jacket,' he shouted. I'd worn it to please Sophie, and now it would get me beaten up.

Frank reached to grab me. I swerved out of the way.

'I don't know what you're talking about.'

Several people in earshot now stopped their stall-browsing to look at us.

Frank lunged towards me and I ran, weaving through the busy street, catching elbows and shoulders, stumbling on shoes, looking over my shoulder to see if I was being followed.

'Sorry. Sorry. Sorry,' I said, as people cursed me.

'Don't let me see you again,' the stallholder shouted as I turned the corner of the street. I didn't stop running until I reached our house.

'You were quick,' said Sophie, meeting me in the hallway when I arrived home. 'What did the doctor say?'

Sweat poured down my face, pooling in the crevice of my neck.

'I didn't see the doctor,' I panted.

She turned and walked towards the kitchen.

'You promised,' she said. I'd worked myself up to go, and I was as disappointed as her.

'But a weird thing happened,' I pleaded. 'A guy accused me of stealing from his van.'

'Did you steal from his van?'

'No, of course not. But not stealing today, in the past. In Luton.'

A serious look appeared on Sophie's face. 'Luton?'

'I've only been to Luton once,' I said.

Her face changed to a smile. 'To steal from vans?' she joked.

'No!'

For the foreseeable future, I'd have to avoid the town centre whenever the market was on, which was every Wednesday and Saturday. Visits to Luton were out of the question, too. Maybe I could grow a beard? Wear a hat?

'He was convinced I'd robbed him. He went crazy. He even said he recognised this stupid jacket.' I pulled it off and threw it to the floor. 'If I hadn't run away, I think he'd have beaten me up there in the street.'

'He wouldn't have,' she said, picking up the jacket, smoothing it and hanging it up on a coat hook. 'And it's not a stupid jacket.'

'He would. That's why I couldn't go into the doctors. He was that angry.'

'If you were going to get beaten up, the doctors would have been the best place to be.'

'Stop joking,' I said. 'And the worse thing was that I'd given him the money for a muffin. He was the one that robbed me.'

Sophie spluttered a laugh.

'Poor baby,' she said. 'Book another appointment.'

The cut on my forehead continued to itch as it healed, and a dull, throbbing ache lived in my skull below it. I didn't notice the ache much if I was busy concentrating on something. If I took painkillers, paracetamol and ibuprofen together every few hours, then I could forget it was there. But in quiet times, when I was trying to relax, the painkillers had less effect and a brain splitting headache would erupt. The pain would shift lower, concentrating behind my eyes, and I'd massage my head to try and make it better. Standing under a warm shower, letting the water cascade over me, soothed the pain. I'd stand there, eyes closed, tilting my head from side to side, letting the water fill my ears and caress my eyelids. As soon as the water stopped, the pain returned.

After the knock on my forehead, and the mighty hangover, I convinced myself my head just needed some time to heal—no point in worrying a doctor with it. There was probably some lingering concussion, and I was dehydrated, always thirsty, drinking litres of water a day. These things didn't last forever. And I could attribute the earthquake, and my scare with the jacket intruder, to my dehydration too. Yes, these things seemed real at the time, but dehydration could make you hallucinate, couldn't it? I'd be fine.

I lied to Sophie, telling her I visited the doctor one lunchtime, they'd checked me over and found nothing wrong.

Sophie's interest in moss continued to grow. She'd disappear on walks with her notebook, backpack, and a little knife she'd bought to scrape moss from surfaces around the neighbourhood. On her return, she planted the moss in the garden.

'I like you watching me the way you do. It makes me feel protected,' said Sophie, as I watched her gardening one evening. I stood on our small patio with a mug of tea for us both.

I loved how she moved. Sometimes smoothly, like a dancer, every movement natural, clean lines, a dolphin gliding through the water, before suddenly becoming a sprite, flitting around, excited and erratic.

'I don't look at you that much, do I?' I said.

'You do. But I like it, so don't worry.'

While Sophie gardened, she talked to the moss. Whenever she knew I was in earshot, she quietened to a whisper, but when I watched her from inside the house, her mouth moved freely, bending down, and conversing with her moss as you would small children, as if the moss was talking back to her. I knew it was common to talk to plants in the belief it helped them grow, and I wondered what moss would like to talk about. But was she talking to moss, or was she talking to Eugene? Sometimes, through an open window, I heard her sing softly to the moss, songs I didn't recognise. She'd sing a few lines and then hum the words she'd forgotten.

'Your tea's getting cold,' I said.

'The mosses all like unique conditions,' she said, walking over, holding moss in her hand. 'This little one likes exposed limestone surfaces.' She showed me a fine-textured sage-coloured moss. 'And this one likes to be sheltered.' She held up a glossy, seaweed green moss, handling it like a rare object in danger of crumbling when touched.

Sophie gently laid her moss on the patio and took her tea, sipping it delicately to test the temperature before tipping back her head and drinking it all, gasping when she'd finished.

'Do you think it's beautiful?' she asked, nodding at the garden.

The moss was thriving in the garden.

She'd created something special.

'It's amazing.'

'You really think so?'

'It's very special.'

I returned to the house.

On the kitchen table, smeared with soil, sat Sophie's notebook, stretching at the binding, swollen with Polaroids, and scribbled notes. She wouldn't mind if I flicked through it.

I opened it up, the pages lightly stuck together by the Polaroid photographs' tacky surface, and marvelled at Sophie's perfect composition and use of light, giving the pictures a timeless quality.

The descriptions of the moss in the notebook were growing in scientific detail: Latin names that sounded like magic spells—*Didymodon sinuosus*, and *Orthotrichum anomalum*, and *Barbula convoluta*, using technical names for the structure of the mosses like seta, capsule, and epiphyte.

And I loved the little poems she wrote about each moss.

Cobalt Green in shade
The faithful walk past daily
Crumbling wall, churchyard

And this one near the back of the book:

Sap and Prussian Green
Cracked concrete under park bench
Hiding from my feet

I admired the annotated black and white illustrations she'd continued to draw of moss under her microscope—carefully crafted, with incredible detail captured in fine lines of ink. She was interested only in accuracy, not interpretation like an artist. There were no nuances of light and shade, just the outline, a cartoon image of a moss. Alien-looking shapes, like triffids: some hairy, some spiky, some elongated, some stubby, some with capsules on the end of long stems.

'You're looking at my book,' Sophie said, standing behind me.

I hadn't noticed her come in.

'I was interested. You don't mind, do you?'

'No. But you should have asked first.'

She washed mud off her hands in the kitchen sink.

'Have you ever studied photography?' I asked, as I looked at a photo of moss sparkling with dew, spots of sunlight flaring over the image.

'Someone taught me the basics once.'

'They taught you well.'

'They taught me a lot of stuff.'

'Who was it?'

'Just a friend.'

The glossy gardening magazines Sophie was fond of were being replaced by moss books and journals regularly dropping through the letterbox. Mosses of the British Isles, Journal of Bryology, and Field Bryology, lay on our living room coffee table, often open at particular pages Sophie would study for ages.

Many of the moss books were old, with worn corners and yellowed pages. I couldn't decide if they were cheap because no one else would want them or expensive because they were rare.

As Sophie gardened one afternoon, I scanned through one of the moss books, fascinated by the detail of some of the illustrations and the scientific wordiness of the text, when the sun brightened the living room, and a ray of light reflected off something on the bookshelf into my eyes.

I walked over for a closer look.

'Where did you come from?' I asked it.

It was a golden fish, curled in a snake-like helix, balanced on its tail, mouth gaping at the top. It gleamed, untarnished, not a speck of dust upon it. I picked it up. It was heavy, solid metal, perhaps brass. I turned it over in my hands—it looked a lot like Sophie's fish tattoo.

Placing it back with my greasy fingerprints upon it, I decided to clean it before asking Sophie where it came from. I brought a duster from the kitchen and rubbed it clean, smiling at the thought a genie might pop out of it and grant me three wishes.

I returned to the sofa and stared at the fish. A pulsing halo of light surrounded it. It drew me into a trance, staring at it shimmering in the sunlight. There was a faint hum coming from somewhere. A headache was growing between my eyes.

Sophie came in from the garden, her head appearing around the door.

'Have you come in for lunch?' I asked.

'Lunch?' She sounded confused.

I looked at the clock on the wall—it was half-past-six in the evening. I must have fallen asleep. But I didn't remember sleeping—I'd been staring at the fish.

'Are you okay?' Sophie asked. 'It looks like you've seen a ghost.'

My headache was painful. I rubbed my forehead.

'I'm fine,' I said. 'Where did the fish come from?' I pointed to the shelves.

'I've had it for ages,' she said. 'I thought I'd put it on display.' She walked over to it. The halo of light surrounding it had disappeared.

'Where did you get it?'

'It was a present.'

'From who?'

Sophie thought a moment, slowly running her finger down the length of the fish, head to tail.

'I don't remember.'

'It's weird.'

'Weird, how?' she asked.

I didn't want to mention the pulsing light, so I shrugged.

'I don't like some of your stuff either, but the fish stays,' she said.

She looked back at me as I continued to massage my head.

'Are you feeling all right?' she said.

'I'll be okay in a minute.'

Sophie went to change out of her gardening clothes.

My headache worsened, and I skipped dinner for an early night, telling Sophie I had a stomach ache. Upstairs, I found our bed covered in new fern-green cotton sheets—a bed of moss. I smoothed my hand over the sheets, feeling their softness, before undressing and gliding into bed naked. The pillowcase smoothed my cheek. The duvet hugged me like a child's cuddly toy. My headache eased, and I slept deeply, better than I had for months.

At work the next day, my head remained clear—I felt refreshed, re-energised, renewed. The day flew by, and I drove home happily, tapping the steering wheel to pop music on the radio.

Arriving home, Sophie was sitting at the kitchen table, reading a moss book, a towel wrapped snug around her body, and another wound like a turban around her head. The aroma of chlorine seeped from her warm, damp body.

'I've dyed my hair,' she said.

I microwaved a chilli con carne leftover from the night before, and we ate. Sophie talked about the moss book she was reading.

'It's written by someone with Native American ancestry. She describes mosses so beautifully, like she's got a genuine connection with them. I feel that connection too.'

When we'd finished dinner, Sophie unwrapped the towel from her head. Damp, her hair looked much darker than normal.

Sophie ruffled her hair with the towel, and as it fluffed-up, catching the light, I realised she'd dyed it green.

'It's green,' I said.

'Uh huh,' she said. 'Like moss.' She looked at me as if daring me to say something. When I didn't, because of shock, she went upstairs, where I heard the hair-drier running.

A little while later, she came back downstairs.

Her hair was the same shade as the moss on the lawn of our garden, the moss from Eugene Gray's grave. She looked a little like something risen from a swamp, a woodland fairy, a nuclear accident, but because she was beautiful, she looked okay—quirky, not monstrous.

'It's good, isn't it?' she said.

'It's different,' I said.

'I fancied a change.'

It would take some getting used to, but I was sort of impressed. When Sophie found something she liked, she committed one hundred percent—that now included transforming herself into moss. I hoped she'd stop short of painting her skin green.

That evening she spent ages in front of the living room mirror admiring her hair, tossing it around, deciding how best to style it, curl it, tie it up.

She came to sit with me and ruffled my hair.

'You should do something with your hair,' she said.

I'd had the same short back and sides hairstyle for years.

'Like what?'

'Grow it longer,' she said. 'It'd suit you.'

'How much longer?' I said, smoothing my hair back into place. Was she telling me she didn't like the way I looked?

'Only a bit. I think it would frame your face better.'

'Don't you like my hair?'

'It's fine, but it could look more organic. It's very neat. There's not a hair out of place, all held perfectly with that glue you put in your hair.'

'It's gel.'

'No one uses gel anymore.'

'I do.'

'Just think about it,' she said.

'I'm going to see my parents on Sunday. Do you want to come?' I asked Sophie, as we were eating breakfast the next day. I imagined the look they'd give when they saw her green hair.

'No thanks.'

I hadn't expected a different answer. Sophie still hadn't shown interest in meeting my parents.

'I've got Bryology Club, and then work, so I can't,' she said.

'We could go on Saturday instead.'

'I'd rather not.'

I finished my cornflakes as Sophie sipped her coffee.

'You should invite your parents to stay soon,' I said, changing tact. 'I'd still like to meet them.'

'No, you wouldn't,' she said flatly.

'Why not?'

'They're not the sort of people that people get on with.'

'What do you mean?'

'They're very into themselves, very selfish. They don't have time for other people.'

'Aren't you being a bit harsh?'

'No, Ben. I haven't talked to them in almost a year now and I don't miss them. They're mean and cruel, and I'm better off without them.'

She stood up and put her coffee mug in the sink.

'Whatever happened can't have been that bad?'

Sophie sighed.

'It's great that you have lovely parents, Ben, and that you get on with them, but I don't need mine. They weren't a good influence on my life. I don't want to see them. Now leave it.'

She stood by the window and stared into the garden.

'But why won't you meet my parents?' I asked.

'They're different from your parents, they're nice.'

'I'm sure they're lovely, but I don't see why I need to meet them. Do they need to vet me? Do you need their permission to see me or something?'

'Of course not.'

'You want to parade me in front of them like some prize you've won? You want me to get dressed up, do my hair and make-up nicely, smile sweetly, and make polite conversation?'

'It's not like that. They just want to meet you.'

'To make sure I'm not a massive freak?'

'No.'

'What would you do if they don't like me?'

'That wouldn't happen.'

'Come on, tell me. What if they hated me?'

'That wouldn't happen.'

'But what if they did?'

'Then I'd ignore them.'

'And you'd be able to do that? You'd be able to say, "Sorry Mummy and Daddy, but Sophie is wonderful, and I don't care what you say." And you'd be okay with that?'

'It would never happen.'

'It could.'

'You can't put off meeting them forever. What if we got married?'

Sophie laughed out loud.

'We've been going out for five minutes. Why are you talking about getting married? Are you mad?'

'Forget I said anything,' I said.

'Gladly.'

I joined Sophie by the window.

'I'm sorry,' I said, reaching out to hug her. 'I don't want to fight about it.'

Sophie shrugged me off. This was our first proper argument, and one I wouldn't win. As I pocketed my disappointment, I noted not to mention her parents again—well, not any time soon.

5

On Sunday, I knocked on my parent's door three times, and tapped four times on the adjacent window. After a moment, a nose pressed against the door's frosted window and two wide eyes surveyed me before the door opened an inch.

'Is Sophie not with you?' asked Mum through the gap. An aroma of fresh-baked pastry wafted from the kitchen.

'She can't make it,' I replied.

Mum unfastened the security chain from the door and ushered me in.

'Quick,' she said. 'Don't let the cold in.' The weather was baking hot with a clear blue sky.

As soon as I was through, she attached the chain and slid a bolt across. She checked through the window to make sure there was no one else there.

'It's just me, Mum,' I said.

She turned and hugged me, her white feathered hair tickling my nose, before stepping back to look at me.

'What happened to your head?' she asked.

'This?' I replied, tracing the cut on my forehead. 'I hit it on a beam. It's fine.'

I went through to the living room where Dad sat on the edge of his chair. Mum had dressed him for the occasion in a crisp white shirt and his silver hair was neatly brushed behind his ears. His beard had even received a trim. Despite his bad knees, he sprang up and hugged me tight.

'Good to see you, Benny,' he said. He pointed at my head. 'Ouch.'

I sat on the sofa opposite Dad as Mum prepared lunch.

'We're having quiche,' shouted Mum from the kitchen.

'It smells great,' I said. Mum had a few staple things she'd cook if people were coming round: quiche or sausage casserole for mains, apple pie or apple crumble for dessert—they were all delicious. The rest of the time my parents lived on baked potatoes with various toppings: baked beans, tuna, grated cheese, canned chopped ham.

Visiting my parents in this house always felt strange—this was not the home I grew up in. They'd moved here after I'd permanently left home after university, and I had no fond childhood memories of the place. No ornaments, keepsakes, or photographs sat on the shelves, walls, or mantlepiece—nothing to give the house personality, nothing to connect it with its owners.

'Just more things to dust,' Mum once said, when I'd asked about her aversion to objects.

When I was growing up, she was forever dusting, running between rooms with a yellow cloth, and a can of furniture polish. Our wooden furniture gleamed, tacky with polished beeswax. And if my little hands accidentally made a mark, she'd fret and clean it straight away. I learnt not to touch anything I didn't have to.

They'd moved to this new-build house because Mum liked the plainness of it. The walls were bright white, the carpets and curtains beige. An igloo would feel cosier. The house had five enormous bedrooms, decorated just as plainly—far too many for the two of them, and they rarely had guests. A long-lost cousin of Dad's visited from New Zealand once, a willowy lady who spent ten minutes each morning popping medication from packets and washing them down with organic milk.

'It must be organic,' she said, in her high-pitched voice, like she'd inhaled helium, 'or it affects my constitution.'

Otherwise, my parents floated around in the space, just the two of them.

'Where's Sophie?' asked Dad. 'Are we ever going to meet her?'

He said it jokily, but I could tell he was disappointed.

'She's working in the shop this afternoon and at her club this morning.'

'What kind of club?'

'A Bryology club.'

'A what?'

'A club for people who like moss.'

'Moss, as in, the green stuff in the garden, moss?'

'Yes.'

'How peculiar,' said Dad, reaching for the biscuit tin he kept hidden under his chair. 'Each to their own.'

He shook the biscuit tin at me. I put up a hand to say no, but he insisted, and I took a shortbread. The crumbs scattered down my front as I bit into it, and I quickly picked at them, placing them in my mouth, before they fell to the carpet and triggered Mum to start vacuuming. She wouldn't just vacuum the crumbs; she'd have to vacuum the entire house—it was one of her rituals.

'We'd come visit you both if it wasn't for Mum,' he said. 'It's a bit far for her to go. You know what she gets like.'

Dad took a gingernut biscuit from his tin.

'How's Mum been?' I whispered, leaning in close.

'Pretty good,' he nodded. 'There're good days and bad.'

She'd become worse in recent years. As a child, I just thought she was quiet and incredibly tidy. When I visited my friend's homes, the mess and clutter they lived among amazed me. And they didn't live in a fog of cleaning spray. Instead, their homes all had different, interesting smells: musty dog or garlic or wet towels.

I didn't pick up on Mum's anxiousness until I was a teenager. Until then I thought it natural that Dad would always be the one to make all the telephone calls, always the one to answer the door or make chit-chat with the neighbours. Dad did the shopping and banking. Mum rarely left the house, and when she did, she often wore sunglasses and a headscarf as if she was a film star in disguise.

But she was a great Mum and she'd do anything for me. I never felt her problems affected my upbringing.

Dad was a hero. He'd never get angry with Mum, even though her behaviour must have been frustrating. He dealt with the responsibility in his calm manner. I could tell Mum loved him deeply, and he loved her back, no matter what.

Looking back, I had a happy childhood and didn't want for anything. And they continued to look after me. I was lucky.

The sound of rattling knives and forks came from the kitchen, and Mum came in to ask for help to set the dining table.

'So, where's Sophie?' asked Mum.

'She's at a moss club,' said Dad. He crunched his gingernut biscuit so loudly I thought he may have broken his teeth.

'A what?'

Dad swallowed his mouthful.

'A club for people who like moss,' he said.

'Moss?' Confusion scrunched her face.

'Yes, Mum,' I said. 'She likes moss.'

Mum looked at Dad with raised eyebrows. He nodded at her.

'We're worried you're embarrassed of us,' said Mum. She looked at Dad to gain consensus. 'You've been living with Sophie for weeks now, and we've not even met her. She could be a serial killer for all we know.' Mum probably considered this a serious possibility.

'You'll meet her soon. I promise.'

'Does she not want to meet us?' said Mum with deep worry on her face. 'Is it because of me?'

'No, Mum, of course not. She's just shy. She'll be here next time. I promise.'

Mum handed me knives and forks, and I arranged them on the table already covered in a neat white tablecloth and set with beige place mats.

Mum served her quiche for lunch. Its soft, golden filling spiked with bacon wobbled slightly as her knife met the buttery, crumbly crust. It was a recipe she'd perfected over years.

I glanced at my phone before we ate to see if Sophie had sent a message. I imagined her in a musty hall, sat in a row of threadbare, rickety chairs staring at a projector screen showing images of moss.

'Are you and Sophie getting along okay?' asked Dad.

'Don't ask things like that, John,' said Mum, giving Dad one of her hard looks.

'It's okay, Mum.' I put my phone away. 'We're getting on fine.'

'*Fine?*' questioned Dad.

I took a bite of quiche.

'She's just been busy lately… with moss,' I said as I chewed.

'Are you treating her nicely?' he said.

'John! Of course he is. How's the quiche?'

'The quiche is great, Mum.'

'Us men are pretty useless when it comes to women. But I can give you some pointers.'

Dad winked at Mum.

'You should be the last person he should ask for advice.' She smiled at him. 'You don't always get it right, you know.'

Dad pulled a sad face.

'But you do try,' she conceded.

I forked quiche into my mouth and imagined Sophie being here. My parents were friendly people, they made anyone feel welcome. They wouldn't pry much or ask too many awkward questions. If I could convince Sophie to come, I knew she'd enjoy it. They'd spoil her. She'd sit at the head of the dining table, radiant and beautiful, making polite conversation, enjoying the food. She'd charm them.

Seeing I'd drifted off into a daydream, Dad said, 'Don't worry about Sophie. It's just the end of the honeymoon period. It happens. Relationships are hard work.'

I finished my food.

'You might as well eat it all up,' said Mum, putting the last of the quiche and salad on my plate.

When finished, my stomach was so full it ached and juddered, as if the food was trying to find a way out, up or down, but the food was so tasty my body wouldn't let it escape.

'What was the name of that girl you used to go out with at university?' asked Dad, wiping crumbs from the corner of his mouth and sitting back in his chair.

'Why are you asking him that, John?' said Mum.

'I'm just trying to remember,' he said. 'Millie?'

'Margaret,' I said. 'Maggie.'

'She was an odd one,' he said.

'John!'

'Well, she was. She was very—' He searched for the right word.

'Direct,' said Mum.

'That's not the word I was looking for. Rude. She was quite rude.'

Maggie had been my one and only girlfriend before Sophie. She'd lived with my flatmate's girlfriend, and we'd met half-way through our first year at university when my flat mate took me along to his girlfriend's house for the evening. Maggie had short, dark hair, a sharp nose, and wore austere black clothing. She was pretty, but her face was set in a permanent scowl.

She curtly introduced herself and looked me up and down before sitting in a corner and remaining silent for most of the evening. But when our respective friends disappeared to have sex, leaving Maggie and me alone to watch a dull film and drink cheap vodka, we talked.

'What are you studying?' I asked.

'I don't know you,' she said. 'I don't know what you'd do with that information.'

In the awkwardness, the quantity and rate of our drinking increased. My eyelids grew heavy, and I was about to fall asleep on the sofa when Maggie slid beside me and kissed me forcefully on the lips. I returned her kiss, and soon her tongue was deep down my throat, almost choking me. We'd pause, but on finding nothing to say, took another drink, and leapt back into the action. It felt like we were kissing for hours. My lips were dry and my jaw ached. Then Maggie suddenly stroked my hard penis through my jeans, and I ejaculated into my underpants. I stopped kissing, removed myself from her grip, and stood up. She looked insulted.

'Where are you going?' she asked.

'I need the toilet,' I said, red-faced.

I drunkenly stumbled to the bathroom, removed my jeans & underpants, and cleaned up the sticky mess as best I could. It had spread down my thighs, painfully sticking leg hairs together, and I couldn't wash it off entirely.

'Are you okay in there?' Maggie shouted through the door.

I said, 'Yes,' in a weird and wobbly high-pitched tone.

I dried myself and shoved my underpants to the bottom of the bathroom bin, covering them over with tissues, cotton wool, and tampon wrappers. When I returned to the living room Maggie had disappeared, but she'd left me a bare, age-yellowed duvet with a wide, brown stain in the centre. Smelling of stale semen, I stretched out on the sofa, covered myself with the duvet, and fell asleep.

The next morning, she woke me by offering a cup of tea and suggested we go out for breakfast.

'The lovebirds are still at it,' she said. 'I can hear them through the wall.'

Over breakfast, in a small cafe across the road, we agreed we'd go out for dinner that night. I'm almost certain she didn't find me attractive, and as she ate her pancakes, I examined her face to satisfy myself she did have the ability to smile.

I was curious to know what sex was like. My peers were coupled-up or shagging around, and Maggie seemed my best hope of experiencing it for myself. Normally, I couldn't talk to women. I flushed and stammered, came across as weird. I'd never dream of walking up to a girl and asking her out—that was something in the realm of impossible. And rather than pluck up the courage, I told myself I was too busy studying and didn't have time for a serious relationship, or that the right girl would come along. But I could talk to Maggie. Maybe Maggie was the right girl? Maybe.

Maggie and I had dinner in an Italian with a loud and jolly Italian owner who walked the tables telling us how delicious his food was in fragmented English, and after a doughy pizza and two bottles of strong House Red, as I hoped, we ended up in bed. It was fierce sex, without preamble. Maggie was firmly in control, placing my body and hands where she wanted them. And when finished, she changed into her pyjamas and fell asleep. I lay awake, my body tingling. For a first time, it was unforgettable.

During the few social events we went to together, Maggie was rude to anyone and everyone. She'd walk off in the middle of conversations or cut off people's sentences. I'd never have introduced her to my parents if they hadn't decided upon a surprise visit to my student flat one Sunday morning when Maggie and I were still asleep. They knocked steadily on the front door for five minutes as I cursed whoever it was, hoping my flatmate would answer, before rousing myself sufficiently to open it.

Mum held a cake tin and Dad struggled with a cardboard box stuffed with cans of food and pasta. I showed them in and Maggie appeared dressed in her black pyjamas, looking furious.

Mum blushed. 'Sorry, we didn't know you had company.'

'Are you going to introduce us?' asked Dad.

'This is Maggie,' I said. And then, despite a look from Maggie that predicted what I'd say and urged me not to, I told my parents she was my girlfriend. My first proper girlfriend.

Maggie's look could have slashed my arteries.

Mum and Dad looked delighted.

'Shall I put the kettle on?' asked Mum nervously.

We all sat down together in the living room, Maggie squirming as my parents quizzed her. She gave vague, clipped answers, before suddenly disappearing to the bedroom, returning fully dressed, and without a word left the house.

'She's just shy,' I said to my wide-eyed, shocked parents.

When my parents had gone, I met up with Maggie that evening. She was in a foul mood.

'I'm not your girlfriend,' she told me. 'I don't belong to you. I don't belong to anyone.'

'I just thought—'

We went to our separate homes that night but continued to meet up. We'd never talked much, but now we barely spoke. She was using me. I was using her, I guess. She always came over to my flat, she didn't want me at hers. During sex she came quickly but let me finish before she dressed and left.

The relationship ended when I saw her leave a crowded bar, arms linked with a tall, thin boy dressed like a vampire. We never spoke again.

I'd still think of Maggie, my first, my only, until I met Sophie. Sophie was amazing in comparison.

Dad continued, 'I'm glad you didn't stay with Maggie. She wasn't very good for you. I hope Sophie's better?'

'John! You can't ask that.'

'I can worry about him, can't I?' he said.

'She's much better than Maggie,' I replied.

'Well, I hope she looks after you. When you had your little episode, your mum and I were so worried. You need to talk to us if things aren't working out. We can help. Let us know if you're stressed. Don't let it build up like it did before. That's why things went wrong.'

'He's okay now, aren't you, Ben? You know we're here if you need us.'

We had an unwritten rule not to talk about my "episode" and acted like it never happened on the understanding that if I felt it coming on again, I'd be honest and tell them.

'I'm fine,' I said. Fine, apart from the headache that was building.

Mum cut us each a slice of warm apple pie. I poured thick, steaming custard over the top, and despite feeling stuffed, devoured it.

Afterwards, I asked whether I could have some painkillers for my head.

'Are you okay, Benny?' asked Mum. 'Are you coming down with something?'

'It's just a headache, Mum.'

She fetched me two tablets and a glass of water.

'Thanks,' I said, gulping them down. 'I should be off now.'

I hugged Mum goodbye, and Dad walked me outside to my car.

'It would be good if we could meet Sophie. It's really worrying your mum we've not seen her,' he said.

I promised I'd arrange something soon. Sophie couldn't hold out forever.

As I drove home, my mobile rang.

'A woman died in the shop,' said Sophie on the other end of the phone. 'Will you come and fetch me?'

When I arrived, Sophie was pacing outside the shop, smoking a cigarette. I'd never seen her smoke before. She smiled when she saw me and took a deep drag, exhaling a long ribbon of grey smoke through her nostrils. She stubbed the cigarette under the heel of her trainer and got in the car.

'Thanks for coming to get me,' she said.

She hunched forward, shivering as if cold. Her hands shook, clasped together.

'What happened?'

'Drive us home,' she said.

As we waited at traffic lights, Sophie said, 'It was Alan's mum. Alan's mum died.'

'The weird guy from the shop?'

She nodded.

'They came in to pick up his regular order and she looked ill, like, really ill. Her face was white, pouring sweat, and she said she felt dizzy, like bath water was sloshing around in her skull.'

I remembered a similar feeling before I'd passed out in the pub.

I placed my hand on Sophie's trembling knee.

'We sat her down. Then she just sort of froze. Her eyes bulged, almost bursting out of their sockets, and her head flopped to the side as if attached by a thread.'

The traffic lights turned green. I removed my hand from Sophie's leg and drove on.

'It was terrifying,' said Sophie. 'Alan was panicking, and Emily slapped his mum on the face trying to wake her.'

Sophie stared through the sunroof at drifting grey clouds.

'I could tell she was dead,' she said. 'Emily called an ambulance, and we locked the shop door.'

Sophie took her cigarette packet from her bag. Her fingers shook as she placed a cigarette between her lips and lit it. Acrid smoke filled the car, and I fumbled to open my window, coughing before the cold air rushed in.

'I'm worried about Alan,' she said.

I didn't know what to say. His life was going to be turned upside-down, and I couldn't imagine how he'd cope with the loss of his mother. 'I'm sure he'll be fine.'

'I don't think he will,' she said. 'He's very sensitive.'

Sophie took a long bath that evening. I called up to her several times to check she was okay.

'Yes, thank you,' she said each time.

When I took her a cup of tea, she was already out of the bath, in bed, and asleep.

Preparing to leave for work the next morning, I asked her if she'd be all right.

'I'm having the day off,' she said, staring vacantly into her coffee.

I hugged her. She was trembling slightly, not visible, but a tiny vibration felt through my body.

'I can stay with you, if you like?' I said. 'I'll call in sick.'

'I'd rather be alone.'

She sounded so sad and helpless.

'If you need anything, call me,' I said.

As sad as it was, Sophie had not been close to Alan's mum, nor really to Alan—they were people who popped into the shop occasionally. But this fresh grief was likely a reminder of Eugene. So, to make sure she was okay, I rang Sophie at lunchtime. She sounded distracted, like I'd disturbed her in the middle of something.

'How are you doing?' I asked.

'Fine.'

'Should I pick up something nice for dinner?'

'No need.'

'Okay, I'll get back to work then,' I said.

'Bye.'

She hung up.

There was an odd smell in the house when I arrived home: cabbagy, sulphurous.

'I made dinner,' said Sophie, appearing in the hallway, her voice brighter than when I'd left her. 'It's ready. Come and sit down.'

Sophie rarely cooked. When she did, it was usually something quick: something she could throw in the oven or microwave and forget about until the timer pinged.

She whistled a tune to herself as she placed a plate in front of me. Pungent steam rose from a huge portion of sprawling spaghetti strands covered in a glossy, rich brown Bolognese sauce. I sniffed it and had to turn my nose from the odour. It was the smell of something rotting.

'It looks great,' I said, poking around with my fork, trying to identify all the ingredients. Sophie smiled opposite me, waiting for me to take a bite.

I stuck my fork deep into the spaghetti and twisted the surrounding strands. Tentatively, I put the fork in my mouth. To my surprise, it tasted like regular Bolognese. I grinned at her, and she began to eat.

As I chewed, grit crunched between my molars and scoured my cheeks. I swallowed the mouthful and drank some water. It left me with a bitter taste. Sophie shoved huge forkfuls into her mouth in rapid succession, sauce coating her chin.

'What's the crunchy stuff?' I asked. Sophie looked at me blankly.

'Have you put moss in this?' I said, placing my fork down on the plate.

'Only a little,' she said through a full mouth of spaghetti. She sucked up a long, loose strand between pursed lips. 'I like it.'

'It's gritty and it tastes weird.' I drank more water, swilling it round my mouth, flushing it through my teeth, and swallowing. The bitterness lingered. 'Sorry. I can't eat this.'

I took the plate and dropped it by the sink. 'I'll leave it here in case you want more.' My hunger was making me angry.

Sophie shrugged and continued eating.

I searched the cupboards for something I could prepare quickly. I banged each one closed as I found nothing to eat.

'What made you want to eat moss? No-one eats moss except reindeer,' I said, my voice raised.

She put down her fork.

'Can you try to be nice, please? I don't need you shouting at me,' she said. 'It's been a crap couple of days.'

I took a deep breath and said sorry, kissing her on the forehead.

'Anyway, reindeer don't eat moss,' she said.

'Yes, they do. They eat Reindeer Moss. I saw it on telly once.'

'Reindeer Moss is actually a lichen.' She picked up her fork and continued to eat.

'What's the difference?' I asked.

Sophie paused until she'd finished her mouthful.

'A moss is a plant. A lichen is a symbiotic partnership of a fungus and either an alga or cyanobacteria or both.'

I nodded, grudgingly impressed.

I found a box of cereal hidden on top of the fridge and poured some into a bowl with milk. Sophie chased the last of her spaghetti around the plate as I sat back at the table.

'I did some research,' she said. 'Moss contains almost all the nutrients you need to live.'

'Almost? What's missing?' I asked. The cereal was stale and chewy. I pushed the bowl away from me.

'Nothing I'd need to worry about,' she said.

That evening, I noticed a deep buzz coming from the

sofa. I squeezed my hand between the cushions and gripped Sophie's vibrating mobile phone.

'Your phone's ringing,' I shouted, hoping she'd hear me. She'd been in the bathroom for ages.

It was Emily calling, so I answered it.

'I've been trying to get hold of Sophie all day,' she said. 'Is she okay?'

Before I replied, Sophie snatched the phone from my hand and ended the call.

'Who was that?' she asked.

I was stunned for a moment.

'Emily. She only wanted to—'

'Don't answer my phone, okay?' Sophie switched her phone off and shoved it in her jeans pocket. 'Okay?'

I nodded.

'Your hair's not green anymore,' I said. She'd dyed it back to a natural-looking colour, slightly more mahogany than her normal chestnut.

'I looked a bit like a witch, didn't you think? So I changed it back.'

'I like it.'

'I like you,' she said, standing on tiptoes and kissing my forehead.

After the Bolognese incident, Sophie told me we'd need to make our own meals. She'd continue eating moss, and if I didn't want it, I'd have to cook my own food.

'That's not very economical,' I said.

She smiled.

'That's a very accountant thing to say,' she replied.

As I prepared my dinner in the evenings, I'd watch Sophie in the garden from the kitchen window. She'd hover over her patch of moss, deciding which moss she'd eat that night.

'It's best eaten fresh,' she said. 'It doesn't store well.'

Sophie would harvest her chosen moss using a small trowel to prise it from the earth. She shook the moss to remove large clumps of soil and rubbed off more with her fingers. Mostly, she'd use a single type of moss, but occasionally she'd blend various mosses together— different colours and textures. After harvesting, Sophie's moss patch looked like a checkerboard, until she filled the gaps with new moss gathered from the neighbourhood. She didn't use chemicals: no fertilisers or pesticides.

'Mosses are so great at absorbing stuff, I wouldn't be able to wash the pesticides away,' she said. 'It's totally organic.'

Sophie washed the moss aggressively in a colander to remove any remaining soil, drained it, and patted it dry with a tea towel, before using it in her next meal.

One day she made herself a chicken salad with lettuce, tomatoes, and grated carrot, with a sprinkling of moss, and balsamic dressing on top.

The next day, she wrapped a cod fillet in a sheet of moss and baked it in the oven. It looked good. It smelt rotten. I opened all the windows.

'You can't seriously enjoy eating that?' I asked.

'Yummy,' replied Sophie, as she forked it into her mouth.

The day after, she ate vegetable soup, cooked low and slow to tenderise a firmer, woodier-textured moss. There was enough left over for dinner the next day, which she ate with a huge chunk of crusty white bread and a glass of red wine.

In the mornings, Sophie filled a blender with bananas, apples, kale, seeds, and moss to make a thick khaki-green smoothie. She drank it down in one go, as if chugging beer, slamming down the cup in triumph.

At the weekend, it disgusted me to catch her

snacking on moss from a plastic tub.

'Just try it,' she said. 'This is a good one.'

I had to admit that Sophie looked well: trimmer, brighter skin, glossier hair. There was a cheerful lilt to her voice, a sparkle in her eye. She even walked differently—bouncier, quicker steps.

'Perhaps you've discovered something with your moss diet,' I said, as Sophie and I cuddled in bed. 'You look good.'

'I feel good,' she said. She stroked my cheek and stared into my eyes. 'Hey, a few of us are going for a drink tomorrow after the Bryology Club meeting. Partners are welcome. You should join us.'

I declined.

'They're nice people,' she pleaded. 'You've always wanted to meet my friends before.'

'I just don't think I'd enjoy it.' I wouldn't have anything in common with them. It would be awkward for all of us.

'Well, don't say I didn't give you the option.'

We kissed goodnight. Her breath smelt of freshly cut flowers, garden mint, and boiled sweets—nothing at all like the moss she was devouring. She rolled and pulled the duvet tight across her.

'Are you going to tell them you're eating moss?' I asked.

She switched off her bedside light and didn't reply.

Sophie travelled to London for Bryology Club on Saturday, and I stayed at home. My head ached, and I spent the morning reading a book and watching an old black and white film. At lunchtime, I took tablets to ease my headache, and fell asleep on the sofa, only waking as Sophie repeatedly tapped me on the knee.

'I slept with someone from Bryology club,' she said.

I sat up and rubbed my eyes. 'What?'

'I said, I slept with someone from the club.'

It felt like someone had punched me from inside my body, somewhere behind the stomach.

'Are you joking?' I asked.

'It was the club chairman, Martin.'

'Martin?'

Sophie reached for my hand, but I shook it off.

'I don't want you to be angry. It won't happen again.'

I jumped up and barged past Sophie to the other side of the room.

'I can't believe this,' I said, shaking my groggy head. 'Why?'

'It just happened. We had a few drinks and went back to his house. We looked at his moss photos and things went from there.'

My stomach was being squeezed. My brain span in my skull like a carousel.

'Things don't just happen!' I screamed. Was this a dream?

She shrugged.

'Does Martin lure a lot of girls into bed with his fucking moss pictures?' I said.

She laughed, then put her hand over her mouth to stop. She was a little drunk.

'Maybe. He's quite ugly, though. And old. And rubbish in bed. You've got nothing to worry about.' Sophie approached with outstretched arms, trying to hold me. I stepped back and bumped into the wall.

'If he's old and ugly, why the fuck did you sleep with him?'

'It just happened,' she repeated.

My body shook. My hands danced wildly in front of me.

'I'm hoping, because I've been honest, you won't

make a big deal out of this,' she said.

I paced the room. My hands opened and closed fists.

'Of course it's a big deal. You've cheated on me.'

'Not really,' she pleaded. 'It was a one-off.'

I took a deep breath and forced myself to stand still.

'You really think this is okay, don't you?' I asked.

'I can tell you're upset.'

'Anyone would be upset! How would you like it if I slept with someone?'

'Like who?' she stifled her laughter.

'Anyone!'

I ran upstairs to the bedroom, pulled the duvet over me, and curled up like a baby.

Sophie shouted up the stairs, 'I thought you'd be grown-up about this.'

Unable to control this intensity of emotion, this barrage of feeling, my cheeks quivered, my eyes watered. I cried. I'd not cried since childhood. Tears came in deep, short bursts, leaving me breathless. I wiped my tears with a pillow. It became humid under the duvet, my skin became clammy, and I wafted the duvet to be swathed in cool air.

Questions flashed through my brain:

Why?

Why did she do it?

Why Martin?

What's wrong with me?

What's wrong with her?

Did she love me?

Did she love me like I loved her?

Did I love her?

Was it my fault?

There was no time to consider each question before the next forced its way in.

I heard Sophie walking up the stairs and held my

breath to stop crying. The floorboards creaked where she watched me from the doorway—a big lump under the duvet. After a moment, I heard her go downstairs again. I gasped for breath, and my tears returned.

Images of Martin and Sophie played in my mind. I pictured Martin, tweed suit covered in moss and dirt, shaggy grey hair, bulbous nose, and wild demon-eyes, his warped penis protruding from loose-fitting trousers, and Sophie knelt in front of him, her lustrous brown hair swaying while he shouts in ecstasy, 'Moss. Moss. Moss. Moss. Moss!'

At some point, I drifted off.

On waking, the sun was setting, and the house was silent. I sensed Sophie had gone. I went downstairs. Sophie was nowhere to be seen. The house felt abandoned and lifeless, the air cold and still. Had she left me? Run away with Martin?

I stared through the kitchen window. Fine drizzle fell from a pink sky. In a daze, I opened the door and walked barefoot across the moss lawn. The various colours and shapes of each section of moss reminded me of plane journeys high over the British countryside, each field coloured by different crops. I stroked the moss with my toes, feeling the damp shaggy-rug texture of some, the scratchiness of others. As I stood upon the moss, water squeezed out like it would from a sponge, the cool liquid ran into the gaps between my toes. I wiped rain from my face and was peeling off my T-shirt to feel the raindrops on my body when Sophie coughed from the kitchen doorway.

'We ran out of coffee.' She waved a jar of coffee at me. 'Do you want a drink?'

I towelled myself dry and changed clothes. We drank our coffee in the living room, staring at the television in silence. I sat on a chair while Sophie curled up on the sofa, huddled around her large mug, steam dampening her face.

I wanted Sophie to say sorry. To apologise, and not stop apologising, until each apology had taken away a tiny bit of hurt with it. But she sat sipping coffee as if nothing had happened.

Occasionally, she'd look over and I ducked my head to hide my bloodshot eyes and red cheeks. I hated her. I hated her and loved her—a confusing, dizzying sensation. I wanted to shout, to start an argument, just to get her talking.

'Hey, Sophie,' I said. 'Who's Eugene?'

She almost dropped her mug into her lap. She sat up and perched on the edge of the sofa.

'How do you know about Eugene?'

'I saw you at the cemetery.'

'You were spying on me?'

'No.'

She glared at me with narrow eyes.

'So, who is he?' I asked.

'None of your business.'

She continued to glare. Her mouth tightly shut, quivering at the corners.

'Did you cheat on him, too?' I asked.

She sprang off the sofa like a cat, a blur, and slapped me across the face. My neck jarred. I bit my tongue. A metallic taste flooded my mouth. I formed a fist. My arm tensed—it wanted to fly.

Sophie shoved me back in my chair, pinning me to where I sat, and held her face close to mine, so our eyelashes touched, and her damp, hot, panting breath blasted my face.

She spat out, 'Fuck. You,' and ran from the room.

I'd hurt Sophie. I'd got one back on her. And it was out in the open that I knew about Eugene. It was good to get the secret out that had gnawed at my insides for weeks.

Maybe I should have thrown her out of the house. But that night, Sophie slept in the spare room's single-bed, surrounded by junk: old clothes, empty suitcases, and cardboard boxes. Through the wall, I heard her fidgeting in bed.

I lay awake, cradling my sore cheek in my palm.

I'd never felt so alone.

On Sunday, Sophie and I lived as ghosts. I'd hear footsteps on the kitchen tiles, the toilet flushing, coughing, cutlery placed in a drawer. I'd catch glimpses of her and she'd be gone.

I lay in bed most of the day, poisoned by a strange numbing drug. I couldn't eat. Instead, I sipped water, its coldness aching in my empty stomach. My cheek was sore and red, but hadn't bruised.

On Monday, I went to work. I forced smiles and feigned laughter as I chatted to colleagues.

'Did you have a good weekend?' they asked.

'Just a quiet one at home,' I said.

'That's nice though sometimes, isn't it?' they said.

At my desk, I replied to emails, listening to music on my headphones, drowning out the office chatter. I played songs I'd not listened to for years, songs I thought would cheer me up, but all the lyrics became about the hurt Sophie had caused. After one particular song, I rushed to the toilet to hide my teary eyes.

At lunchtime, I sought refuge from the office clamour. Behind the office building sat a walled garden. Neat shrubs bordered a square of raked gravel upon which sat four wooden picnic benches. Ivy-covered walls shielded the garden from the wind and captured the sun's warmth. I was alone in the garden. It was like a secret place, visible from the office, but no one seemed to see it but me. I took a seat and ate a sandwich.

As I held my face to the sun, its heat warming my closed eyelids, I tried to push out any thoughts of Sophie. Suddenly, I heard the crunch of gravel and opened my eyes to see a young woman approaching.

'Do you mind if I sit here?' she asked.

I motioned for her to take a seat.

Her short bob of blonde hair shined silver in the bright sunlight. She wore a smart white blouse and black skirt. She sat down, facing me.

'I saw you from upstairs,' she said. 'It looked so sunny, I thought I'd join you. You're Ben, aren't you? I'm Elise, from Customer Services.'

She offered me her hand to shake. It was cool, soft, small, and the handshake gentle, like holding the leaf of a delicate house plant. Elise opened a plastic container and began to eat a salad.

'I've never been out here before,' she said, pausing between mouthfuls. 'It's peaceful.'

As Elise ate, I admired the garden's plants and listened nervously to birds chattering within a bush adorned with orange berries.

With a flutter, a sparrow flew from the bush and perched upon the end of the picnic bench. Elise smiled and I hid my unease at its appearance. The bird studied Elise's food. Elise slowly took a crouton from her salad and placed it on the bench between us. The bird hopped to the crouton, its feet tapping on the wood, so close we could stroke its feathers. It tilted its head, grabbed the crouton in its beak, and flitted away over the wall. We stared after it.

'A few of us are going out for drinks tonight,' said Elise, breaking the silence. 'You should join us. It might cheer you up.'

'Do I look that miserable?' I asked.

'You kind of do, yes.'

At five o'clock, Elise asked me if I was coming to the pub. I said I was. I took my phone from my pocket to text Sophie I'd be back late, then changed my mind. Would she care?

I joined Elise and three colleagues on the brief walk to the pub and as we arrived I offered to buy everyone the first drink.

'No, it's okay. I'll get these,' said Elise.

The five of us sat at a table near the window. Elise and I soon broke into our own conversation as the three others chatted together. We talked about work. We talked about the news. We talked about the weather, and our favourite TV shows, and what food we liked. We talked about holidays and where we'd like to travel. We learned about each other's families and friends and the towns in which we grew up. We talked about how nice it was to meet new people. We shared a bag of salt & vinegar crisps and I licked the grease and salt from my fingers. I already felt like I knew Elise better than I knew Sophie.

As I waited at the bar for another drink, Sophie texted me.

Where are you?

I didn't reply.

The evening passed quickly and the bell rang for last orders.

'One last drink?' I asked the others.

They declined.

'I think we've had enough,' said Elise.

I swayed on my feet when we left the pub. The night

had turned cold. Elise hugged her coat tight around her and I sunk my hands deep in my pockets, doing a little dance to keep warm. I headed towards the nearest taxi rank with Elise. The other three lived nearby and would walk home.

There was just one black cab at the taxi rank.

'Do you want to share it?' asked Elise.

Elise gave the driver her address. I told him I'd go on from there.

It was dark and cool in the back of the taxi. We sat at opposite ends of the back seat. As the taxi turned corners, a sea of beer surged against the rubber walls of my stomach. A dull ache was forming around my temples.

In the taxi's isolation, we found ourselves with nothing else to say—things were suddenly awkward. I noted how Elise sat on her hands, her bare legs stretched out, rising up and down with toes pointed. She bit her bottom lip. Her forehead and nose shined.

'It's just round the corner,' Elise told the taxi driver. She turned to me and said, 'I hope you've enjo—.'

I leaned forward and kissed her. A clumsy kiss, landing in the corner of her mouth, half lips, half cheek. Then the sharp turn of the taxi threw me sideways, and our teeth clashed. She pushed me away with a firm hand against my chest. Her smiling face transformed to stern disapproval.

'It's just here,' she said to the driver.

The taxi came to a slow stop, and Elise handed me a ten-pound note.

'No, I'll pay,' I said.

'Take it.' She pressed the note into my hand and closed my fingers around it. Her small hands were icy cold. 'Goodnight.'

Elise stepped out of the taxi and slammed the door. I

watched her weave through a neat yard of terracotta flowerpots to her front door.

'Where to, mate?' asked the taxi driver.

Elise opened her front door and stepped in. The taxi took me home on the other side of town.

When I arrived home, I stumbled upstairs to the bathroom, and vomited beer, and the soggy remains of crisps, into the toilet. The sound must have woken Sophie, but she didn't come to check on me. I sat, head over the toilet, until I was sure I'd finished.

I lifted my shirt over my head and smelt Elise's perfume clinging to it. I buried my clothes at the bottom of the laundry hamper, piling other dirty clothes on top. The smell of perfume still lingered. I sniffed my forearm—the perfume deep in my skin. I showered with plenty of soap and scrubbed with a brush until my skin turned red. I dried myself and crept to the bedroom. The bed was empty—Sophie had slept in the spare room again. I fell asleep, haunted by the smell of Elise and the cold touch of her small hands.

Expecting to feel the terrible effects of the previous night's alcohol, I woke with only my throat sore from thirst. When I went downstairs for a drink of water, Sophie was at the kitchen table preparing a roll-up cigarette, sprinkling something on top of the tobacco. I almost walked back out—I wasn't ready to see her yet, but I was intrigued. Sophie slept around and now took drugs. What was going on with her?

'Are you smoking cannabis?' I asked. My voice croaked with dryness.

'It's not cannabis,' she said. 'It's moss.'

I sighed. Of course, it was moss. I filled a glass of water.

Sophie licked the cigarette paper and rolled it in to a

neat, tapered cone.

'You were back late last night,' she said. 'Where were you?'

'I went for a drink.'

'And you didn't think to tell me?'

'Why should I?'

'Because I was worried.'

I snorted a laugh.

She pulled a lighter from her jeans pocket and went to the garden. I watched her through the kitchen door.

Sophie lit the cigarette and took a deep drag, blowing the yellow smoke upwards as she exhaled, the breeze carrying it away. She took another drag and immediately coughed out the smoke. Then coughed again, and again, spluttering. Sophie dropped the cigarette and bent over, retching. I rushed out the kitchen door.

'Are you okay?' I asked, stroking her back.

'Water,' she rasped.

I handed her my glass. Sophie was dry heaving. A thin trail of saliva hung from her mouth.

'Drink it.'

She braced herself to stop the coughing, drank it down, and handed me back the glass.

'More, please.' She sounded a little better. I went to refill the glass and handed it back to her.

'Come and sit,' I said, taking her hand and leading her to the kitchen as she leaned on me. It felt good she needed me, if only for a moment.

'I bet you think that was stupid of me?'

'Yes.'

'I know,' she said. 'Perhaps it's not the right type of moss?'

I left Sophie still coughing, though much better, and went to work, dreading the thought of seeing Elise. I felt the eyes of the office upon me as I walked in. People whispered in corners. Muffled laughter passed through closed doors. When colleagues said hello, they did it with sly and knowing looks.

I was making a strong coffee when Elise sidled up.

'Have you recovered from last night?' she asked.

I nodded.

'Sorry, I got carried away,' I murmured.

'That's okay.' Elise grabbed a cup and made a cup of tea while I stirred my coffee. It needed more milk.

'You have a girlfriend, right?' she whispered.

I poured a little more milk into my mug and stirred as Elise waited for an answer. Did I still have a girlfriend?

'Yes,' I said, staring at the whirlpool I'd created in my mug.

'It's okay. You'd drunk too much,' Elise said. 'It's all forgotten.'

'Thanks,' I replied. 'Sorry, again.'

She walked away, smiling over her shoulder as she went.

Sophie was standing in the hallway when I arrived home. A creased white shirt hung loose on her body. Lit by the kitchen light from behind, I could see her slim body through the thin cotton, dark nipples showing. Long grey trousers clung to her hips, bunched around her ankles, bare toes poking out—the clothes I'd been in the day before, the clothes I'd hidden in the laundry basket, the clothes that smelt of Elise.

'Did you think I wouldn't know?' Sophie asked.

She raised the shirt up to her nose and inhaled.

'It's nice, this perfume,' she said. 'It reminds me of my grandma.'

'It's not what it seems,' I said.

'I get it. It's revenge for what I did. It's crude, but it's understandable.'

'But I haven't done anything.'

'Are you sure? At least I was honest with you. Who were you with?'

'Why do you even care?'

'Because I'm your girlfriend.'

I laughed.

'Aren't I?' she asked. She stared at me, awaiting an answer. 'You can't get rid of me. I won't let you.'

Sophie undid the top two buttons of the shirt, revealing her bare chest.

'You still love me,' she said, undoing another button. She unfastened buttons until they were all undone. Staring into my eyes, she slid the shirt off to bare her shoulder.

'I know you love me,' she said.

Sophie peeled the shirt off her other shoulder and let it fall to the ground. She looked beautiful, doe-eyed, wetting her parted lips with her tongue.

With a wiggle of her hips, the trousers fell down. She stepped out of them and slowly swayed towards me.

Sophie threw her hands over my shoulders, moulded her body to mine, breasts squashed against my chest, one leg hooked around mine, and kissed me. She unbuttoned my shirt, unzipped my trousers, and pulled me down onto the hallway floor. Elise's perfume wafted from Sophie's skin.

6

Before Sophie woke, I gathered the Elise-scented clothes lying in the hallway and bundled them into the washing machine. I heaped powder into the machine drawer and flooded it with summer-scented fabric conditioner, before setting it for a long wash with an extra rinse. My head told me I shouldn't feel this guilty. It was Sophie who'd slept with someone else—I hadn't even come close—but guilt, regret, and shame were deep in my guts, making me nauseous.

Sophie brought me a cup of tea as I prepared to leave for work.

'Sit down,' she said, pointing me towards the sofa.

I perched on the sofa's edge, holding my tea, and Sophie sat beside me.

'Do you want me to tell you about Eugene?' she asked.

For a moment, I was stunned. After all the secrecy, why tell me now? Was this and last night's sex her way of making up with me?

'Yes,' I replied, unprepared to hear what she'd say, but needing to hear it.

Rocking gently, she smoothed her knees with her hands and took a deep breath.

'He was my boyfriend before you. He died.'

So, Eugene *had* been her boyfriend.

She put her hand over her face, as if about to cry,

and I patted her leg weakly as comfort.

'It was an accident. A car crash. Very sudden. One minute he was there, and then he wasn't.'

'That's horrible, Sophie. I'm sorry.' My words felt shallow. If he hadn't died, I'd never had met Sophie.

'It was just so weird, debilitating, a limb severed from my body. I couldn't do anything but lie in bed at my parent's house crying. I didn't eat. I refused to talk to anyone—I couldn't even have them in the same room. Why couldn't I have died when he did? It got dark, Ben. Really dark. It took months to get to a point where I could start living life again and then it was mainly to escape my parents. My Dad was cruel. He'd shout, "Just snap out of it," and slap me round the face like I was hysterical. And Mum was no better, screaming at me to pull myself together, like it was that simple, like I could mend myself like a broken doll. One day, I packed a bag and walked out. I sent them a text to tell them not to try and find me, and as far as I know they never did.'

'I'm sorry t—.'

'Let me finish.' A tear escaped her eye. 'I'm not the same person I was when I was with Eugene. I'm broken. I know I am. Bits of me died with Eugene. He took bits of me with him. And now I'm not always a good person. I should never have slept with Martin. That was unforgivable. But I hope you can be okay with it. Because you are a good person. I need a good person to make me a good person. I need to be with you, only you. You know that. That's why you haven't thrown me out.'

'I couldn't throw you out. Where would you go?'

'See? You're a good person. You shouldn't have worried about that and just thrown me out. If I seriously thought you'd slept with someone else, I would have killed you. But I know you wouldn't. You're too good.'

'For a moment I wanted to.'

'But you didn't.' Sophie hugged me, nestling her head against my neck.

'You can talk to me, you know,' I said. 'You can talk about anything. Don't keep everything inside.'

Sophie nodded.

'I promise from now on I'll talk to you more,' she said, kissing me on the cheek.

'Tell me more about Eugene.'

Her eyes widened.

'What was he like?' I asked. I had to know. Eugene was a huge part of her life. He'd shaped her. He was imprinted on her. And if I knew some of him, I'd know more of Sophie.

Sophie paused.

'Where do I start?' Smiling, she took hold of my hand and looked deep into my eyes. 'He was great. Kind, loving, generous, adventurous.' She stroked my hair above my ear. 'But he had a wild streak, this loose craziness that would seize him, and nothing could talk him out of something. He shouldn't have even been driving when he was. He'd borrowed his friend's car to pick up an old record he'd become obsessed with—he couldn't trust the post office to deliver it because it was so fragile—but he didn't even have a driving licence. It was all his fault—speeding in the rain. It was lucky he didn't kill anyone else.' She shook her head. 'He was such an idiot,' she laughed, and wiped away a tear dripping down her cheek. 'He didn't take anything seriously.' She dropped my hand and pulled her t-shirt up at the back. 'We both got these matching fish tattoos on a whim—a symbol of our freedom—swimming free, untamed. Stupid, really.' She covered up the tattoo again and picked up my hand. 'He wasn't like you. He didn't have a good job. He couldn't hold down a job for five minutes. But if he needed the money, he'd always work his natural charm and find one. Then he'd soon get sacked for turning up late, not turning up at all, turning up drunk, or stoned. Always stoned. He must have worked in every restaurant in town, and then if they changed management, he got a job there again. He did waitering, pot-washing, potato-peeling, and if they were crazy enough, they let him serve behind the bar. He wasn't perfect. He did stupid things. He even got arrested once.'

'For what?'

'He pinched some things from the supermarket. He was between jobs and needed food—just a loaf of bread and two cans of beans. Not the easiest things to smuggle out under his coat. They let him off eventually—he worked his charm on them.' She stopped and sniffed. 'Do you really want to hear all this?'

As she'd talked, I'd compared myself to Eugene, rating myself. I was bland and ordinary, lacking Eugene's dangerous edge. Did Sophie like this ordinariness about me, or would she prefer me to be more like Eugene?

'How did you meet?' I asked.

'I knew him from school—he was in the year above. He was this effortlessly cool, pale, skinny boy with scruffy hair, always leaning against a wall and surrounded by his court of friends. As I'd walk by, he'd nod at me and I'd hurry past looking at the floor, blushing. I was a mousy little girl and there was no way he was interested in me. It wasn't until years after we'd left school that we got together. I worked on the checkout at a supermarket and Eugene came in to buy beer. The coolness and confidence I remembered evaporated as he asked me if I wanted to come to a party. He was shy and sweet, fumbling with his hands, struggling to put the beer away in a carrier bag. I said yes.

'At the party, I stuck to his side all night, and we went to a quiet spot in the garden and kissed. I was still living at my parents, and when he took me home, Dad was waiting at the window. I was only fifteen minutes later than I'd promised I'd be home, but Dad was so angry. He hated Eugene from then on—never gave him a chance. If Dad had been nicer to Eugene, I think Eugene would have tried to be less wild, would have tried to meet Dad's high expectations of the man dating his daughter, but he acted the part Dad gave him, the troublemaker corrupting his weak daughter. Dad drove me away from him and closer to Eugene.'

'Did you live together?'

'Never officially. But I slept over at his place a lot. I stayed living at home for Mum's sake. I didn't want to leave her alone with Dad. Dad would tell me I was treating the place like a hotel, but he preferred me under his control, even if he had lost some of it.'

'In Plymouth?'

'Pardon?'

'You're from Plymouth.'

'Sorry, yes.'

'So why is Eugene buried here?'

She hesitated.

'His parents live here,' she said, looking away. She didn't sound convinced of her answer. 'They moved here when he left school. He stayed in Plymouth.'

'Do you ever see them?'

'I never met them. Eugene didn't talk to them much.'

'Didn't you meet them at his funeral?'

'I didn't go.'

'Why not?'

'I couldn't bring myself to do it. All those people there, strangers, mourning him. They didn't know him like I did. I didn't want to mourn with them. And the thought of his mangled body being in that coffin, his face scarred by glass, was too much. The day of the funeral, I went for a walk and lay in the middle of a field, staring up at the clouds remembering things we'd done together and thinking how much I'd miss him.' Sophie stood from the sofa. 'Anyway, I've talked enough about him. It's time I moved on. It's all about the future, you and me.'

'You can talk about him whenever you like, you know?' I said. 'We both had lives before we met. Things like this don't have to be a secret. It's not healthy to keep things to yourself like this.'

'I'm fine. I don't want to talk about the past anymore. I've told you everything. And I don't want to know anything about your life before me, how many girlfriends you've had, where you've been, what you've done—I only want to look forward. Is that okay?'

When we'd first met, we'd shared all sorts of things, but now I understood these were all superficial. Our favourite films and music said little about us. Sophie had no interest in what made me, me. She hadn't shared what made her, her. When she hadn't answered my questions fully, I assumed she'd been teasing me, maintaining her mysterious allure. Now I realised it was evasive. In a way, this chance to bury my own past was an opportunity—I never had to tell Sophie about my psychosis—something I feared would scare her away. But we'd never be as close as I wanted unless we shared everything. Couples shouldn't have secrets, should they?

I noticed I was late for work.

'I have to go,' I said. I needed to get away and think.

'Promise me we won't talk about Eugene ever again,' she said.

Reluctantly, I promised.

Driving to work, my emotions were on a spin-cycle. I couldn't forgive Sophie for cheating on me, yet I wanted to forgive. I believed it had meant nothing to her, and she still wanted me. But I continued to suffer with the same dull ache in my stomach I'd had since she'd told me about Martin, like it was heavy with tar. Even though it had only been three days, I couldn't remember life without this sickness. Time heals. But how much time? If I could know the timescale, maybe things wouldn't seem so awful. I'd tell myself, just another couple of days, and all would be better.

The traffic was slow that morning. There were roadworks, and the temporary traffic lights only let out a few cars at a time.

I loved Sophie. She was not a perfect girlfriend I'd imagined, far from it, but the problems in our relationship, her secrecy, her unwillingness to share her past, had softened, she'd cracked open, if only for a moment. Maybe that crack would remain.

Traffic at a standstill, I put my hand over my mouth as I yawned. Stubble bristled against my palm—I'd forgotten to shave. Looking in the rear-view mirror, my expressionless face stared back at me—like eyes, nose, and lips drawn onto an egg. My boringness suddenly staggered me. My plain visage had no signs of experiences lived, of personality, of meaning. No wonder Sophie wanted to know so little about me—it looked as though there was nothing to know. I ruffled my hair as Sophie liked to do, but it fell flat, smooth, boring. Maybe I should grow it longer, as she suggested?

I pulled a face, trying to give myself some character, a forced smile with tongue sticking out, until I realised the cars in front and behind could see what I was doing. It was no good. I was a giant bore—nothing at all interesting about me. Compared to Eugene and his wild streak, I was plain, vanilla, beige. Did I even have a pulse?

I jumped as the car behind beeped its horn. The lights had changed.

I drove the rest of the journey to work, replaying the morning's conversation in my head. Something was bothering me—I was jealous of Eugene. I needed to be more like him.

At lunchtime, I ate alone at my desk, staring through the window at the street below while chewing on a canteen-bought cold, damp, and tasteless cheese sandwich which oozed with margarine. A strong wind had swept in, throwing a woman's waist-length blonde hair into her eyes, her unfastened coat billowing behind her as she fought to tame her locks. Dancing along the pavement, a newspaper flipped and flapped, losing pages as it went. A pigeon, just outside the window, was buffeted as it tried to fly across to a neighbouring building, its beady orange eyes fixed and determined.

Sophie had described Eugene as so unlike me. He seemed charismatic, energetic, fun. I couldn't describe myself as any of these things. What could I do to become more like Eugene? To become less boring? What did exciting people do?

Down below, a group of women from the office gathered by the building's entrance, stretching, jumping, lunging, preparing to go for a lunchtime run. Elise was one of them, hair in a ponytail, doing star jumps. Perhaps that's what I should do? Exciting people did sports. They wore shorts, and Lycra, and sweated, not too sweaty, just enough to glaze their forehead.

My phone rang. It was Dad.

'You didn't call at the weekend,' he said. 'So, I'm just checking you're all right?'

Elise and her friends jogged away towards the park.

'Sorry for not calling,' I said, putting down my sandwich. 'We were really busy.'

'Oh, what were you up to?'

What should I say?

'Ben?'

'Gardening,' I blurted. 'I've been helping Sophie in the garden. It was exhausting. My back aches.'

Dad told me Mum was having an awful couple of days. She was nervy, unable to sit still for a minute.

'I don't know what's wrong with her, Benny. She won't tell me.'

'Do you need me to come up and help?'

'There's no need for that. She'll come round soon. She always does.'

I stared out of the window at clouds as Dad changed the subject and told me what he'd been watching on television and reading in the newspaper.

'Is something bothering you?' asked Dad, snapping me out of a daze. 'You sound a little withdrawn.'

'I'm fine?'

'Are you sure?'

He always knew when something was up.

'Do you think I'm boring, Dad?'

'Pardon?' he said, shocked. 'No. Of course you're not.'

'But I don't *do* anything.'

'What kind of thing do you think you should be doing?'

'Exciting stuff. Hobbies, interests, running. It feels like I go to work and I come home and that's it. Just a repeating cycle.'

'What's brought this on. Has someone said something? Sophie?'

'No, she hasn't said anything.'

'Then why are you feeling like this?'

I couldn't tell him about everything that had been going on. I didn't want to tell him Sophie had cheated on me, or that I was competing in personality with a dead man.

'You don't sound happy,' said Dad.

I wasn't.

'I'm happy,' I replied.

'I don't know what to suggest,' he said. 'I don't do anything and I don't think I'm boring. Perhaps I am. I've never really thought about it. There's nothing wrong with being boring if you're okay with it yourself. I like building my models and doing puzzle books. I read. I watch television. The important thing is I'm content. But I remember what it's like to be young. There's a lot of pressure, probably more pressure than there's ever been, to appear to be living an exciting life. But here's the thing—life isn't like that. Life can be pretty boring. No, actually, life *is* boring. Better boring than a constant whirlwind where you don't know what'll happen from one minute to the next, where you don't have any time to relax. I'm not saying you are boring, Benny, but if you are, boring is okay.'

'Thanks Dad.'

Once we'd hung up, I crunched on a bruised apple and imagined Dad as I often saw him, sitting there in his chair, absorbed in a sudoku puzzle, happy in his own little numerical world. Maybe Sophie wouldn't mind me turning into a copy of Dad, but I think she wanted, perhaps needed, someone more dynamic.

The office began to fill with people returning from lunch and I got back to work, continuing to worry about my "boring" problem.

At home, I ate a chicken curry at the kitchen table as Sophie sat opposite devouring a moss salad, her hands still covered in mud from working in the garden.

'Are you okay?' asked Sophie between mouthfuls. 'You look worried.'

I put down my knife and fork and took a sip of

water.

'Do you think I'm boring?' I asked.

'What makes you say that?'

'I'm worried I'm boring.'

Sophie paused a moment, studying my face.

'Is this because of what I told you about Eugene?' she said. 'Because you're fine as you are.'

'It's not that,' I replied. 'I think I need a hobby or something.'

'I like you just the way you are. Boring suits you fine.'

'So, you do think I'm boring?'

'I didn't mean it like that. You're not boring. You're steady. Reliable. Calm. That's what I like about you.'

I sounded boring.

Sophie looked around the kitchen in thought, then pointed at my book resting on a stack of moss journals on the kitchen worktop.

'You like reading, right? That's a hobby.'

'I guess.' Reading novels didn't make me as exciting and dangerous as Eugene. The novel I was reading was the beautifully written, yet slow, tale of a milkman pondering whether he was part cat.

'There you go then. You're not boring. Problem solved.'

That night, as I went upstairs to get into my pyjamas, I heard Sophie chatting in the bedroom. I assumed she was on the phone, but when I walked into the room, she was lying on the bed looking at a patch of moss laid flat on her palm. She looked surprised to see me.

'Do you often enjoy pillow talk with your moss?' I asked jokingly.

'I'm not mad, you know?' she said defensively, sitting up and springing from the bed. 'It's good to talk to plants. They grow better if they hear encouraging human voices.'

'Do they?'

'It's well known. They like music too.'

'What kind of music?'

'I suspect different mosses like different things. This one though, I think likes David Bowie.'

'Why David Bowie?'

'That's just what he likes.'

I started shedding my work clothes to change into my pyjamas, and Sophie turned away from me.

'You don't have to look away. You've seen me naked plenty of times.'

'It's not that. I don't want the moss to see.'

'Really?' I laughed. Was she being serious?

'I'm not mad,' she said again, cupping the moss in her hands to hide it and going downstairs.

In the morning, Sophie's phone rang loudly in her green dressing gown pocket.

'Are you answering that?' I asked.

She shook her head and took a large swig of the moss smoothie she'd just finished making. This one was particularly thick, like sludge, and filled the kitchen with the aroma of freshly mown grass.

The phone stopped ringing. She took it out of her pocket and looked at the screen.

'It's just Emily. I'll call her back later.'

It was getting late and Sophie didn't look in a hurry to ready herself for work.

'Aren't you going to the shop today?' I asked.

'I took a day off.'

'On a Wednesday? Why?'

'Just to chill out.'

She gulped down more smoothie.

'I could have taken the day off with you if I'd known. We could have done something together, gone somewhere.' A day together might help us repair our wounded relationship a little.

'Sometimes it's good just to chill out alone. I'll spend some time in the garden.'

Sophie wiped smoothie from her lips with the back of her hand.

'Go to work,' she said. 'You'll be late.'

When I left she was pulling on her wellies, ready to head into the garden.

The next morning, Sophie complained she was feeling poorly.

'I'm going to call in sick,' she said. 'I've got a fever. A day in bed will fix it.'

I went to put my hand on her forehead to feel her temperature, and she swiped my hand away.

'Don't do that,' she said.

The day after that was Friday, Sophie's usual day off. She sprang out of bed and was already working in the garden by the time I'd dressed.

'Feeling better?' I asked.

'Yeah. It must have been one of those twenty-four-hour bugs.'

'I'm going to the library later,' I told Sophie on Saturday morning. 'Do you want me to see what books they have on moss?' She had enough already, but it would save her from buying more.

'I'll come with you,' she said.

'Aren't you working today?'

'I swapped my day off with Emily, so I have the entire day free.'

Before I'd met Sophie, I'd visited the library every weekend. I'd return the book I'd borrowed, choose another, and sit at a reading desk enjoying the first chapters in the library's peaceful surroundings. Now I went every three weeks, perhaps longer if I renewed my latest book over the phone.

I enjoyed the sound of the library—the sound of people attempting to be quiet and books sliding on and off shelves, paperbacks swishing, hardbacks tapping, books being shifted along to make room for returned comrades and glossy new arrivals, the turning and rifling of pages, muted coughs, sighs, sneezes, hushed conversations between public and librarian as if requesting risqué literature sequestered in a secret vault of the library only an elaborate handshake or obscure password would provide access to; and parents in loud, agitated voices, demanding their rebellious children keep quiet. The library was inclusive, with regulars including a retired, moustached man in a crisp blazer who read *The Telegraph*, smoothing its broad pages with his sleeve, reading it from cover to cover; a homeless lady with matted hair flicking through the glossy photos of lifestyle magazines, avoiding the cold outside, cowering at the sight of a librarian, fearing eviction if not fully immersed in her reading; and a teenage couple completing their homework opposite each other, earphones in, their hands occasionally reaching over the table to touch fingertips, smiling. The library smelt musty, acidic, of vanilla and grass; paper, ink, and glue. It was a place I could relax—a place I preferred to visit on my own.

'Are you sure you want to come?' I asked Sophie.

'I fancy getting out of the house,' she said.

Sophie held my hand as we walked to the library.

Today, in a green, lacy, long skirt and white t-shirt, topped off with a white floppy hat and round sunglasses, she looked herbaceous, like her bottom half was wrapped in a flowing sheet of moss. Recently, she'd worn a lot of green clothes. She never dressed entirely in green—she'd wear green trousers with a black top, or a green cardigan over a white vest—but there was usually something green.

'I've been thinking,' she said. 'We should visit your parents soon.'

Surprised, I stopped walking.

'Um, okay.'

I was so pleased, I didn't question her sudden change of mind.

I squeezed her hand tight. 'Thanks,' I said.

'For what?'

'For being cool.'

She squeezed my hand back.

'You're cool.'

We arrived at the library and Sophie disappeared into the vast non-fiction section to look for books on moss. I returned the book I'd finished about the half-cat—it turned out he wasn't part-cat and just really liked cats—and went to the crime section. I didn't normally read crime, but my boringness had continued to nag at me, and if my only hobby was to remain reading, then I should try books more exciting than what I'd normally read. My life needed murder, action, mystery, and adventure. I needed fighting, chases across the rooftops of dangerous cities, blood, and broken bones.

As I scanned the books' spines: *Half Of A Dead Heart*, *The Sorrows*, and *Not Asleep. Dead*, I looked up when soft steps moved down the aisle towards me.

'Hey, Ben.' It was Emily from Sophie's stationery shop, her hair as messy as I remembered, wearing a tie-dyed t-shirt. 'So, you're a crime fan?' She spoke in a mocking, deadpan voice.

'Sort of.'

'Is Sophie with you?'

'She's looking for a book on moss.'

'Moss?' She looked puzzled.

'Yeah, Sophie's suddenly fascinated by moss.' It surprised me Sophie hadn't talked to Emily about it.

'She's a strange one, isn't she?'

I nodded.

'Aren't you working in the shop today?' I asked.

'I'm taking my lunch break early and bringing a book back. I've got someone covering.' Emily picked up a Val McDermid book and glanced at the back cover before putting it down. 'If the shop's quiet, I always have a book nearby to pass the time.' Her expression changed into one of concern. 'I'm glad I've seen you, actually.' She bent down below the height of the bookshelves and urged me to do the same. 'I want to ask you about Sophie leaving the bookshop,' she whispered.

I stared blankly at Emily and shrugged.

'She's not working at the shop anymore,' she said. 'You knew that, right?'

This was a surprise.

'Since when?' I asked.

'She didn't come back after Alan's mum died.'

Why hadn't Sophie told me? Why pretend she was still there? And what was she doing with her time if she wasn't working? Just when I thought our relationship might be getting back on track, something like this happened. She didn't tell me anything—I didn't know her at all.

'You didn't know?' asked Emily.

'I had no idea.'

She looked guilty for having told me.

'She must have her reasons for not saying anything. You can't let her know you found out from me. Promise. She'll hate me.'

'Okay,' I said, my voice shaking and head spinning.

How could Sophie have kept such a big thing from

132

me as quitting her job?

'You need to look after her,' said Emily. 'When her last boyfriend died, she told me she got really ill. I'm worried this thing with Alan's mum has triggered the same feelings. Is she depressed? Is she unwell?'

'Maybe.' Was Sophie ill? Or was this normal Sophie? How could I know?

Emily looked at her watch.

'I need to go. Please promise you won't tell her you heard it from me.'

'I promise.'

Emily darted off moments before Sophie found me, a thick book gripped in her hands.

'This is just the thing I was after,' she said. 'It's a plant identification guide. It hasn't been checked out in ten years.' She looked down at my empty hands. 'Haven't you chosen anything yet? I've been ages.'

I grabbed a book. A heavy hardback covered in plastic frayed at the edges—*It Was There That I Saw You.*

'That's not your normal kind of thing, is it?' asked Sophie, raising her sunglasses and looking at the cover of a dead body splayed out under a full moon.

'I fancied a change.'

'Are you all right?' she asked. 'You look pale.'

'I'm fine,' I said through clenched teeth.

We checked out our books and left the library.

'I need to go to the stationery shop,' I said, wondering what Sophie might say.

'Why?'

I fumbled for an excuse to go.

'I want to buy a new calculator for work.' I already had three in my desk drawer.

'Can't you get one later?'

'It's only around the corner. Let's go now.' I took her hand, and I turned in the shop's direction. She yanked her hand away.

'I'll wait here,' she said.

'Come on, I need your employee discount.'

'No.'

She folded her arms and stood stubbornly.

'What's the matter?' I asked.

'I can't go in there.'

'Why not?'

Sophie looked at the ground and mumbled something incomprehensible before saying, 'I don't work there anymore.'

I tried to look shocked.

'What do you mean?'

'I'm not going back. I hated it.'

'You loved it.'

'I used to love it. Now it's boring. I'll find something else.'

I could tell she didn't believe what she was saying.

'Why didn't you tell me you'd left?'

'I don't have to tell you everything.'

'You barely tell me anything,' I snapped.

'Don't shout at me.' Her body sank, and she removed her sunglasses to wipe a tear from the corner of her eye. 'I'll find another job. I just need a break.'

Angry at myself for shouting at her, I put my arms around her and hugged tight. I needed to calm down, pocket my emotions.

'I'm sorry,' I said.

Heeding Emily's warning that Sophie probably needed time to recover from the shock of Alan's mum's death, I didn't mention her needing a new job.

Over the next week, coming in from busy days at work, Sophie would be lying on the sofa, nestled among cushions, reading one of her moss books, or watching something on television.

'Did you have a good day?' I'd ask.

'Yeah,' she'd shrug. 'I did a bit of gardening.'

The house grew increasingly untidy—empty cups, plates, and magazines everywhere. Dried soil from her boots trailing from the kitchen down the hallway. Bits of moss scattered all over the kitchen, getting deep in the joins of cupboards and the gaps between tiles. When I got home each evening, I cleaned the house.

I washed the dishes, dried them, and put them away.

I did the laundry.

I vacuumed.

I mopped the kitchen.

I scrubbed the bathroom.

I did the grocery shopping on my way home from work.

Sophie even rarely offered to make cups of tea for us both.

She did very little.

Give her time, I said to myself. She may be depressed. Be supportive. It won't last.

Sophie outwardly didn't appear miserable; in fact, she remained smiling and upbeat. But I tried to be cheerful around her, never letting my frustrations escape, pocketing them away nicely.

At the weekend, as I'd finished putting some washing on, I found Sophie scribbling away with a pencil on a thick sheet of paper. She quickly turned it over when she realised I was there, folding her hands across it.

'What are you drawing?' I asked, surprised to find her doing something different to lulling on the sofa.

'Just something silly.'

'Can I see?'

Sophie thought about it for a moment before slowly turning over the paper.

'It's not finished yet. I don't think it's very good,' she said.

I looked over her shoulder to view it.

She'd drawn a man, his body a host of complex, dense textures, finely drawn and shaded with pencil—a man made of moss.

'Is that me?' I asked.

'Do you think it looks like you?'

'Yes.'

'Really?'

'It's clearly me. Me made of moss.'

Sophie took it off the table and held it up for more window light.

'I guess it looks a bit like you.'

The detail was stunning—she had genuine talent.

'How long did that take you?'

'Probably three or four hours over the week.'

'You should frame it.'

'I don't think so.'

'Why not?'

'I don't want it watching me.'

I laughed, but she looked serious.

The eyes were drawn so well they seemed alive and focussed. I wondered if they'd follow you around the room.

'Don't throw it away, though,' I said. 'It's too good.'

When Sophie wasn't in the garden, she tinkered with the drawing for the rest of the weekend. And then, despite my protests, she hid it away somewhere, refusing to display it.

A heady, chemical aroma diffused through the front door as I returned home from work on Monday.

I stepped into the house and Sophie called from the living room, 'Careful of the wet paint.'

The walls of the hallway had transformed from white to a murky green, visually shrinking the space, and banishing light, like a shaded, algae-choked pond.

Shaking my head in disbelief, I carefully peeled off my coat so it didn't touch the paint. Old bedsheets covered the floor, splattered paint spots evidence the painting had been done quickly, messily.

'You've been decorating,' I said.

Sophie came into the hallway.

'Do you like it?' she asked.

I slowly turned three-hundred-and-sixty degrees.

'It's a bit gloomy,' I said, unable to hide my dislike.

She pouted. 'Well, I love it. It might take some getting used to, but you'll definitely like the living room. I've painted in there as well.'

I crept along the centre of the hallway, avoiding touching the walls, the soles of my shoes sticking to tacky spots of paint.

Each wall was a different colour green, the shades brighter than the paint in the hallway, but clashing together: one luminous like a workman's fluorescent jacket, one British Racing Green like an old sports car, one a vivid green I imagined children painting with, and the other was a washed-out green, so pale it may have been white reflecting the green of the surrounding walls. The ceiling remained bright white. A large shaggy rug lay in the centre of the room like a splayed green sheep.

'It's different,' I said, astonished.

'I've got pictures to put up too.'

'Photos of moss?'

'Yes.'

I looked around the room, deciding if there was anything I liked about her decorating. It would send someone like Mum into physical convulsions.

'Why didn't you tell me you were going to do this?' I

asked.

'If you really don't like it, we can change it, but I think it'll grow on you.'

Grow on me? Like moss growing on me? Suffocating me with its tiny leaves?

'You shouldn't just change things,' I said. 'I live here too. This is my house.'

'Don't you mean it's *our* house?' Sophie stood with hands on her hips. 'I'm not a lodger, Ben. I'm your girlfriend. I thought we'd moved past our bit of trouble or is this your house you can throw me out of whenever you like?'

'No.'

'That's what it feels like. I try to do something to make it feel a little homelier, I spend all day painting, and you act like this.'

'I'm sorry.'

Sophie walked out of the room, and I heard the back door to the garden slam.

I walked around the living room, folding up the sheets that had protected the carpet and sofa.

She wasn't gone for long, returning looking upset and defeated.

'I shouldn't have shouted at you,' I said, sorry for getting angry at her again.

She came over and we hugged.

'I'm sorry for not telling you about the decorating. The idea leapt into my head and I went straight to the shop and bought every green colour paint they had.'

Sophie's eyes were sparkling.

'I can't explain it, but I find pure excitement in moss, learning about moss, looking at moss. I wanted this place to reflect that joy.'

She looked up at me, imploring me to understand.

'I know it's geeky,' said Sophie. 'I know moss is a

weird thing to be into. But I'm in love with it.'

After her manic painting spree, Sophie became strangely withdrawn for the rest of the week. She rarely changed from her pyjamas and grunted when I asked her questions. She moved sluggishly, only sliding off the sofa if she really needed to. As it was such a complete change, I wondered how much my dislike of her decorating had affected her, or whether it was a slump connected to grief, or something even worse. Whatever the case, I wanted to get her out of the house, away from her moss, and hopefully spark some life into her.

'Do you want to go for a walk in the park?' I asked on Saturday morning.

'Not really.'

I continued to ask a few more times over the next hour until Sophie, sick of me asking, reluctantly agreed.

She took ages to get ready. Unable to decide what the weather was doing, she dithered over what clothes and shoes to wear, until eventually we walked to the park hand-in-hand on a cloudless afternoon, her huge sun hat knocking into my face whenever she turned to look at something.

'Do you really need a hat today?' I asked.

'Yes, it's definitely a hat day,' she said, pulling it lower on her head.

As we walked Sophie brightened, occasionally skipping, humming a song I didn't recognise.

When we arrived at the park, Sophie smiled, tugged my hand, and led me into a wood.

'Where are we going?' I asked.

'You'll see.'

Sophie held my hand tight, frequently turning and grinning at me, as we stumbled through leaves, twigs snapping beneath our shoes. The cool air smelt damp, green, of decomposing leaves and logs slowly decaying under cream-coloured fungus.

Sophie stopped.

'This is the place,' she said.

'Why here?'

'Look,' she said, pointing to the trunk of a stout tree. 'Moss.'

Of course. The tree trunks were thick with it. And dotted around the place were strange, circular mounds of earth covered in moss like little cushioned stools.

'I'm glad you suggested we come out. I've wanted to show you this place for ages. It's amazing, isn't it?' she said, walking up to a broad, gnarled oak and stroking the moss. She looked up into its canopy as if seeking the tree's eyes to gain its approval. 'Do you like it, Ben?'

'What are these?' I asked, pointing at one of the mounds.

'I don't know, but I think they're magical. I think they're where the fairies and elves sit for important woodland meetings when not flitting around, hiding in the leaves, watching, and whispering.' Did Sophie believe in fairies now? She saw my expression and laughed. 'I'm kidding. It's a nice spot though, isn't it?'

I nodded.

'Shall we keep walking?' Goose bumps had risen on my bare arms from the cold.

'Can we stay here a few minutes?' she asked.

Sophie skipped from tree to tree, mound to mound. The moss all looked alike to me, but to Sophie there was something unique about each one that required close observation. She explored each moss with her fingertips and lingered over a few that required more probing.

I wandered over to a hollow, fallen trunk, so wide I could have climbed inside. Peering into the space, I wondered if anything lived in it, half-expecting to see the bright eyes of a rabbit or badger. I sat on it, its loose bark spongy beneath me, the trunk creaking with my weight as I bounced up and down as if sitting on the edge of a trampoline, testing it to see if it would break.

Sophie took a few plastic bags out of her pocket and began choosing moss to collect.

To satisfy her moss-eating habit, the samples she took were bigger than the ones she'd taken when she first started collecting, yet she left enough on the trees that it could grow back and remain healthy.

'I should have brought my book to read,' I said, growing bored. I hadn't progressed through my crime novel much. Its grisly prologue had left me feeling queasy.

'Sorry. I'll be done soon,' Sophie said, looking up from where she was peeling moss from the base of a tree.

She placed the moss in a bag, sealed it, and put it in her pocket.

'I'm finished,' she said.

Sophie came to sit beside me on the trunk. It sank to the ground like the heavy end of a see-saw. She put her hand on my leg.

'Fancy it?' she said with a suggestive wink.

She really had brightened up.

'Here?' I said. 'It's a bit public.'

'I can't see any public.' She rubbed her hand on my thigh. 'Shall we?'

'We can't. Not here.'

'Go on.'

I stood up.

'Let's keep walking,' I said.

'You're so boring,' she said, grabbing my hand.

There it was again. That word. *Boring.* I was boring.

'Okay,' I said. 'Let's do it.'

'Really?' Her eyes widened.

'Yes.'

'In the woods?'

'You just said you wanted to?'

She laughed.

'I was joking. We're not teenagers.'

Sophie stood up off the log.

'If you're feeling horny, I guess I could give you a hand job, if you like?' she whispered, her hand stretching out towards my trouser zip.

I stepped back.

'No, it's okay,' I said, my boldness subsiding.

We left the wood for the open space of the park. Sophie grabbed my hand and held it tight.

'Are you okay?' she asked. 'You're not sulking, are you?'

In a playground, children slipped down the polished slide and demanded their parents push harder on the swings, stretching their legs as far as they could on the ascent, tucking them back on the descent; clambering over wooden obstacles, dropping from monkey bars half way, complaining their arms weren't long enough. Laughing, squealing, screaming, calling in pre-pubescent shrill.

'Do you ever want kids?' I asked Sophie.

As soon as the question was out, I knew I shouldn't have asked. It was too early in our relationship. The question was too serious, too adult. I hoped she hadn't heard me.

'Probably not,' she said.

'Oh.'

I'd never given much thought to parenthood. But I assumed it would happen one day. That's what normal people did. It was a natural, human thing to do.

We dropped each other's hands and stuffed them deep into our pockets.

'Why not?' I said.

'I don't think I'd be a good mum.'

'That's nonsense.'

'And the thought of all that pain, blood, and shit isn't for me.'

I should have finished the conversation, but this had real implications for my future—a childless future. My parents would never become grandparents, and they'd make great grandparents. It was sad.

'We'd have beautiful children,' I said. It was corny.

'That's probably true. They say beauty skips a generation,' she said, poking me in the cheek with her finger.

'Hey,' I laughed.

'Why are we even talking about this? We've only been going out a few months. I haven't decided whether I like you yet.'

'I like you,' I said.

'I know,' said Sophie, trying to stuff her hand into my pocket to take hold of my hand again. 'What's not to like?'

We walked past an elderly woman, three black musclebound dogs running around her legs, as she tossed them treats from her pocket. She smiled at us as we passed.

'Why don't we get a dog?' I asked Sophie.

'A dog instead of a child?'

'I didn't mean it like that.'

'No, thank you. It would wee all over my moss.'

'We could fence off the moss.'

'I don't want a dog, Ben. Why do you want a dog suddenly? Why are you talking about kids? What's got into you?'

'I've always liked the idea of having a dog.'

'Have you ever had a dog before?'

'No.'

'Well, I have. And they're demanding. They eat a lot. They shit a lot, and you have to pick it up and carry it around in little plastic bags. They smell. They make your house smell. They get sick a lot, go to the vets, and die, and it's very sad, and you feel miserable for weeks, until you buy a new dog, and repeat the same thing. We're young, Ben. We could go through five, six, seven dogs in a lifetime. Why subject ourselves to all that pain?'

'I think it would be nice.'

'No.'

'Just think about it, please.'

We walked in silence until we approached the café where we'd met on our first date.

'Coffee?' I asked.

Sophie nodded.

The cafe was quiet, only another couple sat by the window, immersed in reading newspapers, huge coffee mugs in hand.

They'd freshened the décor since we'd last been here. On each table sat a glass vase of small, white plastic flowers and the available food and drink was chalked on a blackboard behind the heads of the baristas, all male, all with bushy beards, tattoos, and piercings in their ears and nose. We ordered our coffees at the counter. The prices had risen.

They'd rearranged the tables so we couldn't sit exactly where we had those few months ago, but I chose the table closest to it, a reminder of the happy day Sophie and I first got together, and waited for someone to bring our drinks.

Music blasted from a speaker on the counter, something rocky.

'You like this song, don't you?' said Sophie.

'Do I?' I didn't recognise it at all.

'I'm sure you said it's one of your favourites.'

'I think you've got me confused with someone else,' I said apologetically. Perhaps Eugene?

Sophie looked down at the table, blushing under her hat.

'Maybe,' she said.

'Do you remember our first date?' I asked, changing the subject.

'Of course.'

'Do you remember you said you didn't recognise me at first?'

She thought for a moment. 'It was dark in here and you didn't look the same. You were wearing clothes I didn't expect you to wear.'

'What did you expect me to wear?'

'Just a different sort of clothes.'

'Like a denim jacket?'

She smiled. 'Maybe.'

'I thought you were going to change your mind and run away. You looked as though you'd made a mistake.'

'I was nervous.'

'You were so beautiful. I couldn't believe why you'd be interested in me. I couldn't believe my luck.'

'Don't be silly,' she said. 'You're beautiful as well.'

I stared into her eyes for a few moments until she looked away.

'Do you love me, Sophie?' I asked.

'Of course.'

'But you never say it. You never say, I love you.'

'I'm just not into saying things like that. You know I do.'

'It'd be nice to hear it.'

'You need to stop watching so many rom-coms.'

One of the bearded men brought us our coffees and

told us to, 'Enjoy,' giving a little bright-eyed nod to Sophie as he left.

'You're amazing,' she said, looking me in the eye. 'Do you know what I like about you? You never really talk about how you feel. You say you love me every now and again, but you never go into why, or what it means to you. And I like it that way. It's uncomplicated. I know you love me, but I don't want you gushing lovey-dovey stuff in my ear or bringing me flowers and presents all the time. I don't want any of that nonsense.'

I sipped my coffee, found it too hot, and licked milk froth from my top lip. How could Sophie be so passionate and yet so unromantic? Sophie was right. I wasn't great at talking about my feelings. But I wanted to be better, or how else could I prove my love for her and stop her straying again.

Sophie reached deep into her pocket and took out some of the moss she'd collected from the wood. As I watched in amazement, she tore it into little fragments, sprinkled it over her coffee, and stirred it in with her spoon. Why couldn't she enjoy a coffee without adding moss to it? The coffee was expensive, excellent coffee.

Sophie placed down her spoon and sipped her drink.

'Delicious,' she said.

We fell silent and looked through the window at the park. A family on bicycles rode past the window, their little girl wobbling into the path of a runner who leapt into a bush at the last moment to avoid a clash. A father and son flew a small drone, which lurched unsteadily in the breeze, the boy frowning in concentration over the controls as his dad animatedly shouted instructions. I excused myself and went to find the toilet.

When I returned, Sophie was staring at two elderly women enjoying a conversation sitting a few tables across from ours. One was older and more shrunken than the other, both wearing similar pink, knitted bobble hats. They could have been mother and daughter.

'I'm sorry,' Sophie said to the women, interrupting their chat. 'Are you talking about me?'

They stopped talking.

'No. Should we be?' the younger one asked, surprised at the interruption.

'Do you have a problem with me?' said Sophie.

I sat down and tugged at Sophie's sleeve.

'What are you doing, Sophie?'

Sophie pulled her arm away.

'These ladies were talking about me, and I want to know what they have to say.'

'They weren't talking about you.'

'I saw them looking at me and laughing.'

In a frail and wobbly voice, the older of the two ladies said, 'I can assure you we weren't talking about you. We're just trying to enjoy a nice cup of coffee.'

'Come on, Ben,' said Sophie, standing up and trying to guide me away. 'Let's go.'

'But my coffee…' My drink was almost untouched.

I stood reluctantly, and as I did a tide rose in my skull, pushing behind my eyes, creating a wave of nausea that turned to a stab of pain in the centre of my forehead. I spread my legs to steady myself. The headaches had eased recently—I hadn't even thought about them. Why had one come back so suddenly?

Sophie jabbed her pointed finger towards each of the ladies in turn. 'I'll be keeping an eye out for you two.'

The ladies leant back in fear. The baristas watched from behind their counter, and the couple by the window peered at us above their newspapers.

'Is everything okay there?' asked the barista who'd brought our coffees.

'Don't worry, we're going,' Sophie snapped at him.

Sophie took my hand and led me stumbling out the door. She glared back at the women before the door shut behind us.

Instantly, the fresh air improved my head—woolly, but pain free.

After we'd walked a little way from the cafe, I asked Sophie what she thought she was doing terrifying old women.

'I know I heard them talking about me.'

'What were they saying?'

'I don't want to say.'

'Why not?'

'It was upsetting.'

Maybe they'd seen the moss in her coffee?

'Even if they were talking about you, you scared them.'

'They'll get over it. Stupid busybodies.'

I stopped and held Sophie by the shoulders.

'Tell me what they said? It can't be that bad.'

She shook me off and stormed across the road.

'Sophie!'

A car slammed on its brakes, swerving to avoid hitting her. Sophie stuck up her middle finger to the driver as he drove away, swearing, his thick, hairy arm stretched out of the window returning her gesture. I chased after her.

Sophie refused to talk as I caught up with her and walked by her side on the short distance home. But as soon as we stepped in the house, she said, 'We should go on more walks,' kissing me on the cheek, looking genuinely happy.

7

The banging, rattling, and scraping of metal trays, mixing bowls, spoons, and spatulas came from the kitchen.

'What are you doing?' I shouted to Sophie from the living room.

'Baking a cake.'

What had prompted her to bake? She'd never made a cake before.

I left her alone to get on with it. About half an hour later, the delicious aroma of warm sponge filled the house, and soon after, Sophie handed me a plate with a wedge of sponge cake fresh out of the oven, glossy and moist, speckled with brown flecks, and a thick layer of raspberry jam in the middle.

'Are these flecks of moss?' I asked.

'Might be.'

I held the cake close to my nose, detecting the slight smell of sulphur.

'No, thanks,' I said, passing the plate back to her.

Sophie looked as if she might cry.

'I promise it tastes good.' She held the plate out to me, pleading wide-eyed. 'Try a piece.'

I took the plate and slowly lifted the cake to my mouth. Closing my eyes, I nibbled it.

'You need to take a bigger bite than that,' she said. 'You won't be able to taste it properly.'

Reluctantly, I took a bigger bite and chewed it well,

turning it into a gooey paste on my tongue before daring to swallow it, expecting the grittiness and earthiness of moss, but finding none. It tasted good. Like an ordinary sponge cake, but with a delicious saltiness.

I took another bite. Sophie beamed.

'It's great.'

She clapped her hands.

'Thank you,' she said, and kissed me on the forehead. 'I'm going to take it with me tomorrow.'

'Where to?'

'To Bryology club.'

The cake dropped from my hand to the floor.

Sophie hadn't mentioned the club for ages, not since telling me she'd slept with Martin the Moss Man.

'You can't be serious?' I said. 'Not after what happened.'

'Why should that stop me?'

'Because I don't want you to see *him* again.'

'So, what if I do see *him*? I told you it wouldn't happen again.'

'But he'll try it on.'

'Probably.'

'Please don't go,' I pleaded.

'Don't you trust me?' She looked at me with hard eyes. 'I trust you not to go near the slut with the nice perfume again.'

She'd acted like she'd forgotten all about it. Obviously not.

'That's different,' I said.

'How?'

'I didn't sleep with her.'

Sophie gently took my hand.

'Come with me,' she said.

'To Moss Club?'

'It'll stop you worrying.'

I imagined sitting alongside Sophie, Martin stealing glances at us from his chairman's seat, wiping nervous sweat from his brow, trying to keep order of proceedings, as I put my hand on Sophie's knee, giving it a little squeeze.

'I don't think so,' I said.

'I've offered you a solution. It's up to you if you take it or not,' said Sophie, dropping my hand. 'But don't worry. It won't happen again.'

'How do you know?'

'Because I care about you.' She kissed me on top of my head. 'How about you meet me afterwards? We could go for a drink?'

'Okay,' I said, stooping to clear up the cake from the floor. 'Good idea.'

Repeatedly waking in the night, I worried about Sophie's return to Moss Club as she slept soundly beside me, lying on her back, her chest gently rising and falling.

Before she left for the club, Sophie told me how to reach the community centre where it was held.

'Try not to worry,' she called over her shoulder, as I waved her goodbye from the front door, still in my pyjamas. 'I won't do anything with Martin.'

The mention of his name heightened the sickening feeling I'd been experiencing all night.

Yawning, I returned to bed and lay there in the moss green sheets, staring at the ceiling, worrying I should have gone with her.

When Sophie and Martin saw each other, would they act casual, avoid being alone together, not let the other members catch on they'd slept together? Or was Martin going to follow Sophie around like a dog, laugh inanely at everything she said, try to get her alone for a quiet word, *What does it mean, Sophie? Are we an item now?* Would she rebuff him softly or firmly, or rebuff him at all? Maybe Martin's magnetism would be too strong and pull her using his tractor-beam into his dirty, mossy arms.

I closed my eyes and tried to sleep. After a good sleep, things always seemed better—new connections made in the brain, annoyance and stress re-routed. But behind my eyelids Sophie and Martin were having sex in a community centre toilet.

After a few minutes, I sat up and threw the duvet off me. I needed to snap out of it. Sophie said she wouldn't do it again—it had been a mistake.

I changed out of my pyjamas, and as I got dressed, a Pound coin slipped from my trousers' pocket, and rolled beneath the bed. I got on my knees and peered beneath the bed to find it.

The coin glowed in the dim light, surrounded by loose hair and a thick layer of dust on the carpet. I lay flat on the floor and slid under the bed, stretching my arm until I grabbed the coin. Under Sophie's side of the bed sat the cardboard box she'd hidden there when she first moved in. I'd forgotten all about it.

I slid back out, walked to the other side of the bed, dragged the box from beneath it, and heaved it onto the duvet. A film of dust had settled on its lid since Sophie kicked it under the bed, so she'd probably not looked in it recently.

Sophie had asked me never to look in it. But, perhaps childishly, because I'd been told not to, and because I knew it could tell me things about her she'd never tell me herself, I now had an urge to look in it. Sophie would never know if I peeked.

I carefully lifted the lid without disturbing the dust.

The front door burst open, rattling the walls, and Sophie shouted, 'I forgot my purse.'

Slamming the box lid shut, I dropped the box onto

the carpet with a floor shaking thud. I tried to kick the box under the bed, but pain flashed through the side of my foot—it was too heavy. As Sophie thundered up the stairs I bent down and shoved the box farther under the bed, and, standing quickly, whacked my head on the bed frame. Eyes watering, I stumbled to my side of the room and tried to act natural.

'What was that noise?' Sophie asked, appearing in the doorway.

'I was getting changed,' I said, sweat trickling down my neck into the collar of my t-shirt, head throbbing, foot bruising.

She raised an eyebrow, went to her bedside table, and took her purse.

'I've got to rush now. I'm going to be really late,' she said, and left.

'I'll meet you after the club,' I shouted after her.

Afraid to open the box again, I looked under the bed and saw finger marks imprinted on its dusty lid. I found a dry flannel in the bathroom, quickly removed the evidence from the lid, and rinsed the flannel in the sink, leaving it to dry on the side of the bath. I straightened the box so it sat in exactly the same position I'd found it—a patch of carpet paler, less dusty than the rest, and made a note to vacuum beneath the bed.

As I washed my face and brushed my teeth, I asked myself, did I really want to know what was in the box? Looking in the box was a betrayal of trust, and I needed to learn to trust Sophie, no matter how hard that might be.

Downstairs, in the kitchen, I discovered Sophie's cake, wrapped in silver foil, still sitting on the worktop. She must have been so excited about returning to the club, she'd forgotten her purse *and* cake.

As I made myself a coffee, the cake enticed me with

153

its aroma. Could I have cake for breakfast? I peeled open the foil, took a sharp knife from the drawer, and cut myself a tiny slither. As I bit into it, crumbs scattered across my chin and down my jumper, nesting in the gaps between the weave. It was tastier than I remembered. I cut myself a thicker wedge, put it on a plate, and took it to the living room. I ate it while sipping my coffee and reading the crime book I'd chosen from the library.

As I read, now gripped by the story of a serial killer stalking young women he believed to be his cruel dead mother, my stomach bubbled and groaned, like it was shifting from side to side, rising and falling. I rested my hand on it to still it—it was probably gas. But as the murderer strangled his fifth victim, the bubbling grew uncomfortable. A sharp pain dug into the walls of my stomach, and I lurched for the bathroom, arriving on the toilet just before my bowels emptied in a torrent.

Recovering with deep breaths, face clammy, and body shivering, a tide of vomit then rose in my throat, and I turned to be sick in the sink.

It was the cake that had done this, the moss in the cake.

I couldn't move from the bathroom. Every time I thought there was nothing left in me, more came out. Brown liquid, then green, then clear. I drank cold water from the tap and immediately threw it up again. Was I dying? It was too soon to tell. But dying would've been a relief.

When nothing had erupted from me in a while, I slumped to the floor clutching my empty stomach, and with my face against the cold radiator, fell asleep.

I felt much better when I woke. Standing stiffly, I stretched and looked in the bathroom mirror. The ridges of the radiator had left deep impressions on my cheek. My eyes were small and bloodshot. I wiped a white crust from around my lips with a damp flannel.

My watch said five o'clock. I was an hour late meeting Sophie.

I hurried downstairs to find my phone. She hadn't called.

I imagined Sophie waiting outside Bryology Club in the cold, tapping her foot, tutting loudly, glancing at her watch.

Has he not come for you? Martin would say. *He's no good for you. Come home with me. I'd never stand you up. My beauty. My love. I've got some lovely moss to show you in my bedroom; thick, and lush, and vibrant.*

Tremors of panic started in my hands and ran up my arms. I called Sophie's phone. She didn't answer.

I ran to find my trainers and forced them on without undoing the laces. I grabbed my coat and keys and stumbled out of the door just as Sophie was walking up the driveway.

'What happened to you?' she asked.

I held the door open for her, and she breezed past me into the house.

'I was sick,' I said.

'You could have let me know.'

'I fell asleep.'

She shook her head like she didn't believe me.

'It was your cake. It poisoned me.'

'Nonsense,' she laughed.

Sophie went to the kitchen and peered beneath the foil covering the cake.

'I didn't realise I'd forgotten it until the coffee break,' she said.

'You need to throw it away.'

'Moss isn't poisonous. It can't make you ill.'

I stood in front of her, noses almost touching.

'Look at me,' I said. 'I'm not well. Look how pale I

am.' I blew my breath on her.

'You smell of sick,' she said, recoiling.

She looked up in thought.

'I guess the moss could have been contaminated while growing. Maybe it got sprayed with something?'

'Where did you find it?'

'The old factory down the road. There's loads of moss there.'

The factory was a graffiti-covered ruin, walls crumbling, given to the wild.

'What did they used to make there?'

'I don't know. Paint, I think.'

Sophie sniffed the cake, shrugged, and slid it from its plate into the bin.

'What a waste,' she said. 'But the moss did look a little orange round the edges. I'll avoid that in the future.'

Feeling weak and cold, I sat down and hugged my arms around me.

Sophie laid her hand on my head.

'You're burning up,' she said.

'I'll be all right. I'm much better than I was.'

Sophie frowned.

'How was Moss Club?' I asked. 'Was Martin there? Did he say anything to you?'

'He asked me out.'

I knew something terrible like that would happen.

'And you said?'

Sophie fixed me with a fierce stare.

'No, of course.'

Relief washed over me.

'And Martin was okay with that?'

'I told him you knew about me sleeping with him. That surprised him. I think he thought we were having a secret affair. He kept asking if you were angry. I think he thinks you'd beat him up.' She laughed.

'I would.'

Sophie laughed again.

'I would,' I repeated, though I'd never fought anyone, unless a playground scuffle over a squashed bag of crisps counted.

'Well, you don't need to beat him up. I've scared him off. He's worried his wife will find out. We're just fellow bryologists now.' She stroked my cheek. 'Anyway, you look awful. Why don't you go to bed?'

As I walked up the stairs, my stomach lurched, and I just made it to the bathroom before I was sick again.

When I came downstairs later that evening, tired and achy, but stomach settled, I found Sophie hunched over her laptop—a clunky, ancient thing, its black plastic lid covered in stickers of rainbows and cats.

'I'm starting a blog,' she said, keen to share the news. 'One of the girls at the club writes a blog and I thought it was a good idea. I'm writing down all my moss recipes.' She looked at me to see my reaction.

'You just poisoned me with cake,' I said, rubbing my stomach.

'I obviously won't make that mistake again.' She looked down at her screen before continuing to clack away on the keys. 'Some bloggers become really successful, you know. They appear on TV, open restaurant chains, sell branded kitchenware—all sorts.'

'Is that what you want to do? Be on TV?'

'One step at a time. But why not? Once people learn how great moss is, they'll want to make programmes about it.'

Sophie was the kind of fresh-faced young woman successful blogs often featured, and moss was no weirder than some of the stuff people ate. Recently, I'd seen a food programme with people tasting cheese, rotten and

squirming with maggots, and I'd read of people eating
Dead Sea mud, believing it would filter toxins from their
bodies and make their skin glow. But if her plan was to
make money from blogging, rather than a proper job, she
was kidding herself—it seemed so unlikely.

'Do you want to read what I've done?' she asked,
passing me her laptop.

EDIBLE MOSS

*Have you ever stopped and really looked around you? Nestled
within the cracks of paving slabs, decorating tree trunks, and atop
limestone walls, you'll see moss. Moss is everywhere—succulent,
vibrant, and delicious. This blog is for adventurous eaters looking
for a nutritious and flavoursome food waiting to be explored.*

Underneath the paragraph was a photo I'd taken of
Sophie a couple of months ago: summer-tanned skin, a
healthy flush to her cheeks, eyes wide and bright, and a
broad smile showing white teeth. The difference to her
current appearance was shocking—I didn't realise how
gaunt and pale she'd become.

'You look great in this photo,' I commented.

Her cheeks had now hollowed, like they'd been
sucked in, and her skin, especially her chin, was pimply.
Maybe she'd been working too hard in the garden and
was exhausted?

'Don't I always look great?' she laughed. 'Look at one
of the recipes.' Sophie pointed with a bony finger to a list
on the side of the screen. *When did she get so thin?*

I clicked on a page for spaghetti Bolognese.

'I've been photographing all my meals with the
Polaroid camera, and then I scan them onto the
computer. The pictures look good, don't they?'

The spaghetti Bolognese was positioned perfectly on
a plain white plate, a few torn basil leaves making it fresh

and inviting.

'It looks very professional,' I said.

Below the photo, Sophie had written the recipe—simple and easy to follow. She'd recommended the best mosses to use and the places they could be found, including drawings of the moss for easy identification. They were far more advanced than the sketches she'd initially done under the microscope.

'Did you do these drawings?'

'Yes.'

They were as impressive as her drawing of me made from moss, but this time in colour. Shades of green, yellow, and brown really made the moss jump out of the computer screen.

'We had someone come to the club to give us tips on drawing moss. I think I've really improved.'

I passed the laptop back to Sophie.

'I'm impressed,' I said. Some people may have been willing to cook this stuff.

'I'm adding a few more recipes before making it live on the internet. Then I'll promote it to other bloggers. Hopefully, they'll share it to their followers, and soon enough I'll be a culinary moss expert, famous lifestyle blogger, darling of the Sunday paper supplements and *This Morning*, and I won't need to get some horrible job.'

'Sounds like you've got it all planned out,' I said. 'But you might need a job until you become successful. These things take time.'

'Don't be patronising,' she replied.

'I wasn't.' I was being realistic.

'Don't you believe in me?'

'I do, but—'

'Just have a little faith. That's all I ask.'

She glared at me.

'Okay,' I said, holding up my hands in surrender.

'Sorry.'

Sophie spent the rest of the evening finishing her website, and with a triumphant hit of a key, and a huge smile, she set it live to the world.

'My blog has had two-hundred hits already. People are writing comments.' She read one out as I lay in our bed, slowly waking up. '"Looks delicious. I'm making it tonight!"'

After a shower, I went down for breakfast to find Sophie sitting at the kitchen table, grinning excitedly.

'Now I've had almost five-hundred views. Someone's drunk one of my smoothies and left a comment. "Deliciously healthy. Will make again."'

I was pleased for her. And surprised. How had people stumbled on her website?

'And someone's asking for tips on how to grow moss so I'm adding another section—a gardening section.'

She started tapping away on her laptop.

'If you're getting all these website views, you need to put adverts on it to make money,' I suggested.

'I don't want to clutter it up with big, ugly adverts.'

'But that's how bloggers make money.'

'It's not all about money. I'm trying to help people live a healthier life and raise awareness of moss. Besides, once the blog's successful then I'll make money from my expertise, not adverts. And I've got plenty of money. I'm not struggling. I'm paying my way, aren't I?'

She didn't seem to lack money.

Sophie asked me to take photos of her in the sunny garden as she posed with spades, trowels, and watering cans. She changed outfits to make it look as though the photos were taken at different times, as if she was often photographed while gardening. She smeared mud on her hands and cheeks to look as if she'd been toiling hard.

And by the evening, Sophie had created a gardening section for her blog.

'I'm really pleased with it,' she said, closing the lid of her laptop. 'And one of my followers wants to interview me tomorrow for their health blog. I'm going to meet them.'

'*Meet* them? In real life?'

'Yes.'

'But these internet people can be anyone. They could be dangerous. Where are you meeting?'

'I'm meeting a health blogger in a vegan café. Are they going to murder me with a coconut latte and tofu salad?' she laughed.

'You never know,' I said. Perhaps I needed to stop reading my crime novel—maybe it was making me paranoid.

After dinner, I spoke to Dad on the phone.

Dad told me he and Mum were well.

'She's been settled the last week,' he said. 'She's started a new jigsaw—elephants at a watering hole—two-thousand pieces. It's taking up most of the dining table.'

Once absorbed in a jigsaw, she was always relaxed.

'Are you still worried about being boring?' asked Dad. 'Because I was wondering if you had anything exciting planned, perhaps a holiday?'

'Nothing planned at the moment.'

'It would be good for you to get away,' he said. 'You work hard, you deserve a holiday. Your mum and I always liked Wales. Have you thought about Wales?'

Wales? Exciting?

'I'll suggest it to Sophie,' I replied.

Sophie left early the next morning to meet her blogger for breakfast. She'd put on a nice summer dress and spent more time than usual applying make-up at the bedroom mirror.

As I readied myself for work, the stiff springs of the letter box screeched, and something dropped to the doormat. It was earlier than the post normally arrived, but I found a letter lying there.

I picked up the white, blank envelope—no addressee written on it, no sender, no stamp. Curious, I tore it open and removed the folded note inside. Unfolding the beige paper revealed a black & white outline of a horse, like something from a child's colouring book. And over the other side of the page, in big, black marker-pen capital letters was written,

WHAT HAVE YOU DONE WITH HER?

I looked through the door's window, but no-one was there.

Cautiously, I opened the door and peered into the empty street, before closing it quickly and pulling the security chain across.

Who'd written it? Perhaps Martin the Moss Man? Maybe he'd taken Sophie's knock-back more seriously than she'd thought. But why would he be asking where she was? And how was I supposed to answer if they'd run away?

I stared at the letter; the words creeping me out.

WHAT
HAVE
YOU
DONE
WITH
HER?

I needed to leave for work but now hesitated to go. What

if the person who'd left the note was staking out the house, waiting for me to leave, either to attack me or break in when I'd gone?

Over a coffee, I convinced myself it was probably kids playing a joke on their way to school. Who else would have the outline of a horse on a sinister letter? I placed the letter on the kitchen table so Sophie would see it when she arrived home and prepared to leave, securing all the windows and back door, and giving the front door a push on my way out to check it was locked thoroughly.

Walking up the driveway to the car, I suddenly tripped, falling heavily onto my outstretched hands. I lay like that for a moment, wondering what had just happened, examining grit embedded in my palm, before getting to my feet.

At ankle height, a taut piece of brown string stretched across the driveway, tied to fence posts. I looked around. No one was smirking at my misfortune from a distance. The same person who posted the letter must have done this. Why would they do such a thing?

I untied one end of the string so it fell slack on the floor, wound it up, and left it to one side.

As I drove to work, I repeatedly checked in the rear-view mirror to see if anyone was following. I avoided the short-cut through the quiet industrial estate—preferring to stick to the busy main road.

At work, I thought about the string and the letter—it must have been kids.

But after work, picking a few things up in the supermarket, I became suspicious of people trailing me. A young mum holding the hand of her toddler son, suddenly turned to look at tinned beans when I caught her eye. And a pony-tailed man, a stallion decorating the back of his leather motorcycle jacket, kept walking the same aisles as me.

I shopped quickly, paid, and left, cursing myself as I drove home for forgetting things I needed.

On my return home, as I was about to pull into the driveway, I braked hard, noticing the string had been retied in the same place as before. Again, I looked around—the culprit wasn't in sight.

Quickly, I got out of the car, easily untied both ends of the string, and pocketed it. Checking that there was still no one watching, I parked the car, took the shopping into the house, and waited by the closed front door to spy anyone appearing.

After five minutes, a trail of water ran between my shoes as the frozen items melted in my shopping bags, and I left the door to put the food away.

When finished, I took the string from my pocket and studied it, thinking it might offer me clues to who had put it across the driveway.

I wound it round my hand and stroked it. The string was coarse and dry. I unwound it, then wound it again, tighter, so it pressed into my palm, skin bulging between the strands. First a letter and then the string—what next? A flaming bag of dog shit through the letterbox? Car tires slashed? Or a good old-fashioned knife through the chest when I next left the house?

Sophie returned soon after, rushing upstairs to the bathroom as soon as she arrived.

The toilet flushed, and through the toilet door she shouted she'd take a shower.

When she came down, hair wet, and dressed in different clothes, she seemed twitchy, looking at the floor, avoiding eye contact, as if she was hiding something.

A dull, heavy sensation hit me. My throat dried and narrowed, and I swallowed saliva past a hard lump. Had she cheated on me again?

She glanced at me from the corner of her eye. Her look said she knew I suspected something was wrong.

'How was your interview with the health blogger this morning?' I asked. The question came out more interrogating than I'd hoped.

'Fine.'

'Fine?'

'I was with her all day. She asked lots of questions. She thinks I could start a moss revolution.'

Sophie looked anywhere but at me.

'When will she put the interview on her blog?'

'Soon. She's going to let me know.'

What was Sophie hiding?

'What's the blog called?'

'*Susan's Healthy Day.*'

The title sounded so earnest.

'And will you be seeing *Susan* again?'

'No, I don't think so.'

Sophie scurried from the room and went upstairs to dry her hair. I thought I could hear her crying above the blast of the hair dryer.

Unable to sit still, I leapt from the sofa and paced the living room, fists balled tight, jaw clenched so hard my teeth ached in my gums. I knew she'd cheated again—I just knew it. Why would she cheat again? And this time with a woman? My head began to ache. Why hadn't Sophie come straight out and told me like she'd done before? Was it because of how I'd reacted last time?

Crying into my hand, I rubbed away the tears away before they ran down my cheeks and stained them. I hated myself for crying. I hated her for making me cry. I hated I couldn't pocket the hurt.

As my headache worsened, I lay on the sofa and nestled my head in the cushions

I must have passed out because I woke with a stiff neck, face still buried in the cushions. It took me a moment to remember what had happened with Sophie, before the hurt came back in a tidal wave.

Struggling up, I looked in the mirror at my puffy eyes.

I went to the kitchen to fetch water and painkillers for my still aching head and found Sophie working on her laptop. Her eyes were red, and blotches stained her cheeks. She sniffed and greeted me when she saw me.

'You've been crying,' I said.

'Yep. So, have you.'

'You've cheated on me again,' I said calmly, as fact, and poured a glass of water, downing it in one go.

'Not really,' she said.

I slammed the glass down on the worktop.

'What does that mean?'

'I just thought she was being nice.'

'But you've slept with her?'

'We kissed.'

'Oh, you just kissed.' I couldn't control my anger. 'Well, that's okay then!'

'We kissed a lot.'

'Why, Sophie? Why would you do that?'

'She was saying such nice things about the blog, and then she was saying nice things about me, and then we just started kissing. It won't happen again. I'm not even into girls.' She cried loudly, burying her face in her hands. 'I'm sorry. I don't want to ruin everything.'

Sophie seemed genuinely upset. When she'd cheated on me before, she'd presented it matter-of-factly, but this time there was real remorse.

'I won't do it again,' she said.

'That's what you said last time.'

How many times would I let her do this to me? What

was she capable of next? Despite appearing remorseful, she didn't seem to be able to say no.

Sophie stood up from the table and came over to hug me.

I shrugged her off.

'Leave me alone,' I said, leaving the room.

I spent the afternoon sitting in the living room staring at the green walls, mentally creating two lists: reasons I should end it with Sophie and reasons I shouldn't.

Reasons I should end it:
She keeps cheating on me.
She's secretive.
She refuses to get another job.
She picks fights with random people when we go out together.
She eats moss.
She hasn't got over her dead boyfriend.
Her dead boyfriend was better than me.

Reasons to stay with her:
I love her.
She makes me laugh.
She's beautiful.
The sex is amazing.
I can't imagine life without her.
I'd be lonely without her.
I am nothing without her.

I thought back to a night at university when Maggie kissed a girl in the club, a girl as pale and severe-looking as her—someone she knew from her course. They held their cigarettes to the side and kissed. Maggie coolly looking sideways to me, gauging my reaction. I was aroused. They were beautiful, like two black swans kissing. When Maggie saw I wasn't annoyed or cross, she broke off the kiss. The other girl disappeared into the crowd and Maggie and I sat in a dark corner for the rest of the night, silent, watching the crowd dancing wildly.

Sophie was impulsive, but a perhaps a kiss, a kiss with a girl, was harmless, wasn't it? She'd come home to me. She wanted to be with me.

That night, we slept in the same bed, but there was a huge, cold canyon between our bodies, our backs turned to one another.

The creak of floorboards stirred me out of sleep as Sophie crept back towards the bed on tiptoes. Where had she been? The sun was only just rising, and when she noticed me awake, she stopped moving.

You were fidgeting a lot in your sleep,' she said, before I could ask where she'd been. 'You woke me up'

'Maybe I was dreaming,' I yawned.

'Of what?'

'I don't remember.'

'About yesterday—are you angry about it?'

'Yes.'

'Please don't be.'

'You're kissing other people.'

Sophie looked down at the floor.

'When's the last time we properly kissed?' I asked. 'When's the last time we had sex?'

Sophie shrugged. 'I can't remember.'

'Don't you fancy me?' I asked. Maybe she'd gone off me totally—I'd reached maximum boring and she required excitement elsewhere.

'Of course I do,' she said.

She sat on the bed and stretched over to kiss me as I lay against the pillow. Our lips touched, and I forgave her

168

almost instantly. My list of reasons to break up with her erased by her soft mouth and sweet breath. I couldn't live without her.

Sophie climbed over and straddled me.

'It's my time of the month,' she said, frowning. 'But I can give you a hand job if you like?'

Did Sophie always think she could make things better with sex?

'Grab a tissue,' she said.

Blood rushed to my penis in excitement, ignoring my wish to stop this.

A box of tissues lay on my bedside table. I pulled a tissue from the box.

'Is one tissue going to be enough?' she asked. 'We've not had sex for a while. There might be a lot to come out.'

I took another tissue in case.

'Pyjamas off,' she commanded.

I pulled my pyjama bottoms down to my knees and she grabbed them, pulling them all the way off, throwing them to the floor. My freed penis stood erect in the cool air of the bedroom. Sophie folded her warm hand around it and moved it slowly up and down. I closed my eyes, imagining my penis tight inside her. As my breathing rate increased, so did her hand, until I came, and smothered my shuddering penis with the tissues, panting for breath.

'I bet that felt good,' she said.

Sophie went to make us tea, and I carried the sticky tissues to the bathroom, flushing them down the toilet. I felt dirty. She'd given me sex just to keep me happy, to keep me from throwing her out—hustling her way out of trouble. And it had worked. But I didn't want to let her do that again.

'Do you fancy a holiday?' I asked Sophie over breakfast.

I'd been staring into my bowl of cornflakes, eating so slowly they'd become a soggy, orange goo.

'It's a nice idea, but I can't afford one without a job,' she said.

I hadn't considered that.

'I'll pay,' I offered.

'You can't do that.'

'Why not?'

'Because holidays are expensive.'

'It'll be my treat. I need a holiday. *We* need a holiday.'

If we could get away for a bit, away from the house, the garden, the moss, Bryology club, Eugene, and health bloggers, we could work on our relationship. I could convince her she didn't need to cheat on me—I could be enough for her. But we needed to be together with nothing getting in the way.

'Where do you want to go?'

'I haven't really thought about it,' I said. 'Maybe Wales?'

'Wales?' Sophie laughed with surprise. 'I thought you were going to suggest somewhere hot and exotic. Maybe somewhere romantic. Why Wales?'

On second thoughts, there was a high risk of moss in Wales. A sandy tropical beach would likely be a moss desert.

'It doesn't have to be Wales.'

'Why don't you save your money?' she said. 'When I start making money, we'll go on holiday.'

Dropping my spoon into my bowl, I left the table and sulked away to the living room.

I was about to open the curtains and let some sunlight in when I heard the crisp sound of gravel like someone was standing right outside on the other side of the window.

Peeping through the curtains, I noticed someone's

breath had misted the glass, and a hooded figure, dressed in black, leapt away from the window. Shocked, I also jumped back before steadying myself and flinging the curtains wide open.

'Hey!' I shouted through the glass.

The short and skinny figure fled, slipping on the driveway's loose stones as they ran to the road.

Bursting through the front door, I ran in bare feet, still in pyjamas, to the pavement.

'What's going on?' Sophie called from the open doorway.

Distant footsteps slapped against the pavement, and the figure's silhouette turned the corner of the street. I'd never catch them, even with shoes on. As I watched the corner, wondering who'd been here, and what they'd hoped to see, I shivered in the cold and returned to the house.

Sophie waited for me in her pyjamas at the door.

'They've gone,' I said. 'Hopefully I've scared them off.'

'Who's gone?'

'There was someone watching us through the window.'

'Creepy,' she said, looking over my shoulder at the street. 'Who do you think it was?'

Could it be the same person who left the letter? That tied the string?

'I didn't see their face. But I think it was a woman.'

'A woman? Do you think it was a burglar?'

'Perhaps. Or it could be the same person who wrote the note.'

'What note?'

After the shock of Sophie's second betrayal, I hadn't yet told her about the strange letter and string booby trap.

I found the note and showed it to her.

She stared at it for a while, studying the words and horse picture on the reverse, as I told her about the string tied across the driveway.

'It's just kids,' she concluded.

'But why target me?'

'Kids get up to strange things nowadays. You probably did strange things as a kid. I remember my friends and I posting empty crisp packets through a woman's letterbox every day for an entire school term. Ready Salted, Cheese & Onion, Prawn Cocktail, Pickled Onion. The woman probably went insane. We only did it because she looked at us funny once.'

'But it feels more personal, more sinister than just kids. Have you noticed anyone follow you?' I asked.

'What? Like a stalker?'

'Maybe.'

'No. Why are you asking?'

'Perhaps Martin from Moss Club did this?'

Sophie laughed.

'I thought you said it was a woman?'

'It could have been a man. How tall is Martin?'

'Over six foot.'

'It wasn't Martin then,' I said, imagining him as a massive moss monolith.

I wandered around the house checking the windows were closed and doors locked. It felt like we'd been invaded—that merely by peering in, the figure at the window had stolen something.

At lunchtime, I looked online for a CCTV camera to put in the front window.

Until the camera arrived two days later, I was on edge. The whole time I was in the house, I'd run to the window, hearing noises outside, seeing nothing. And when I had to go out, I was convinced I'd return to find the house broken in to.

With some swearing, and accidentally giving myself a thin, itchy cut to my finger, I installed the camera in the corner of the living room window. With an excellent view of the driveway and the street beyond, triggered by movement, the camera recorded everything passing by—cars, people walking their dogs, potential burglars, pesky kids. I could watch the footage from my laptop and pored over the speeded-up footage at breakfast that whole week. I saw a succession of neighbours, postmen and postwomen, cats, a squirrel, Sophie leaving the house, me heading to work. Sophie went out more than I thought. I'd assumed she stayed in the house most of the time, working in the garden, tinkering with her website, or lazing about. But she left regularly, at least twice a day, wearing a backpack, returning within an hour. Where was she going?

'Are you spying on me?' she asked, surprised when I asked her about it.

'I saw it on the camera.'

'So, you *are* spying on me?'

'That's not what it's for. I just happened to see you.'

She looked at my face as if studying for signs I was telling the truth.

'I'm going on my moss walks,' she said. 'You already know I go out looking for moss.'

'I didn't know you went so often.' I thought it was an occasional thing, a couple of times a week.

'Where do you think I get all this moss from to eat? I've got to pick it fresh.'

The most important thing was that the potential invader hadn't returned. No more booby traps were left. If it had been a burglar, they'd moved on to another target. Still, the thought nagged at me that someone was watching us. I was paranoid about the windows being closed properly and the doors locked, the shed and garden gate secure. I still twitched the curtains whenever I thought I heard something outside.

On Saturday, Sophie sat at her laptop for hours, staring at the screen, the silence punctuated by tapping on her keyboard and jerking the mouse around. Her eyes were narrow with dark bags beneath. She'd tilt her head, forehead wrinkled in concentration, studying what she'd done, then stab the delete key, taking out her frustrations on it.

'What are you up to?' I asked.

'I'm doing a presentation at the club,' she snapped. 'It's called *Mosses where I live*. I've got to finish it for tomorrow.'

'Tomorrow?' I said, surprised. 'But we're supposed to be seeing my parents. It's Mum's birthday. You promised you'd come.' I'd told Sophie about the visit days ago. She'd even helped me to choose Mum's presents.

'Did I?' She looked puzzled. 'Sorry. I can't.'

'But you need to come. Mum will freak out.'

'Sorry, I forgot about it. I'll come another time.'

I glared at her, but she didn't lift her eyes from her laptop.

'Sophie, please.'

'No.'

I stamped my foot and she looked up.

'Really?' she said with a withering look.

I sulked out of the room to go and calm down.

How would I explain to my parents why Sophie hadn't come to visit again? I'd have to be honest—moss came first—it was important to Sophie. I could take some of Sophie's drawings to show Mum. I could show her photographs of the garden. She'd like that. She'd see that Sophie was serious about moss. It wasn't just a poor excuse not to come.

After a few minutes, I'd pocketed my anger, then went back to the kitchen to make myself a cup of tea. Sophie was still tapping away.

'You're spending a lot of time on it,' I said.

'It's stressing me out a bit if you can't tell.' She tapped her fingernails on the side of her laptop.

'I'm sure it's fine.'

'I don't want to identify things wrongly. They'll pick me up on it.'

'They can't expect you to be an expert.'

'Why not? What do you think I've been doing reading all these books?' She waved at the piles of books and magazines surrounding her. 'I'm trying to become an expert. That's what I want to be. I don't want to look foolish,' she sighed.

'You can practice your presentation on me if you like.'

Sophie frowned.

'Maybe when it's finished.'

She continued to work, and trying not to disturb her, I took my book to the garden, and lay on my front on the moss beneath the oak tree, the warmth of the sun passing through the tree's canopy. The moss was soft and spongy, my elbows sinking deep into it as I propped myself up to read. Lawnmowers hummed in surrounding gardens, and the air was fresh and fragrant with the smell of cut grass. The texture of the moss, tiny fronds densely packed, made my bare toes tingle.

Reading about the detective closing in on the serial killer made my eyelids heavy. I closed my book, lay my head on the ground, and shut my eyes.

The fence at the back of the garden creaked loudly and I looked towards the noise. There was someone there in the shade, hands gripping the top of the fence, pulling them up so they could spy on me from the alleyway on the other side.

'Hey!' I shouted, jumping up.

The spy dropped down, and I heard them stumble and run as I approached the fence. I pulled myself up, but they had vanished.

I lowered myself down, swearing as a splinter pierced my thumb, and I returned to the house.

'Someone was watching me in the garden,' I told Sophie animatedly. She was still working on her presentation and looked angry at the interruption. 'I chased them off.'

'It's kids again,' she said, waving me away. 'I need to finish this.'

'But I'm getting really worried now. What if it's not kids? What if it's more serious?'

'Well, you scared whoever it was away, so don't worry about it.'

I left Sophie to get on with her work, and dug out the splinter from my thumb, worrying over who was spying on us. Why wasn't she taking this seriously?

Sprinting across the moss while watching the fence, I fetched my book from the garden. I locked the door to the garden behind me and went to the living room. Perhaps I shouldn't be reading things like this? Rather than thinking it was kids messing about, I thought the worst: stranglers, kidnappers, knife-wielding psychopaths.

I put the book to one side and checked the CCTV footage on my laptop for the spy passing the house— nothing. To distract myself, I switched on the television—an antiques show. Then I wrapped Mum's birthday present—a jigsaw of a woodland scene, which, with all the trees being the same shades of green, looked difficult to complete—the type she liked. I signed her card with both my name and Sophie's because I didn't want to interrupt Sophie to sign it herself. I'd leave to visit my parents when Sophie left for Moss Club in the morning.

That evening, Sophie whispered her presentation to herself over and over. And when I went into the kitchen, she was delivering her presentation to an invisible audience, carefully rehearsing her body language.

'Why don't you take a rest?' I said.

'Not yet. I need to get this right.'

Sophie didn't eat anything for dinner and couldn't sleep that night, spending a few early morning hours out of bed, pacing downstairs, muttering her presentation. She disturbed me climbing back into bed as soft dawn light filtered through the curtains, and she woke again an hour later, flicking through clothes in her wardrobe, and turning out drawers, trying to decide what to wear.

After covering the floor in clothes, she chose jeans, a white blouse, and a smart grey jacket. With a nervous tremor in her voice, she asked me how she looked. She appeared confident and intelligent.

'Wait, I have some glasses,' she said, unfolding them and putting them on.

They suited her. I nodded my approval.

'Where did you get the glasses from? You look like a sexy professor.'

Sophie smiled and relaxed a little.

'I've always had them.'

'You've never put them on.'

'I get by without.' She studied herself in the mirror. 'Should I wear them?'

'They make you look clever.'

'Are you saying I'm not clever?' she said, glaring.

'I didn't mean it like that.'

She laughed.

'I was only joking, Ben. But are they too much?'

'No. I don't think so.'

Sophie gathered her things for Moss Club and I offered her a lift, worried the person who'd watched the house might decide to follow her.

'I can look after myself,' she said, 'And I need the fresh air to relax me a bit.'

'Good luck,' I said as she left.

As I started the car to drive to my parents, Dad called my phone.

'Your mum's not great today,' he said. 'Can you postpone your visit?'

'What's the matter?'

'She's had her pills and gone back to bed.' He sighed. 'To be honest, she was worried about you coming today.'

Mum always looked forward to my visits.

'She's thinking about all sorts of strange things.'

'Like what?'

'Silly things.'

'Silly how?'

He paused.

'Your Mum thinks Sophie might be planning to kill us all.'

I laughed in shock.

'Of course she isn't,' I said.

'I know that, but your Mum's got this idea in her head.'

'But Sophie can't make it today—I was just coming alone.'

'Oh.'

'She's got an important moss thing to do.'

'More important than meeting us for the first time? More important than your Mum's birthday?'

'She says sorry.'

Dad mumbled something.

'I'll come and help calm Mum,' I said.

'I think it's best to leave her when she's like this. She's having a bad day today. She'll be fine tomorrow.'

Reluctantly, I agreed to put off my trip.

'Wish her a happy birthday,' I said.

Sophie had to visit my parents soon. I wouldn't let her say no. Mum's sanity was at stake. Sophie had to show them how nice she was.

Returning to the house, I kicked off my shoes and I picked up my library book. I read at the kitchen table as the serial killer evaded the detective again and slashed his way through another hapless victim. Spooked by Mum's idea of Sophie murdering us all, I imagined my face on the victim's bloody body, Sophie's face on the maniac killer. I shut the book. It wasn't doing me any good, making me paranoid, putting absurd ideas in my head—it had to go. Maybe I was too boring for this kind of thing. I'd stick to gentler books. I decided to return my crime book to the library unfinished.

Walking back from the library, a new book in my hand, a novel about a man giving up his former life to live alone in the wilderness, I saw Emily from the stationery shop heading my way. When close, she broke into a run, her frizzy hair bouncing, and with both hands shoved me hard on the chest, sending me stumbling backwards into a wall.

'What are you doing?' I cried.

She panted—tiny beads of sweat hanging on her top lip and forehead.

'Sophie says you don't want me talking to her,' said Emily.

What was she was talking about?

'She says you think I'm a bad influence. How am I a bad influence?'

'I never said that.'

'Yes, you did. All men are the same. You want to keep her all to yourself. Wrap her in cotton wool. Stop her seeing friends. Stop her doing anything so she's completely reliant on you. It's abuse. You're an abuser.'

'I never——.'

Emily shoved me again, and the back of my head bounced painfully off the wall. She ran away, crying in loud bursts.

'Have you been watching me? Did you post that letter through the door?' I shouted after her, rubbing my sore head.

Arriving home, Sophie was back early from Moss Club. She was sitting in the living room, head slumped, a damp tissue drying her eyes.

'Did the presentation go well?' I asked tentatively.

'It went okay,' she sniffed. 'But I found out what happened to Alan's mum.'

I knelt down in front of her and Sophie wrapped her arms around me, drawing me close, pressing her head tightly to my chest so my shirt buttons dug into my skin. I held her as she sobbed.

'Alan's mum had osteoporosis,' she said, releasing her grip slightly. 'She knew all about it and went to the doctor regularly, took medication, ate healthily to keep her bones strong—she knew she had to be careful. But despite all that, the bone that attaches the spine to the head, the Atlas bone, just crumbled and gave way.'

My hand involuntarily went to the back of my neck and rubbed it.

'Her head fell so suddenly and so hard it snapped her spinal cord,' she said, shaking, beginning to cry. 'Why do such horrible things happen? Why are people always dying?'

I held her tightly as she sobbed. I could feel the solid lumps of her spine under my hands. She felt worryingly small, fragile, much thinner than she'd been. I tried to remember the last time I'd seen her naked. She changed clothes when I wasn't looking, wore pyjamas in bed, and wrapped herself in large towels after showers. Why hadn't I realised she was shrinking?

'How about I make you dinner tonight to cheer you up?' I offered.

'No, it's okay. I've got some of last night's dinner to finish.' Sophie referred to the pasta she'd made with a basil and moss pesto.

'Are you sure?'

'Just cuddle me.' I tightened my grip so her nose pressed against my neck, inhaling deeply.

'You smell nice,' she said.

She was sniffing the aftershave she'd bought me. I'd worn it to smell nice for Mum's birthday.

Sophie cried for a long time. I grew stiff and fidgety, but each time I tried to move, she held my arms around her. Finally, she took a deep breath and released me.

'Sorry,' she said. 'It's just so sad.'

'Who told you about Alan's mum?' I asked.

'I bumped into Emily.'

So Sophie *had* spoken to Emily. Maybe Sophie had said those horrible things about me?

'Alan came into the shop with his aunt and told Emily the story,' she said. 'He'd been looking for me.'

'It must have been strange going into the shop where his mum died.'

'Emily said Alan doesn't seem right. He's gone into himself. And his aunt seems kind, but it looks as though she's not coping. He's special. He could be a lot to deal with.'

'I'm sure he'll be fine,' I said. 'How's Emily?'

'She's upset.'

'Why don't you invite her over for dinner or something?' I could show her I wasn't an abuser.

'I don't think so.' Sophie shook her head.

'I thought you were friends?'

'We were, but I don't want to see her anymore.'

Sophie stood up. 'I'm going to get another tissue.'

She began walking away.

'I saw Emily as well, on my way home,' I said.

'Really?' Sophie stopped, intrigued.

'She pushed me against a wall.'

Sophie put her hand to her mouth in surprise.

'Sorry,' she said. 'I think that's my fault. I had to make an excuse to not see her anymore.'

'She thinks I'm some sort of abuser.'

Sophie laughed.

'You? An abuser?'

'That's what she thinks.'

'That's not what I told her.'

'What if she tells other people? What if she attacks me again?'

'You said she pushed you, not attacked.'

'I hit my head.' I turned to show Sophie the back of my head, pointing at where it'd hit the wall. 'It hurts.'

She came over, turned the back of my head to her, and prodded around. I flinched when she hit the spot.

'I can't see anything there,' she said. 'There's no blood, no lump.'

'Anyway, why don't you want to see her anymore?' I asked.

'She had a go at me for eating moss, said I looked too thin—emaciated, she said. I don't need someone like that around me.'

'Maybe she has a point.'

'Don't you start having a go at me about it. I'm a

healthy weight.'

Sophie nodded towards my stomach.

'What about that?' she said.

'What about it?' I looked down at my stomach.

'It's getting bigger.'

Sophie was upset, saying things she didn't mean—I needed to leave her alone for a bit.

'I'm going to clean the bathroom,' I said as an excuse to leave. I went upstairs, hoping she'd cheer up.

In the bathroom, I took off my t-shirt and looked at my pale torso in the mirror. I lay my hands on my stomach. It was soft, like warm dough spreading beneath my fingers. A roll of fat hung over my belt. I sucked in my stomach and held my shoulders back. I could just see my ribs below what I'd heard described as man boobs. When did this begin? I hadn't noticed getting bigger. I wore the same sized clothes I'd always worn since reaching adulthood.

I put my t-shirt back on, and now conscious of my weight gain, realised how much I'd filled out, how my stomach and nipples pushed at the fabric. I used the widest hole on my belt, my thighs pushed against my jeans. And when I jogged up or downstairs, my breasts wobbled. Sophie was so thin, a stick, a bean pole—I was obese in comparison. Now I was fat *and* boring. What did Sophie see in me at all?

Later, Sophie apologised for insulting me.

'There's nothing wrong with you,' she said, ruffling my hair as she liked to do. 'I've just had a bad day, I was lashing out.'

I gave her a kiss.

'By the way, I'm not going back to the club again,' she said. 'They can get lost.'

'I thought you said the presentation went okay?'

'It went amazingly. They loved it. Then Violet, the

silly hag, told everyone about my website. She told them about my recipes, and how I encouraged everyone to eat moss, and said I was encouraging the mass destruction of mosses in the wild. I told them I had a gardening section too so people could grow their own moss, but they didn't want to hear it.'

'So they kicked you out?'

'No, I left,' she snapped. 'They were calling me "stupid" for eating moss—even Martin didn't defend me, the fucker. They all ganged up on me. So they can fuck off.'

'Come here,' I said, offering her a hug.

She shrugged me off.

'Anyway, I've got a plan. I won't let them get me down. I'm starting my own moss club. An online one. I've got thousands of visitors to the website now, loads of people will want to join.'

Sophie spent the evening creating a new section of her website for her new digital moss club. She tapped heavily on her keyboard, as if nailing the coffin closed on her former club mates. When finished, she looked triumphant.

'That'll show them,' she said.

As I ate porridge for breakfast, Sophie crunched on square crackers of dried moss and studied her laptop.

'I've had a few members sign up overnight. Not as many as I'd hoped,' she said, looking downcast.

'You only set it up yesterday. Give it time.'

'I don't know. Maybe people aren't interested in moss like I am? They're just looking for quick ways to lose weight—they don't care about the moss.'

'Be patient. They'll sign up eventually,' I said, trying my best to be encouraging.

'I really need like-minded people to talk to about

moss.'

'Talk to me about it.'

'You're not interested.'

'I might be.'

'But you don't care about moss. Not *really* care about it like I do. Not like I thought the people at Bryology Club do.'

'I care about *you*, though.'

'But you've never understood my love of moss. You don't understand who I am.'

'I do.'

'You don't, Ben.'

Sophie put her last cracker in her mouth and crunched loudly.

'Okay, tell me who you are,' I said. If I didn't understand her, it was because she never told me about herself.

Sophie shook her head.

'It's probably a good thing you don't understand me. You might not like me if you understood me.'

'I would.'

'I'm not so sure.'

'Don't be like this,' I said.

Sophie took a deep breath.

'Sorry, I'm not feeling great about myself at the moment, Ben. I'm having an off-day. I'm still annoyed at the club. It's left a massive hole in my life.'

I left Sophie to herself and got ready to go to the shops before work. I needed to talk to her about coming to visit Mum, but now didn't seem the time.

In the supermarket, I stayed away from crisps, biscuits, and chocolate. Avoided sausages, bacon and burgers, fried chicken and ready meals. I planned to eat healthily, eat all the things I knew I should eat but didn't—plenty of vegetables and whole grains. Instead of chips, brown rice. Fruit rather than sweets. I'd skip desserts. I'd always been slim—'hollow legs,' Mum used to say—but that had changed.

Leaving the supermarket, holding shopping bags in both hands, I saw Alan. He was alone, his bright red jacket replaced with a black one, his fringe hanging down beneath his hood, and acne blistered and sore. He ran towards me, and I dropped my shopping, a bag of rice splitting and scattering grains, a pot of natural yogurt splattering glossy and white on the pavement, as his fists delivered tiny, angry jabs to my chest. I blocked his hands with my palms, like I was sparring with a toddler.

'What have you done with her?' he cried in his squeaky adolescent voice.

'Stop it Alan.' My hands were getting sore.

He sweated, his acne on fire, fringe swinging in time with his punches.

People stood around watching, no-one intervened.

I didn't want to be seen to be beating up a teenager. Alan was smaller than me, shorter, wiry, just a boy, so I let him continue punching, hoping he'd tire before I did.

'What's the matter, Alan?' I asked. 'Calm down.' His right hand flew upwards and caught my lip, smashing it against my teeth. I shoved him hard and he stumbled, then fell onto his bottom, landing heavily.

A man stepped between us.

'That's enough, mate?' he said to me, as the tang of blood flooded my mouth. 'Back off.'

I stepped away. Alan remained seated.

'What have you done with Sophie?' he asked, panting.

'Nothing.'

'Why isn't she at the shop anymore?'

'She quit, Alan. She didn't want to work there.'

He looked confused.

'She's at home,' I said. 'Nothing's happened to her.'

He shook his head, 'No, no, no,' and stood. He eyed the man waiting to separate us, and the watching crowd, and ran, tripping on a raised paving slab, falling to his knees.

Someone laughed.

'Alan, come back,' I called after him. 'Did you post a letter through our door? Did you tie the string across the driveway?' But he didn't look back as he stumbled away, limping.

After gathering my shopping and heading towards home, I wondered whether the world was out to get me. Walking the streets wasn't safe anymore—there was always someone attacking me, and I was being spied upon in my home and garden.

'What's happened to your lip?' asked Sophie when I arrived home.

I was heavy with exhaustion, wanting to crawl into bed and hide beneath the duvet until it felt safe to come out. My lip was tender and swollen.

'Alan did it,' I said.

'Alan? My Alan from the shop?'

I nodded.

'He's upset you're not working there anymore.'

'But why he would attack you?'

Sophie grabbed my head with both hands and turned my face towards her. 'Don't squirm. Let me see,' she said.

I pulled away.

'First Emily and now Alan—who else is coming for me?' On the way home, I'd imagined assailants lying in wait behind corners, crouched in bushes, ready to spring. 'And I think it was Alan watching the house. It was him that left the note and the string.'

'He wouldn't do that.'

'You didn't see him, Sophie. He was crazed. He'd probably do anything.'

'Even if he did, grief makes you do silly things, Ben. You're not badly hurt.' She looked out of the window into the garden. 'Grief never goes away, but the pain gets a little better,' she mumbled.

'You should find him, explain why you're not at the shop anymore, calm him down.'

'I wouldn't know *how* to find him.'

'Emily might.'

'I told you, I don't want to talk to her again.'

Sophie opened the freezer and handed me a bag of frozen peas.

'Put this on your lip.'

I held the bag to my lips, the cold an instant relief, soreness shortly subsiding to a tingle.

'Now Emily and Alan have got the anger out of their system, I'm sure you're safe,' said Sophie. 'I'll protect you.'

8

'Can I borrow twenty quid?' Sophie asked sweetly as I was about to leave for work on Monday morning.

'What for?'

'I've got no money left.'

It'd been weeks since Sophie had left her job at the shop, and it seemed she'd stopped looking for anything else, occupying herself with her moss website and gardening. People were slowly signing up to her online moss club, learning and discussing moss, but I could tell she wasn't happy with it—the spark was missing behind her eyes.

If Susan had written an article about Sophie on her blog, Sophie never mentioned it, and there didn't seem to be other bloggers interested. I wasn't sorry about that. And no-one called on her moss expertise as she'd expected.

Sophie spent little on food because she bulked out most of her meals with moss, but moss books and journals still regularly dropped through the letter box, and at some point, she was always going to run out of money.

'You need to find another job,' I told her bluntly.

'I'm looking,' she said. 'I look every day. There's not a lot out there at the moment.'

'Where are you looking?'

'Online.'

All she ever looked at online was her own website or sites related to moss. Her project this week appeared to be printing out pictures of moss from the internet, placing them on the living room carpet, and arranging them in a big collage, moving the pictures repeatedly before finding a position which pleased her. Every time she added a new image, she couldn't simply slip it in. Instead, she had to rearrange all the others surrounding it. It was like a jigsaw puzzle that had no solution.

Sophie followed her passions as I worked to pay for the house we lived in. I appreciated she'd needed time away from work to recover from the death of Alan's mum and the feelings stirred up about Eugene, but now, weeks later, with Sophie smiling in front of me asking for a handout, it was hard not to feel like I was being used.

'There must be jobs in other shops?' I said.

'I don't want to work in a shop anymore.'

'You could do it temporarily until you find something else.'

'I'll hold out for a job I want.'

'What kind of job are you after?'

She thought for a moment.

'Perhaps something outdoors,' she said, 'like gardening.'

That would suit her brilliantly.

'I'll help you look if you like.'

'I don't need any help, thank you,' she said. 'I'm quite capable of finding my own job.' She smiled more broadly, a forced smile. 'Can I have those twenty pounds or not?'

I took out my wallet and reluctantly removed the only money I had in it: two ten-Pound notes.

'You can have this on condition you promise to visit my parents with me soon.'

'That's blackmail.'

'Maybe. But Mum really wants to meet you.'

Sophie paused in thought.

'Okay, I already said I would before, and I promise,' she said, taking the money from my hand and kissing me on the lips.

Later, at work, as I stared at a spreadsheet, worrying about Mum, worrying about Sophie, a ringing started in my ears—an electronic ring rather than the dinging of a bell, accompanied by a light vibration from my forehead to the back of my skull, like an electric current was being applied to my head.

The ringing started off quietly, almost inaudible among the everyday background noise of office chatter and clacking keyboards, but it soon grew louder, and the vibrations stronger. I couldn't concentrate on my screen and went to get a glass of water.

Elise was in the kitchen.

'I haven't seen you for a while,' she said. 'How have you been?'

The noise in my ears fogged over her words.

With tiny tremors shaking my hands, I quickly ran a glass of water and gulped it down as Elise awkwardly waited for an answer.

'Thirsty?' she asked.

The ringing eased a little as the chilly water seemed to flow through my body, cooling my blood and nervous system, steadying my hands.

'Sorry, I needed it. My head feels funny.'

'You look pale,' she said, holding her small, soft hand to my forehead. We briefly stared into each other's eyes before both turning away, embarrassed. I looked around the office to see if anyone had spotted us having that intimate moment, but they were all busy looking at their computers or phones.

'You don't have a temperature,' she said, stepping back. 'Anyway, how's life? How's your girlfriend?' Why was she asking me about Sophie? 'What's her name again?'

'Sophie.'

'What does Sophie do? Is she an accountant like you?'

'No,' I laughed. What could I say Sophie did? 'She studies moss.'

'Moss? Like a student?'

'Sort of.'

'That's interesting.'

'She thinks so.'

'Don't you?'

'Not really.'

'She probably thinks what you do is boring.'

'It is,' I said.

'Well, don't say that too loudly around here.' She laughed.

The ringing increased in volume again, and I rubbed my forehead.

'You should go home if you're not well,' said Elise.

'I think I will,' I replied.

As Elise walked away, the waft of her perfume brought back memories, not of Elise, but of Sophie wriggling out of my perfumed clothes.

Arriving home, I took a bath. With my head under the surface, and ears full of warm soapy water, the ringing dulled in pitch, but the vibrations strengthened, feeling as though they rippled the bath water.

In frustration that I wasn't feeling better, I banged the back of my head against the bath and suddenly the noise and vibration stopped. I lifted my head from the water to nothing but the sound of drips from my hair and the sloshing of bath water around my body.

The week passed without my head feeling funny again, but Sophie's outstretched hand received money from my wallet on Wednesday, Thursday, and Saturday. In total, I'd given her ninety pounds.

On Sunday morning, I engineered a trip to a garden centre to encourage Sophie to apply for a job there.

During the week, when Sophie had been out of eyesight, I'd spent hours searching job websites for something suitable for her. With her shop experience and new love of moss gardening, the job at the garden centre was perfect. I told Sophie I wanted to find Mum a plant to cheer her up, an extra birthday present alongside those I hadn't yet given her, and I needed Sophie to help me choose. Dad had called earlier to say Mum had calmed down a little. She wasn't quite right yet, but we could visit next weekend.

'And Sophie's definitely coming this time?' he said. 'Because you've said Sophie's coming before. That'd be even harder on your mum.'

Sophie had promised to come. And with no moss club to attend, she didn't have an excuse.

'She'll be there,' I said.

Sophie was keen to visit the garden centre—she wanted to find out whether they sold moss.

On the drive there, as Sophie inspected her appearance in the rear-view mirror, again wearing her enormous sun hat, she told me how she'd closed down her online moss club.

'Barely anyone's signed up and the ones who have are nutters. I'm better off alone,' she said.

In between looking for jobs for Sophie, I'd visited her website. A barrage of negative comments had appeared from people, mainly men, rubbishing Sophie's recipes and her conviction that moss was good for you. Comments ranged from the eloquent, *Moss tastes like shit*, to, *I'm very concerned about people eating moss. Moss has no proven nutritional or medical benefits and yet people with serious conditions, instead of listening to the expert advice of their doctors, believe moss will cure a range of ills. Always follow medical advice before trying fad foods.*

Sophie hadn't mentioned the comments. Either they upset her and she didn't want to talk about it or she was oblivious to how passionately some people felt against what she was doing.

'Without the club I can focus on my garden and recipes,' she said.

We drove around the large garden centre carpark twice until we found a free parking space. It was so narrow I had to squeeze myself out, holding my breath, door knocking against the car beside, with Sophie wincing as she watched. When I was out, I checked for damage, and luckily found none. I really needed to slim down.

The sliding doors to the garden centre opened and blasted us with warm, tropical air. Dozens of elderly people, many accompanied by their middle-aged children, pootled around the shelves and displays, admiring the sharpness of secateurs, and the patterns on pots; the gauge of gardening gloves, and suitability of seeds for their garden's growing conditions.

The queue at the garden centre's coffee shop was so long it looped around the lawnmower section.

'I hope they don't run out of teacakes like they did last week,' I heard someone say.

Sophie found some dried moss used for lining hanging flower baskets.

'Inedible,' she said, chewing on a bit she broke off, spitting it discreetly to the floor.

We found the house plants.

'I need something simple,' I said. 'Mum doesn't like things cluttering the house. It needs to be low maintenance.'

'How about this?' said Sophie, pointing to a foot-tall cactus, green with fine brown spikes up its length.

'It looks a bit unfriendly.'

'It looks like a penis,' she said, laughing.

We meandered through the plant displays. I felt the leaves between my thumb and finger, leaned in close to smell the flowers, and read the tags to learn what growing conditions they liked, while imagining how they'd look in my parents bare living room.

'I'm going to look at watering cans,' said Sophie, looking bored. She disappeared to another section of the garden centre.

Eventually, I settled on a simple plant with red-tinged leaves. It looked hard to kill and came in a terracotta point painted with tortoises.

I picked it up and was about to find someone who could give me a job application form for Sophie when I heard a commotion from the other side of the garden centre. Things were being thrown about. A man was talking loudly and firmly. A woman was shrieking. It was Sophie! The plant slipped from my hands. The pot smashed, and dozens of startled eyes turned in my direction. With the soil scattered, and the plant lying like a discarded weed, I ran towards the noise.

I skidded to a halt when I saw Sophie standing by a display of powdered weed killer boxes, garden centre employees surrounding her in a semi-circle. She pulled a box from a shelf and threw it to the floor. Its sides split, and a puff of white powder escaped, settling over the other damaged boxes already lying there.

'You shouldn't be selling this stuff,' she yelled at a uniformed member of staff as he motioned for her to calm. 'Moss has a right to life.'

I moved in closer. The boxes on the floor were

labelled "Moss Remover" or "Moss Killer" depending on the brand, "For greener lawns free of moss."

A small crowd of on-lookers gathered.

'Moss is beautiful,' Sophie shrieked. 'Why would anyone want to destroy moss?' She was crying. Her arms waved frantically.

I was numb with embarrassment.

A tall, spindly man, like a twig in a suit, appeared, and dialled a short number into his mobile phone.

'Police.'

'Don't,' I said, stepping in front of him, pleading. 'I'll calm her down.'

'You know her?' he asked.

'I'm her boyfriend,' I said uncomfortably. 'Sorry, she's not herself.'

He looked stern and unsympathetic but put his hand over his phone's mouthpiece.

'You'll have to pay for the damage.'

'No problem,' I said, reaching into my back pocket and holding out my wallet.

He told me to calm her down, then spoke into his phone, saying it had been a mistake and no one needed to come down.

'Sophie,' I said as she prepared to sweep an entire stack of boxes to the floor. 'Sophie, we need to go.'

She stopped, looked at me, and then at the mess at her feet, shaking white powder off her trainers.

'I can't let them sell this stuff,' she sobbed.

'They've promised to get rid of it.' I nodded at the twig in the suit. 'They'll put it all in the bin.' He looked at me perplexed, before realising he needed to join in.

'Of course we will,' he said dryly, his nodding so exaggerated I thought he might snap his neck like Alan's mum.

Sophie looked at him, eyes narrowed, questioning his

sincerity.

'Okay,' she said, before leaping and stamping heavily on the boxes she'd thrown to the floor. An explosion of white powder burst into the air. I shut my eyes, hid my face with my hands, and spluttered on the dust. When the powder settled, it looked as though Sophie was sculpted from plaster. The air tasted bitter. The people who'd gathered around coughed as they brushed themselves down.

Sophie cleared her throat. 'I'm finished,' she said, walking a trail through the powder and taking my hand. 'Let's go.'

We walked together to the carpark, followed by the twig and two of his dusty and intimidating staff. Once Sophie was sitting in the car, arms crossed in anger, glaring at our escorts, I walked with the twig in the suit back to the check-out. What he charged me was extortionate, but I handed over my credit card without argument.

'Don't come back here,' he said as I left the building. 'Ever.'

Driving home, Sophie and I were silent. I clasped my jaw tight, stopping anger from cascading out and yelling how embarrassed I was, how crazy she'd been, how scary. She stared out the window the entire way home, biting her nails.

When we arrived home, Sophie went to the living room, picked up a moss book, and collapsed onto the sofa. The white dust still covering her puffed up in the air.

She noticed me looking at her and turned away.

'What?' she said.

'Nothing.'

Dust shook out of my hair as I coughed, and I went for a shower.

As the warm water ran white down my body, my legs, and in-between my toes, I worried about what she'd do next. What other craziness could moss inspire? Moss seemed to have infected all her thoughts and decisions. She was a moss fanatic. At some point, would I receive a call telling me she'd been arrested?

'I bet you think that was mad?' said Sophie, as I towelled myself dry. 'I'm sorry. I don't know what came over me. People kill moss—I'll have to live with it. People kill forests. People kill animals. People kill other people. So why not moss? I don't like it, but that's the way it is.'

Sophie gave me a hug, coating my damp, clean body with white powder again.

'Do you forgive me?' she asked, stroking my bare chest.

'Yes,' I said through my teeth. I had a headache coming on.

To clear my head, I left Sophie gardening and went for a long walk by myself—three laps around the park. A decent walk wasn't something I'd been on recently, but I needed space from Sophie, some time to pocket the anger still bothering me from the garden centre.

By the third brisk lap, I was tiring, but felt much better, and rested to watch a duck feeding frenzy from a distance as two children tore and threw white bread into a pond. I left when a swan appeared from the reeds.

Returning home, I saw the lady from next door outside her house. She'd introduced herself when I first moved in, but I couldn't remember her name. Jean? Jane? She dropped a rubbish bag into her bin, which landed with a heavy crunch as it hit the bottom.

'Good morning,' she said perkily as I fumbled with my door keys. She was in her forties, with dark, pixie cut hair, and despite it being Sunday, wore a business suit and heels. We saw each other rarely, only nodding 'hello' if we passed while leaving or returning home. Her husband was much older, broad, tall, and grey. I'd seen him only once. She came to lean on the fence that separated her driveway from ours.

'I'm glad I've seen you,' she said. 'I wanted a quick word.'

Her wide smile didn't distract from the serious look in her eyes. She motioned for me to come close and leant in low and conspiratorially.

'We've noticed your girlfriend is sneaking into our garden at night,' she whispered. She looked over my shoulder to check we weren't being listened to. 'We think she's stealing plants.'

I dropped my keys in surprise.

'We haven't said anything to her,' she continued. 'We wanted to tell you about it, in case, well, we wanted to check…' she was trying to find the right words. 'Maybe there's something wrong with her?'

I bent to pick up my keys and squeezed them hard into my palm. My face warmed from blushing and I scratched the back of my head, prickling with tiny beads of sweat.

'I'm sorry,' I said. 'I'll speak to her. Tell her not to do it again.' Adding as an afterthought, 'She's not usually mental.' I laughed nervously.

'If she wants any plant clippings, she's welcome to them. We're not keen gardeners, she can have what she likes.'

'She collects moss,' I said.

'Pardon?'

'She was probably looking for moss.'

'How fascinating?' she said. 'Does she do that for a living? Is she some kind of biologist?'

'No, it's just a hobby.'

She nodded slowly as she considered this, tapping her fingernails on the fence.

'Well, tell her she doesn't need to prowl about. She can come around anytime to look at our moss. There's plenty of it. It's a bit of a nuisance, actually.'

'Okay. Thank you,' I replied.

She turned to leave before spinning back around on her heels and waving her finger at me, a tight smile on her face.

'Just tell her she should let us know first,' she said.

She disappeared through her front door.

Sophie was pacing the hallway, looking agitated as I entered our house.

'Some old man told me to stop taking moss from the church wall,' she said, stamping from one end of the short hallway to the other, hands balled into fists. 'He said I was damaging it.'

'What church?'

She waved her hands in its direction.

'The one down the road,' she said. 'I went there while you were out.'

Sophie continued to march up and down the hallway. I'd never seen her so furious.

'I told him to mind his business.' She was shaking with anger. 'I bet he reports me to the vicar. Stupid old busybody. It's not illegal.'

She stopped still and stared at me, looking for a reaction.

Cautiously, I said, 'Maybe he has a point?'

Her eyes narrowed and I felt myself shrink.

'I mean, he's not the only one complaining,' I continued.

'Who else!?' she snapped.

'The lady next door stopped me just now.' My voice

quivered. 'They noticed you sneaking into their garden and stealing moss.'

Sophie placed her hands on her hips and glared.

'It was embarrassing,' I said. 'You can't trespass on people's property just to get moss.'

'It'll grow back,' she shouted. 'That's what moss does. Why's everyone so bothered by this?'

Sophie started pacing again and I backed against the wall to let her pass.

'She's not worried about the moss,' I said. 'She just doesn't want you going into their garden. You're invading their privacy.'

'What? They think I'm interested in what they get up to? I don't care if they fuck in their kitchen.'

'What?'

'I saw them fucking in their kitchen. He had her bent over the sink.'

A squeal of surprise escaped me.

'Anyway, forget them,' said Sophie. 'The man at the church tried to hit me with his stick.'

'There are plenty of other places to get moss,' I suggested. 'Just avoid the church.'

'But the church moss is delicious. You can taste the history in it. Think of all the things it's seen. All the funerals, marriages, christenings. All the joy and sorrow. Life and death. Imagine all the people that've walked past it, brushed against it, stepped on it over the years—the moss has seen so much. Its flavour's sophisticated, like a good wine, or cheese.'

'That's crazy.'

'No, it's not,' said Sophie. 'If you weren't so stubborn, you'd taste it and find out. Moss absorbs things from the atmosphere, from the environment. It absorbs chemicals, sights, sounds, touch, emotions. There's so much people don't know about moss. Think how little we still know about the human body. Think how little we know about how the brain works.'

I unlaced my shoes, kicked them into a corner, and edged past Sophie into the living room, slumping on to the sofa with an enormous sigh. The conversation was exhausting. Sophie followed and stood in front of me, arms crossed.

'Why don't you ask the church for permission?' I said. 'If you say you're studying the moss, the vicar might let you take some.'

'I shouldn't have to ask. The moss doesn't belong to them. It's moss. It's free.'

'You're being unreasonable.'

Sophie flung her arms out wide.

'Why are you always against me?' she shouted. 'Why do you always take their side?'

'I don't,' I said, sitting as far back against the cushions as I could as she leaned towards me.

'Yes, you do. Why can't you be more like—?'

Sophie cut herself short, almost gagging on a name. Who was she going to say? Eugene? Martin from Moss Club?

'Forget it,' she said, walking away. 'I don't need you to agree with me.'

Later that evening, I yelled to Sophie in the garden to tell her I was going to the shop to get bread. She'd been gardening, keeping her distance from me since we'd talked.

She mumbled something incoherent, and I left her tending to her moss.

On the way to the shops, I passed the old church, built of grey stone, a tilting spire at one end, and a stubby bell tower at the other.

The wall Sophie was accused of damaging was

blackened by passing traffic and leaned unsteadily over the pavement as if a gale or hard shove would topple it. It was almost bare of moss. Only tiny, spread out clusters in dark recesses were visible. But looking closely, the stones were dotted with small, beige patches of exposed limestone where Sophie may have prised moss from its grip. I picked at a patch with my fingernail and the stone flaked and crumbled, a hairline crack appearing, fracturing the rock. The moss had been holding the stones together.

Curious to see the extent of Sophie's damage, I passed through a rusted iron gateway and entered the churchyard. The wall deadened the sound of cars passing on the road, creating an eerie quiet, and the air carried the aroma of damp, rotting leaves. On this side of the wall, I saw the same patches of exposed stone. I could see why the old man had spoken to Sophie—the wall looked naked without its moss.

I turned from the wall and walked among the ancient broken gravestones, engravings weathered away, the roots of broad oak and horse chestnut trees bursting from the ground in a twisted web over where bodies lay. This graveyard was unlike the neatly rowed cemetery where Eugene was buried. It looked as though no one had been laid to rest here for decades.

Looking closely at the gravestones, I could see more light-coloured patches where Sophie had removed moss. And there were bare patches among the grass and weeds where she may have torn moss from the soil. Sophie had almost stripped the churchyard bare.

I sat on a creaky wooden bench, which tilted to one side with my weight. Was Sophie really using so much moss? This wasn't just moss to study or plant in the garden—was she eating it all? She was a hypocrite to have gone so crazy over moss-killer when she was destroying so much herself.

A thumbnail-sized black beetle appeared on the bench beside me, unsure of its direction, scuttling towards me and then away to the far end of the bench where it sensed a big drop to the floor and drew back from the precipice.

I held my palm out and gently swept the beetle into my hand, lowering it to the ground. The beetle stayed still for a moment, then walked off, tickling my skin, into the long grass.

I continued to the shop, noticing spots along the way where it looked as though Sophie had removed moss: the bare earth around a bus stop sign, the bald spots on the bark of a tree, the naked fence of a shady alley that I risked walking along despite fear of another attack from Alan or Emily. This walk used to be greener, pleasanter.

It was getting dark when I returned home. Sophie was in the kitchen nursing a steaming cup of foul-smelling herbal moss tea.

'I went to the church,' I said, putting the bread away in the cupboard next to another barely used loaf. The vapour of her tea stung my eyes. 'The wall looks pretty bad.'

She stared into the garden.

'I know. Maybe I took too much,' she said remorsefully, having had time to think. 'But I always try to leave a bit to grow back.'

We were both silent for a moment before Sophie turned with a smile.

'It's fine,' she said. 'There's still plenty of moss round here. There's the park, moss on pavements, driveways, roads, roofs. People's gardens are full of it. I'll just be careful not to cause as much damage when I take it.'

'You can't take moss from people's property,' I said. 'They'll call the Police.'

'Come with me.'

'What?'

'You can keep a lookout.'

'No,' I said. 'You're being ridiculous. No one needs that much moss.'

'I do. Once I've washed it and removed all the soil, there's not a lot to eat.'

'But you're destroying the environment.'

'I'm not. Look in our garden—it's thriving. Every type of moss I've discovered, I've planted. I'm protecting it. Out there, people hate moss. They hate it spoiling their immaculate driveways and manicured lawns. They hate moss clumping on their roof tiles and climbing their garden ornaments. They treat moss like a weed, something alien, something dirty. Don't tell me I'm destroying moss. I'm giving it a purpose—a future.'

As I was about to go to bed, Sophie appeared wearing all black, a rucksack on her back, hair in a tight bun, and eye shadow like black clouds around her eyes.

'Why are you dressed like that?' I asked. 'You look like an assassin.'

'Are you coming or not?'

She had been serious. She was going on a night raid for moss.

I considered for a moment. I wanted her to be safe but didn't want to encourage her.

'No,' I replied.

'Fine.' She looked disappointed. 'Don't wait up.'

She slammed the door as she left the house.

As soon as she'd gone, I regretted my decision—Sophie wasn't thinking right and could land herself in serious trouble. I opened the door and stepped out to the moonlit pavement in bare feet. She'd vanished from view.

'Sophie,' I shouted, but she'd gone.

I put on my shoes and coat, guessed she'd turned left towards the wider, leafier streets, and chased after her. As I ran, my shoes slapping in fresh puddles, footsteps echoing in the chilly, dark, empty streets, I looked out for her, stopping often to rest and call her phone. It rang without an answer. I bounced on tiptoes, peering over fences and walls, and pushed my head through dense hedges, thorns scratching my face. I followed the slightest rustle and creak, ducked as two bats chased moths overhead, and jumped as two cats mewled and hissed in a violent flurry. Suddenly, I thought I heard Sophie's footsteps and ran around a corner, startling a dog walker and almost tripping over his tiny dog.

'Sorry,' I said, backing away.

After an hour, as I sat on a curb, resting, frustrated, deciding where to look next, the starless sky drizzled, and I returned home.

Fighting back yawns and holding my eyelids open, I waited up, hoping Sophie would return soon. I needed to know she was safe. I imagined her breaking a leg while scaling a garden wall, being cruelly savaged by guard dogs, or arrested and locked in a cold Police cell. Drinking strong coffee, I turned the television on loud, and walked around the house. On the kitchen table, I flicked through photographs of moss she'd left scattered. Perhaps these were the mosses she was collecting more of at this moment? They didn't offer clues to where she might be. Did Sophie care about studying moss anymore? Did she care what type it was as long as there was plenty of it to eat?

Eventually, sleep caught me, and I woke as Sophie dropped her bulging rucksack and a full black bin bag on the carpet. She lay down with me on the sofa and rested her damp head against my chest. I held her tight, glad she was safe. The clock said it was three in the morning. Mud splattered her legs and dirt was rubbed onto her elbows and knees. Tiny brown leaves were buried in her hair. I picked a few leaves free, showing them to her before dropping them on the carpet.

'That'll last me a week.' She nodded towards the bags.

I wanted to tell her how worried I'd been, how angry I was at her recklessness, but I was just thankful to have her back.

'I'm sorry for not coming with you,' I said.

'Don't worry. I was fine. Go to bed. I'm going to make a snack.'

We left the sofa and I wearily climbed the stairs. I fell asleep again quickly, only stirring as Sophie slipped under the duvet next to me.

I woke a little later as Sophie sprang from bed and ran to the bathroom. She retched and vomit splashed into the toilet. After a pause, Sophie flushed the toilet, ran the tap, spat water, and staggered back to bed. In the pale light of the streetlamp passing through the curtains, her complexion was a yellowy-green.

'Are you all right?' I asked, as she collapsed back into bed. 'You were sick.'

'It happens.'

'Are you being sick a lot?'

'Every now and again.'

'You need to stop eating moss.'

She rolled away from me.

'The moss is making you sick,' I said.

We slept later than usual, and I decided I'd call in sick to work—the first time I'd ever done it. I couldn't face staring at spreadsheets all day with this little quality sleep.

I was first to rise and brought Sophie a cup of tea—a regular cup of tea, without moss. When I woke her to tell her I'd made it, she grunted, rolled over, and returned to sleep. It was then I noticed loose hair covering her pillow, like her hair was falling out.

I stared at the back of her head. It may have been the way she'd been lying on it, but her hair looked thin—her scalp shone, pale and glossy through fine strands of her chestnut hair.

I went back downstairs, and it was another hour until I heard her get in the shower.

When she came downstairs, she put on her boots, and headed straight into the garden, bringing back a bunch of fertile, moist-looking moss covered in protruding stalks, rinsing it under the cold tap, then whizzing it up in her blender.

Sophie still looked yellow from last night. Her skin sagged beneath her eyes, and her mouth drooped at the corners.

'You don't look well,' I said.

'I'm not feeling great. I'm making a smoothie. That'll sort me out.'

'Maybe have something more substantial? Treat yourself to a bacon sandwich.'

'No thanks,' she said. 'I'm not eating meat anymore. Hadn't you noticed?'

I'd paid little attention to what food she was adding moss to now.

'I think I'm a little anaemic. Time of the month. I'll take some iron tablets.'

'Maybe you should lay off the moss for a few days.'

'The moss has got nothing to do with it,' she snapped.

Sophie took a cucumber, courgette, and banana out of the fridge, sliced them, and placed them in the blender. She sniffed a carton of apple juice before pouring it in, and added two handfuls of kale, and finally her moss. She screwed the lid on firmly, flicked the switch, and the motor buzzed into action, dark green chaos splattering and circling in the blender.

At first, when Sophie had first brought home the moss from Eugene's grave, her interest in moss seemed mundane, the same interest one might have in roses, or bonsai trees, or general gardening. The suddenness of her fascination with moss had been surprising, but understandable—it was a connection to Eugene. It was odd to eat moss, but other than my accidental poisoning, and the fact Sophie had lost a bit of weight, it hadn't seemed harmful, until now. She shouldn't be vomiting. Perhaps it was a bug she'd picked up—but I was convinced it was the moss.

And as well as the physical illness, there was no denying Sophie had been acting oddly. Could moss be poisoning her brain and her body?

Sophie turned off the blender and poured the slimy contents into a pint glass. She gulped it down and wiped her mouth.

'Delicious,' she said before coughing, holding her hands to her mouth and running to the bathroom to be sick.

I summoned my courage and called my boss to say I wasn't coming into work.

'It's probably one of those twenty-four-hour things,' I said in a strained voice, trying to sound convincingly ill.

My boss didn't even question it, telling me to get well soon.

'Why are you still here?' Sophie asked me.

'I'm pulling I sickie.'

'Why?'

'I'm tired,' I said, rubbing my eyes. 'I didn't get much sleep.'

I watched Sophie closely for the rest of the day. She displayed an almost manic energy, flitting from task to task in the garden, unable to rest, and when we spoke, her eyes were wide, and pupils darting. She wasn't well— I was reminded of myself when I'd experienced my psychosis—though she didn't seem to be seeing things.

I'd never really recovered from my psychosis, unsure if I ever got back to normal—assuming I'd been normal in the first place. But what was normal? How could I know my thoughts and feelings, emotions and sensations were those experienced by normal people?

Immediately after my illness, I'd constantly analysed myself, checking for signals of my psychosis repeating. And I'd replay conversations with people, obsessing over how I appeared to them—my facial expressions and posture—did they see my illness? Normal people didn't blush when you talked to them, did they? They weren't that shy. They didn't get covered in cold sweat as they waited in shopping queues, anxious about talking to the person on checkout. They were bold. They went out and had fun, met people for dinner and drinks. I wanted to be like that, but I'd lost my confidence, constantly fearing a decline into mental collapse. If I thought of something funny, I'd questioned whether it was the thinking of a diseased mind. Or if I found something sad, was I overly sensitive?

Despite that, every Monday morning I'd arrived at the office and functioned as required.

Over the years since my incident, some days were good and some days were bad. And on the day I first met Sophie, when she bounded over to me in the park, I'd never felt lower. I'd been staring at my feet, watching one weighty step after another, as if trapped in mud, wondering at the pointlessness of it all. All around me in the park were cheerful people. I wanted some of their joy, their laughter—to grab it and gobble it up. But it was as if a heavy cloak lay across my shoulders, numbing the outside, keeping any positive feelings at bay. If there had been a hole I could jump down into and disappear, end it all with no pain, I would have jumped.

I had no friends, no life—trapped in my own little bubble. And Sophie appeared like a miracle drug. One small dose and she became my confidence, my happiness, my chance to start afresh. Sophie was more than a girlfriend—she was a cure.

And now, to protect myself, I had to protect her. I didn't want to be that shadow person again, that frail neurotic in existential crisis. That liar to my parents and colleagues when they asked why I looked and sounded so glum and I told them I was fine.

If Sophie felt anything like I'd done back then, I had to save Sophie like she'd saved me.

9

It was time for Sophie to face reality and see what moss was doing to her. She'd been upstairs by herself for a while, so I went to find her.

'Who's this slut?' she asked as I entered the bedroom. Sophie sat cross-legged on the bed, photographs scattered around her, eyes red and watery, cheeks blotched from tears. She held out a photo for me to see. It was Maggie.

'An old girlfriend,' I replied. 'From university.'

Sophie had found my box of old photographs in the wardrobe. A friend had taken the photograph as Maggie and I had sat side by side in the Student Union bar, forcing smiles, my arm hanging drunkenly over Maggie's shoulder.

'Are you okay?' I asked.

Sophie sniffed and rubbed her eyes, a tissue scrunched in her hand.

'Why have you kept a photo of her?'

'I just never threw it out,' I shrugged.

'It's not normal to keep photos of old girlfriends.'

Sophie studied the photograph.

'You look happy,' she said. 'Was she your first love?'

'She was my first girlfriend.'

'Did you love her?'

'I thought I did. I didn't know any better.'

'Perhaps you only *think* you love me? Would you

know if you really loved someone?'

'I love you,' I said.

'I'm not sure you do. Would you do anything for me? Would you sacrifice yourself for me? Is it that kind of love?'

I paused. Did that kind of love actually exist? Would I do anything for Sophie?

'I didn't think so,' she said.

'I—.'

Sophie tossed the photograph aside and picked up another.

'How about you? Would you do anything for me?' I asked.

Sophie looked into my eyes and slowly tore the new photograph in half. The ripping sound went through me like a chainsaw. I seized the photo from her hand, the two halves still loosely joined at the bottom.

'What do you think you're doing?' I shouted.

This photograph showed Maggie, her face now parted down the middle, holding a glass of red wine, and sucking on a roll-up cigarette. I'd not seen it for almost a decade, but it was for me to throw away—not Sophie.

'Why does it bother you?' she asked, snatching up another photo.

'You shouldn't go through my stuff,' I said. But that wasn't all—it was like she was feeding my memories through a shredder.

Sophie stared at me with a strange intensity.

'*I'm* your girlfriend now. You should only have photos of me.'

'They're just old photos. I haven't seen them for years.'

With wild, sweeping arms, Sophie scattered the photographs surrounding her to the floor, and I jumped towards her, anger surging—electric and untamed. I wanted to hit her, to slap her hard around the face. I raised my hand, and Sophie threw herself back against the pillows, shielding her face with her hands.

'You were going to hit me,' she said, startled eyes peeking through the gaps of her fingers.

I backed away, trembling arms clasped to my sides. This wasn't me—I didn't hit people.

I staggered to the bathroom, locked the door, and slumped to the floor, my back against the tiled wall. Head in my hands, I stared at the chequered lino, replaying the scene: Sophie's gloomy face, tearstains, and dewy eyes, photographs strewn like windblown leaves, shivers of adrenaline, annoyance whipped to anger, Sophie cowering like a frightened puppy, and shame—no-one had ever made me that furious. I'd promised myself I'd try to help her and failed at the first opportunity.

I stared at my guilty, shaking hands, so nearly weapons, and slapped myself. The loud thwack bounced off the tiles. My cheek flushed warm as blood rose to the surface. I slapped again. Harder. Then again. I bit the edge of my tongue and winced. My jaw ached. I cried in loud, wet sobs. Sophie walked to the other side of the closed door, and I held my breath. Her breathing short and sharp. The door creaked as she leant against it, and I braced for what she might say. She sighed, and her footsteps moved downstairs. I inhaled the damp bathroom air again.

A headache soon developed, and I rubbed at the dizzying pain between my eyes. Every time I thought I was rid of them, they returned.

As I laid my head on the floor, the bathtub groaned as if someone just stepped in it, and I saw the dark, upright shape of a person hidden behind the white shower curtain.

'It's not been a good day, has it?' a man rasped.

My feet scrabbled on the floor as I panicked, trying to stand. I slid the lock from the door and fought to pull it open. It wouldn't budge.

Had the person who watched me from the garden and living room window broken into the house?

Was it the ghost of the elderly man who'd died here?

'Don't worry, Ben. It's only me.'

'Who?' I said, voice quivering, looking over my shoulder, wrestling with the door handle, putting my full weight behind it. It was stuck fast. 'What are you doing here?'

'It's me. Eugene Gray.'

I gave up on the door, grabbed my electric toothbrush from a pot on the sink, and held it at arm's length, ready to defend myself.

'Eugene's dead,' I said.

Sweat ran down the back of my neck.

'Yes.'

'So, this is a dream?' Or had my fragile hold on sanity slipped?

'Perhaps,' he said. 'You're definitely imagining me.'

My headache had vanished, and the light in the bathroom was soft and hazy, thinner than normal light.

'Come out from there,' I said.

'I can't do that. Once you see my face, I disappear. Do you want me to disappear?'

I wanted to know why I was dreaming about him.

'Not yet.'

'Then I'll stay.'

I lowered the toothbrush.

'So, what's your plan?' Eugene asked.

'Plan for what?'

'A plan to help Sophie. In the past, they'd have dragged her to a mental hospital, put her in a straitjacket, and scrambled her brain with electricity, electrodes stuck to her temples. There's no good reason to eat moss. You've tasted it, right? And now this jealousy thing. That's not like Sophie, is it? The moss is distorting her mind.'

'I know,' I said. 'But I don't know what to do.'

'Tell her straight. Tell her it needs to stop. Be forceful.'

'I've tried that,' I replied, recalling how I'd almost hit her.

'You've never been forceful. You got angry just now, but angry isn't the same as forceful. Let her see you're serious, that you're worried about her, that she needs to listen to you.'

'She won't listen.'

'You're a good guy, Ben. Don't lose patience. She's stubborn, so keep trying.' His voice transformed to a dark rumble. 'But if you ever hit her, you'll regret it. Do you understand?'

'I never meant to——'

'I won't be nice.'

His warning was clear.

'And if she won't listen to me?'

'You don't want to know.'

His dark shape was fading.

'One more thing before you go,' I said. There was something I'd been wondering. Something I felt guilty for suspecting ever since Dad mentioned Mum's worries, ever since I started reading that stupid crime novel. Had Sophie's explanation of a car accident causing Eugene's death been too simple? 'Did Sophie have something to do with your death?' I asked.

'I don't know.'

His voice was growing fainter.

'Do you know how you died?'

'No.'

216

'Was it sudden? Slow? Did you feel anything?'

'I just died.' His voice was now a whisper. 'I woke up in my bed as normal but had the feeling I was dead. And I was.'

'So, it wasn't a car crash?'

There was silence, and I pulled back the shower curtain to an empty bathtub.

I woke curled on the bathroom floor and sat up, rubbing at the impression of the lino marking my cheek. The toothbrush sat in its normal place by the sink.

My head ached again. I took painkillers from the bathroom cabinet and washed them down with water drunk straight from the tap.

I left the bathroom, went to my bedside drawer, and rummaged through used batteries, bookmarks, cufflinks, blunt pencils, and pens, until, at the back, I found a bent, silver packet of pink pills. Despite my doctor's advice, I'd weened myself off them, leaving this single pack, in case of emergencies. I knew they didn't usually work immediately, but maybe if I took a few? I sat on the bed and paused for a moment. The painkillers would fix my aching head, these pills could numb my distress. I'd hoped never to use them again. But familiar feelings were stirring—the heavy cloak was draped over my shoulders. I couldn't pocket these thoughts. Popping out three pills, I swallowed them dry. They worked their way down my throat, dissolving.

I picked photographs off the floor. They were jumbled, many upside-down. I piled them together, trying not to look at them—now was not the time to reminisce. But I caught glimpses of Maggie, Mum and Dad, old school friends, family days out, grandparents.

I lay face down on the soft bed, eyes closed, as my headache eased.

Maybe Sophie had a right to be upset—why had I

been keeping things from my past? She was jealous—that was natural, wasn't it? I should look to the future, my future with Sophie—that's how I'd fix all this.

A little while later, Sophie appeared with a mug of tea.

'I'm sorry,' she said softly. 'I shouldn't have been like that.' Sophie sat herself down on the edge of the bed and I propped myself up against the pillows. She passed me the mug. 'I can't help getting jealous,' she said. 'You're special, and I want you all to myself. I worry you'll leave me for someone else.'

She ruffled my hair, which soothed my aching head a little.

'I know that seems ridiculous and I've no right to be jealous,' she said. 'I'm the one who's cheated. But life without you scares me.'

Sophie looked at me to say something as I blew on my tea to cool it.

'I know you're angry,' she continued. 'I'll leave you alone.'

I wasn't angry—I was worried. Worried about her, about me, about us.

Sophie stood and went to leave, but stopped. Her eyes moved to beneath the bed.

'I know I went through your stuff, but please don't look through my box,' she said.

I hadn't even thought about it.

Sophie came back to the bed, knelt down, and looked at her box. She was quiet for a moment, then sprang up.

'Have you been through it already?'

'No,' I answered quickly, defensively.

'It's got finger-marks in the dust.'

I should have cleaned it more carefully.

'What did you see in it?' she shouted.

'Nothing.'

'You're lying.'

Sophie grabbed my wrist and squeezed it tight, her thumb pressing hard on my veins, as I desperately tried to stop spilling my hot tea over me.

'Tell me,' she said.

'I didn't see anything.'

She looked at me with hard, probing eyes. I stared back, unblinking.

'You can't go through my things,' she said, dropping my arm.

What was she hiding?

'I won't,' I said, rubbing my sore wrist.

Sophie pulled the box from under the bed and took it with her downstairs. I was shaking, in desperate need of a way to calm the atmosphere between us.

At sunset, I went to the garden and opened the lid of the barbecue. I screwed up several balls of old newspaper, placed them neatly on the barbecue grill, and lit them with a long match. As I lit the last ball, the heat scolded my fingertips. I blew on them to cool them, as the flames leapt and warmed my face. I took one of my photographs, Maggie, with heavy mascara and cold eyes, looking sternly into the camera lens, and dropped it into the fire. The flames caught the photo in one corner, and it curled slowly, a green hue to the flame, flaking to ash.

Over my shoulder, I noticed Sophie watching from the living room window. She waved and smiled before drawing the curtains and disappearing behind the fabric.

I burned all my photos of Maggie, dropping them one by one into the flames, waiting for one to be consumed before I fed in the next. With all the photos of Maggie burnt, a strange enthusiasm to keep the fire burning took hold, and I began on the rest. Photos of my parents, friends from university, from school, from work, landscape photographs of woods, and sea, and mountains; and holiday snaps of beaches, pools, and sun-baked ancient ruins; all went into the fire. The smoke curled into the starless night sky. Burning them was a release—I had a new life now—a future in which I could save Sophie.

That evening, without a word, Sophie joined me on the sofa, and we spent a silent night cuddling in front of the television. She held me tight, her bones hard and prominent through her woollen jumper, and pressed her nose against my chest, inhaling the acrid smoke on my clothes. I stroked and teased her thinning hair, revealing a white scalp, and brushed my fingers against her cheek— the skin, once lustrous, was now dull and grey, waxy like cheese. She fell asleep in my lap, nostrils flaring gently with each shallow breath.

'You've got to eat properly,' I whispered in her ear.

Sophie stirred and looked at me through half-closed eyes.

'Can you carry me to bed?'

'I'll try,' I said.

Sophie clung to my neck and wrapped her legs around my waist. She was surprisingly light, as though she had a bird's hollow bones. I carried her upstairs and perched her on the bed. Sophie changed into a vest to sleep in, her fish tattoo visible upon her shoulder. It had shrivelled and warped since I'd first seen it all those months ago—thinner, more twisted, more eel than fish.

We covered ourselves in the duvet. Sophie slept as worry kept me awake. How could you know if someone was too skinny? Did she need proper help? As Eugene suggested, did I just need to be more forceful? Was I capable of forcefulness without the anger that now terrified me? I reached into my drawer to take another pink pill. I grew drowsy and my head sank deep into the pillow.

Sophie was not in bed beside me as I woke in darkness. The illuminated face of the bedside clock said 2:03am. I heard the distant click of the door to the garden being closed quietly and carefully, and I went to the window.

Through a gap in the curtain, I saw Sophie creep across the lawn in her bedclothes and trainers. I rubbed my eyes to wake them. She disappeared inside the shed and returned with a spade. Stood in the centre of the moss-covered lawn, Sophie stared at the ground beneath her, before stabbing the spade into the moss, moving along, and repeating the action, until she'd marked out a large rectangle. Her movements were thoughtful, precise, quick, and quiet. She paused a moment, put down the spade, shook off her trainers, and peeled off her clothes—her thin body as white as a church candle, ribs so prominent they could burst from her chest, stomach sucked-in like someone had removed her insides. Still, she was beautiful, ethereal in the moonlight. My penis stirred, aroused, and I touched it through my pyjamas. Her head turned to the window, and I stepped back, almost toppling back onto the bed. I took a deep breath, and when I looked again, she'd slipped under the moss as if it were a blanket, stretched out on her back, head sticking out at one end, and her arms holding the moss close to her naked body. I imagined the sensation—the cool, damp earth on her back, the moss carpet soft and springy beneath her hands. Then I shivered, imagining the tickle of earthworms, woodlice, and centipedes sharing the space with her. As she twisted and wriggled with a face of bliss, Sophie caressed the moss the way her hands explored my back during sex. I was being cheated on with moss. I raised my hand to bang on the window but left it resting on the glass. My penis became flaccid.

And as I watched in wonder, goose bumps rose on my arms, and I hugged myself tight to keep warm.

Sophie was now having sex with moss. Why did she need me anymore? I'd lost her completely to moss.

After a short while, Sophie pulled herself from under the moss and brushed loose soil from her. She flattened the moss blanket upon the earth, then tapped it down with her feet. As she collected her clothes and made her way to the back door, I returned to bed and lay in a state of shock, pretending to sleep. Moments later, the mattress bounced as she silently climbed into bed.

Sophie was already out of bed when I woke the next morning. As I stretched and rolled over, the memories of yesterday and her night-time adventure stirring in my mind, stomach sinking, I heard her talking in the kitchen, her words unclear. The pauses in-between speech suggested she was talking to someone on the phone.

Small, gritty particles on the bed pressed into my skin and I lifted the duvet to reveal the white bedsheet covered with crumbs of dry, dark soil. I rubbed at a brown stain—unlikely to come out—brushed the soil off me and walked to the bathroom.

When I'd finished in the shower, Sophie had stripped the bedsheets.

The washing machine span and rattled as I made my way downstairs. Sophie was sitting at the kitchen table, looking at her laptop.

'Who were you talking to earlier?' I asked.

'No one,' she replied, without looking up.

'I heard you talking, like you were on the phone.'

'I was probably talking to myself.' Sophie tapped at the keyboard, nails clacking on the keys. 'I do that.'

'Did you sleep well?' I ventured.

Sophie looked up.

'Fine, thanks,' she said.

'You were restless.'

'Was I?' She looked back at the computer. 'I didn't notice. I slept like a baby.'

I'd decided not to mention what I'd seen her do in the night. After yesterday's fighting, I didn't want to start a confrontation, and I needed to tread carefully if I had any hope of winning her back.

'What are you working on?' I asked.

'I'm replying to someone from the website. She wants some advice.'

I thought she'd mostly given up on her website.

'Advice on what?'

'She says the moss is cleansing her, but she isn't feeling great yet.'

'Cleansing?'

'You know? She's going to the toilet a lot.'

'Is she being sick?'

'Sometimes.'

'Like you?'

'I feel good.'

'You don't look good.' This morning, her skin was so pale I could see veins pulsing in her neck, almost feel her blood circulating.

'Do I comment on your appearance?' she asked.

'No, but—.'

'But nothing. It's my body and you don't have the right to tell me what to do with it.'

She looked at me sternly.

This wasn't how I'd fix her.

'I worry about you,' I said.

'You don't need to.'

'You're so skinny.'

Sophie slapped her hand on the table.

'I'm not anorexic, if that's what you think. I'm eating.

223

I'm eating a lot. I don't look in the mirror and think I'm some fat heifer who needs to starve herself. Stop going on about it.'

I apologised and began to make myself a coffee. Further talk about her weight would only make her angrier.

'So, what are you telling your website friend?' I asked over my shoulder.

'That I find eating little, but often, helps—don't have big meals.'

'If she's being sick, shouldn't you be telling her to go to a doctor?'

'She'll get over it.'

'You don't know that.'

'What's a doctor going to tell her? They'll just tell her to stop eating moss. They won't take the time to understand, and they'll say the easiest thing, the thing that gets the patient out the door the quickest. And what good will that do? She'll ignore them. I'm giving her great advice.' Sophie continued her typing. 'Can you make me a tea if you're boiling the kettle?'

'Normal tea?' I asked, hopefully.

'No. The moss tea, in the green pot.' She'd cut open regular tea bags, inserted dried moss, and sealed them back up with a thin line of glue.

I made us both a drink. The rank moss tea soon swamped the delicious aroma of my coffee.

'Here's your cup of swamp water,' I joked, placing Sophie's drink beside her.

'Aren't you going to work again today?' she asked.

'I'm going to have another day at home.'

She didn't ask why, and just stared at her laptop.

To escape the smell menacing the kitchen, I stepped out into the garden. The weak sun peeked between clouds as the cold slabs of the patio chilled my bare feet and the coffee warmed my hands. I stretched my arms wide, lifting my face to the sun, breathing in the sweet scent of the cool, damp morning air.

Sophie's denial of her weight loss and sickness had made up my mind. There was a walk-in medical centre in town—I'd go there for advice on Sophie. I'd fix her, then fix our relationship.

I gazed out on the lawn. Because Sophie had other sources of moss to harvest and eat, it looked full and vibrant, tamed by Sophie into a neat, undulating moss patchwork. The moss was cold and moist under my toes as I walked onto the lawn. Where Sophie had lain in sexual bliss in the night, the moss was raised and lumpy where it hadn't quite flattened down. It was such an inviting, lush, vivid green it almost tempted me to copy Sophie and lay beneath it. I put my coffee cup aside and sat upon the raised moss, then laid on my back, stretching my legs, hands interlaced behind my head. The moss moulded snugly to the contours of my body, hugging me close, more comfortable than our mattress. Eyes closed, I listened to the breeze stirring the bushes, the creaking of the wooden fence, a dog snuffling in a neighbouring garden, cars whooshing past on the road; the distant, repetitive bangs of someone's building project. I turned on my side and curled up, ear to the ground, soft moss against my cheek. I listened to my blood rushing, like the sound of the sea, and heard my heart beating sluggishly, barely beating at all. Two fingers on my neck found my carotid artery—my pulse's rhythm was much quicker than my heartbeat. I placed my palm on the moss. It wasn't my heartbeat at all—it was the moss. I got to my knees and pressed my other ear against the moss. Yes, the moss had a heartbeat.

'What are you doing?' asked Sophie.

I scrambled to my feet. Sophie, standing on the patio,

hands on her hips, looked at me questioningly.

'Admiring your moss,' I said.

Sophie looked doubtful.

'You'll damage it if you stay there much longer.'

I stepped off the raised moss.

'This bit's different to the rest.' I pointed.

'It's a special type.'

'I think it's pulsing.'

Sophie's eyes widened. She ran to the moss, knelt, and put her ear to the ground as I'd done.

'Yes,' she said. 'Yes, yes, yes.'

'You can hear it?'

She turned her head to listen with her other ear.

'What is it?' I asked.

'It's just—' She concentrated on what she could hear. 'It's just growing very well.' She paused. 'This kind of moss has a powerful root system. You can hear it moving water and nutrients around. That's what that noise is.'

'That's weird, isn't it? I didn't think moss had roots?'

She stood up.

'Are you a moss expert all of a sudden?' she asked.

'No. I must have read it in one of the books you leave lying everywhere.'

'Well, this one's different. It's the miracle of life.' A soft sob escaped from her, and she teared up. 'Sorry, it's very exciting.'

I finished my coffee and ate toast as Sophie fussed around the garden tidying and watering, paying special attention to the raised moss.

'Bye,' I said, as I was about to leave for the medical centre.

Sophie was lying next to the raised moss with her arm draped over it as if it were a sleeping body, listening to the ground.

'Okay,' she said, not bothering to ask where I was

going.

Noise struck me as the walk-in centre's automatic door slid open: boisterous chatter, crying babies; a man, hand clamped over his jaw, moaning to one of the receptionists through the side of his mouth about his terrible toothache. The seats were all taken, with people instead sitting on the shiny, grey floor, or leaning against the yellow walls. A receptionist, holding a phone against her ear and leafing through paperwork, glanced at me and shrugged, as if to say if my problem wasn't serious, don't bother.

I stepped away from the reception desk. To the right, a small boy, with scruffy red hair and chocolate smeared around his mouth, was spinning a rotating leaflet stand round and round, just slow enough that I could read some of the titles: *Diabetes*, *Heart Health*, *Foot Care*, *Pregnancy*, and there, flying past in a blur was, *Eating Disorders*. The boy saw me looking at the leaflets and span the stand faster.

'Alfie! Leave that alone,' came the shout of the boy's mum sitting nearby, leg outstretched, a bag of defrosting oven chips held to her knee, dripping water on the floor.

Alfie grinned and kept spinning. I tried to snatch the leaflet as the stand whirled round, but it was too fast, and my knuckles grazed the stand.

'Please can you—?'

The boy laughed and continued to spin, putting all his effort into it, threatening to spill the leaflets from their slots.

With both hands, I grabbed the stand, and it jarred to a stop. Alfie looked stunned, stepped back, ran to his mum, and cried. I took the leaflet and left before his mum could shout at me.

I read the leaflet on a bench outside the centre's

entrance, breathing in the cigarette smoke of a woman in a wheelchair, a strange medical device fastened to the back of her chair emitting a shrill beep every fifteen seconds which made her jump.

I checked through the leaflet's list of eating disorder symptoms. Sophie didn't appear to worry about her weight or body shape. Now she no longer attended Moss Club, she didn't socialise, but that wasn't about avoiding food. Sophie ate plenty. She didn't take laxatives or make herself sick. She didn't exercise excessively. But Sophie's moss consumption had become a strict habit and I could describe her mood of late as erratic. She was tired, vomiting, and her weight seemed too low.

Eating moss didn't fit into the brief descriptions of anorexia nervosa, bulimia, or binge eating. The only thing the leaflet referred to were the vague, 'other specified feeding or eating disorders.'

In the section, 'What to do if you're worried about a friend or family member,' it said, 'Keeping quiet does not help. Eating disorders thrive on secrecy.'

I had to confront Sophie and somehow get through to her. She'd be defensive, we'd fight, but it was the illness speaking, nothing else. We'd get over this.

As I folded the leaflet and placed it in my pocket, footsteps ran up behind me, and someone dumped a pile of damp leaves over my head. I leapt from the bench to see Alan, dressed again in black, laughing like a hyena, pursued across the hospital carpark by a giant of a man who mouthed, 'Sorry' at me, and then shouted, 'Come back here, Alan.'

I brushed the leaves from me. They'd gone deep into my hair, down my back, and left small brown smears on my coat. The beeps of the woman smoking in the wheelchair had become more frequent and random, like Morse code, and with a look of concern she stubbed out her cigarette on the arm of her chair, and guided herself back inside. I walked home, looking over my shoulder to make sure Alan wasn't following me, now convinced Alan had been the secret note writer, booby trap layer, and spy.

Sophie greeted me with a broad smile when I arrived back, and before I could tell her about Alan, or talk about her eating disorder, she led me upstairs. As I lay on the bed, wondering what I'd done to deserve this, Sophie removed my clothes and silently kissed me all over. I closed my eyes, enjoying the surprise of where the kisses would land. She reached over to my bedside table and picked up the bottle of aftershave she'd bought me.

'You don't use this much,' she said, taking off the lid, and spraying it across my chest, pressing her nose against me, and inhaling the aroma. 'That's better.'

Sophie removed her clothes and slid her skeletal frame on top of me.

I watched her gently moaning, eyes shut tight, as she stroked my chest, her bony hips gaining pace, until she shuddered.

'Eugene,' she cried.

In that moment, I came—a confusing mix of ecstasy and horror. She didn't seem to realise what she'd said.

She climbed off to spoon in front of me, and I lay there, stunned, as she nestled into my body.

'That was great,' she said, breathless.

It's natural to grieve. Dead boyfriends take time to get over. She didn't mean to say it. She probably wasn't thinking about Eugene in bed.

But—.

Her eyes had been closed.

Had she been imagining him?

10

Things were amazing between us for the rest of the week. I went back to work, and on my return home in the evenings, Sophie was smiley and energetic. We kissed and cuddled on the sofa like when we'd first met, Sophie not tapping away on her laptop or head buried in a moss book. And we had sex every night. Burning my photographs seemed to have made her more secure, and Sophie's night-time visit beneath the moss, and her cry of Eugene in bed, became almost like something I'd imagined—nothing more than beautiful Sophie being a little quirky.

Sophie continued to live off moss, consuming vast amounts of it in complex salads and murky smoothies, and despite her bony body being painful to look at and awkward to touch, she didn't seem to get thinner. In fact, there was a little colour in her cheeks and she had more energy than she'd had in weeks. But it wasn't normal—I couldn't ignore it—Sophie needed to eat proper food.

Whether it was her cheerfulness or my cowardliness, every time I went to mention her eating disorder, something stopped me. I promised myself I'd say something, but an ideal opportunity wouldn't arise, and I feared ruining our fragile happiness.

I'd only had a few mild headaches. Maybe stress had been bringing on the worst ones, and now I was more relaxed, they'd eased. But as soon as I felt a headache coming on, I'd panic and swallow pills, double the amount I should take, wary that Eugene's ghost may be waiting in the shadows, ready to spring if the pain got worse.

Sophie spent each day tending to her moss. Where she'd disappeared under the moss blanket that night, the ground appeared to rising higher, like dough. In the evening, she'd sprinkle her watering can over the rectangular mound, smoothing it with her hands. She used her wristwatch to time the pulses, recording how many there were per minute. Then, before it grew dark, from every angle of the garden, and close-up, Sophie took Polaroid photographs of the raised moss, stuck them in her notebook, and dated the page.

'The heartbeat's getting steadier, stronger,' she told me one evening.

'It's not a heart, though, is it?' I said. 'You told me it was the roots, but you keep saying it's a heart.'

'You know what I mean.'

The weekend came and Sophie told me she was going out for a long walk to look for moss. I looked out the window at the grey weather and decided to stay home.

She kissed me goodbye, and I watched her walk up the road with her backpack, waterproof jacket, and wellies. She gave me an excited little wave as she turned the corner.

In the living room drawer, I found the photographs I'd had printed earlier in the week of Sophie and me when we'd first met. I chose my favourite photo: a selfie, taken with my outstretched arm, our cheeks touching, both smiling, and I slipped it into a plain, silver frame. In the photo, Sophie's skin was blushed and healthy, her hair fuller and glossier, eyes brighter than they were now. I hoped she'd see how much she'd changed, to convince her to eat better. It was my subtle, cowardly way of approaching the issue with her.

I yanked open the shed door to find a hook and nail to hang the photo. The narrow metal shelves on one side strained with boxes and spray bottles of organic fertiliser, trowels and forks, watering cans, and other gardening paraphernalia. The rest of the shed was strewn with various tools, and plastic sacks neatly labelled in Sophie's handwriting as different kinds of soil, compost, and peat. My bicycle, tyres flat, and spiders' webs between the wheel spokes, was pressed up against the shed wall— unused since Sophie had arrived.

Aiming for where I expected the nails to be, I cleared a path through the mess to the shelf. Dragging a sack of compost aside, disturbing a wiry spider who scuttled away, I spotted something in the corner, hiding— Sophie's secret box.

I stood a while, nervously scratching my head, deciding what to do. Then moving aside the lawnmower, strimmer, rake, bucket, and brush, I lifted the heavy box, placed it at my feet in the centre of the shed and stared down on it. Sophie wouldn't be home for at least a couple of hours if her previous moss foraging trips were anything to go by. If I opened it, she'd never forgive me. And things had been so good recently. But a strange, tingling curiosity ran through my body like an electric current. A voice was saying, 'Open it. Open it. Open it.' Whatever she was hiding couldn't be that bad. Perhaps she didn't want me to know she'd been an obese teenager with bad acne, or an awkward tomboy with basin-cut hair? Wasn't it about time I knew more about her?

I carried the box through the garden to the house, placed it on the kitchen table, and tapped my fingers on the lid, contemplating what to do. Until, with a finger drum roll, I opened it.

The contents of the box were so full they sprang

above the rim. On top, I found Sophie's drawing of me made of moss. It was as great as I remembered it, a shame she'd hidden it away—she should have framed it.

Beneath the drawing, ornate with purple flowers and golden vines, was a birthday card. I picked it up and held it, rubbing the raised letters of the Happy Birthday greeting with my thumbs. A card—such a private thing. *Happy 21st, my beautiful Sophie*, it read inside. *Love Nana*. I put the card aside. Other birthday cards lay beneath, with jokes about drinking gin, getting old, the uselessness of men, some with pictures of dogs, or cats, and more with intricate, brightly coloured flowers, signed by people she'd never mentioned: Laura, Jenny, James, Sarah, Matt. Where were these people now? There was a card signed in beautiful, looping script from Mother and Father. I placed them all aside in a pile on the table.

Under the cards were old bank statements from when Sophie must have been a teenager. Sophie's address marked as Luton. Luton? Luton was only half an hour's drive away. She'd told me she'd always lived in Plymouth. I took a bank statement, folded it, and tucked it into my jean's pocket. Sophie wouldn't notice it missing. Perhaps her parents still lived in Luton at this address? It could be useful.

I heard a creak from the hallway and froze.

'Hello,' I said, in a pinched, panicked voice.

My pulse raced as I scrabbled around, putting everything back in the box. In my haste, cards and paper slipped from beneath my fingers and floated to the floor. I abandoned them and slammed on the lid. It wouldn't fit.

'Sophie?' I called.

I could head her off, divert her away from the kitchen until I'd properly tidied and hidden the box. I stuck my head into the hallway. No-one was there.

'Hello,' I said again.

Silence.

It must have been the groans of an old house. Or a guilty conscience.

I returned to the kitchen table. If I stopped now and took the box back to the shed, Sophie wouldn't know I'd gone through it. I'd broken her trust, broken my promise not to look. But the box was a little museum of Sophie— a biography, a journal, a memoir—she would never tell me more about her life than the box could. And she hadn't been out of the house long. Surely, she wouldn't be back for ages yet? Guilt gnawing, intrigue spurring me on, I lifted the lid of the box, removed what I'd already seen, and continued searching.

Receipts for a used car, a silver watch, and a tattoo from a parlour in Brighton, nestled among insurance documents and credit card statements with the same Luton address, GCSE and A-level results from a Luton school—she'd got straight A's, payslips from a Luton café, more birthday cards, a child's drawing that had, *Sofee*, written in blue crayon next to a crude, long-haired stick figure in a yellow dress, and a grey squiggle that could be a dolphin, maybe a horse. And beneath all this, at the bottom of the box, were photographs.

Here was the photograph of me I'd glimpsed under the lid of the box when Sophie had first moved into the house all those weeks ago. She must have shoved it to the bottom so I wouldn't see it again. Me, facing the camera, cloudless sky, and a park's parched grass and leafy trees in the background. I stared at it for a while. Why couldn't I remember when she'd taken it?

But—

Wait a minute—

That's not—

I never—

I stood wide-mouthed in confusion.

How didn't I see it immediately? The man in the photograph wasn't me. It looked a lot like me, yes, scarily like me, my doppelgänger, my clone, but it definitely wasn't me. The person in the photo had a younger, fresher face; messier and longer hair, narrower eyes, thicker eyebrows. I'd never tanned as deep. I'd never owned a striped t-shirt like that.

The photo trembled in my hand. I felt light-headed. Who was this man? I dropped the photo on the table and picked up another.

Here was the man who wasn't me, resting on a blue towel on a sandy beach, sweat glazing his forehead, sunburnt nose, his laugh revealing neat, yellowed teeth. On his bare chest was the tattoo of a snake, just like Sophie's, like the gleaming ornament on our bookshelf. I placed it side-by-side with the first photo.

I looked at another. The man had his arm around Sophie's slim waist. A stab of heartbreak struck me, like I'd stumbled on an affair. How could Sophie react so badly to my photos of Maggie when she had these hidden away? In this photo, fresh-faced Sophie, eyes younger and brighter, wore a loose white blouse. The man was beaming. They were in a restaurant, with a white tablecloth, lit candles, and a glittery cocktail bar in the background. On the empty, sauce-streaked plates, her knife and fork were positioned at six o'clock, his at four. Sophie was raising a glass of sparkling wine as a toast to the camera. There was a ring on her finger, a starburst of light around the diamond embedded in it.

The next photo showed them both at a football game, wearing matching orange scarves and hats, pale with cold, gripping steaming polystyrene coffee cups in gloved hands.

In the following one, Sophie and the man were

beside a fairground carousel, each with an ice cream, creamy drips running down their cones, painted horses blurred in the background as the carousel span, a young girl running past, blonde ponytail trailing behind her.

Then, here was the man who wasn't me wearing my denim jacket. The jacket Sophie claimed she'd found in a charity shop, worn and faded in exactly the same places.

This must be Eugene Gray. It couldn't be anyone else. Was Sophie with me only because I looked like Eugene?

I couldn't breathe, my stomach so heavy it could fall to the floor. I spread all the photos in front of me and stared at them. Every time Sophie looked at me, she saw her dead boyfriend. The denim jacket she bought, the aftershave I'd worn, each time she rearranged my windblown hair; it was to make me more like Eugene. When we had sex, it was Eugene she had sex with. When we cuddled, she cuddled Eugene. She didn't want me to meet her family because they'd known Eugene; she knew what they'd say—I'd have discovered I was a substitute. When she disguised herself with enormous hats or by sweeping her hair over her face, it was to stop her being recognised by people who knew her, people who would have recognised me as Eugene or his double. The drawing of me made of moss was Eugene made of moss. And that time I was chased in the market—had it been Eugene that'd stolen from that man?

I was being used. Did she love me at all, or did she just see Eugene and ignore the rest? Why didn't I realise? I was a sucker, a mug, a chump, a loser, an idiot.

Emptying the remaining contents of Sophie's box onto the table, I threw the box into the corner. Countless more photos had fallen out, but I turned away, unable to bear seeing more.

Sophie's moss rinsing sieves sat on the worktop. I

picked one up, swung my foot, and kicked it hard to the other side of the kitchen. It clanged against the wall, leaving a large dent in its side. I crossed the room and kicked it again.

Opening the cupboard where we kept cups and mugs, I took a mug Sophie liked, a green one, and with a cry, launched it at the wall. It thumped upon the plaster and shattered against the tiled floor. Porcelain shards were strewn to each corner of the kitchen. The paint on the wall was chipped where it'd hit. I took another mug and aimed for the same spot. Then smashed another into the corner of the room.

I opened another cupboard and smashed glasses, plates, bowls. Then emptied the cutlery drawer to the floor, scattering forks, knives, and spoons across the kitchen. Grasping a sharp knife, I ran my finger delicately along the blade, leaving a fine white line of broken skin without drawing blood, before stabbing it into the kitchen worktop. I knocked over the chairs, swinging one against the wall, crashing a hole in the plaster.

Why had I looked in the box? She was very clear—do not look in the box.

I rested against the wall and slid down until seated on the floor, ceramic shards biting into the backs of my thighs.

'But I love her,' I said to the floor. But why did I love someone who had lied to me so often? Should I love someone like that?

I was still on the floor when Sophie returned.

'Hi,' she called from the hall.

She stopped in the kitchen's doorway.

'What the—?' She placed her hand over her mouth and scanned the room. 'What have you done, Ben?'

I looked at the destruction like it was the first time I'd

237

seen it. The floor was a jagged landscape. Broken glass and crockery glinted in the sunlight coming through the window.

'I know about Eugene,' I said.

Sophie straightened and looked at me seriously.

'You've known about him for a while.'

She picked up a large piece of broken plate by her feet.

'Yes,' I nodded. 'But I didn't know he's identical to me.'

She dropped the piece of plate. It smashed into tiny fragments.

'Did you go in my box?' Her eyes were bulging. 'Did you?'

Her look moved to the table where the contents of her box lay.

'Yes.'

Her eyes watered.

'You promised you wouldn't. You promised.' Sophie lunged at me. 'How fucking dare you?!'

She grabbed two fistfuls of my hair and pulled. Pain exploded across my head as hair and skin lifted from my skull. I tried to prise her fingers open but she held tight and yanked. I yelled. Eventually, she let go, taking some of my hair away in her closed fist. She retreated and I rubbed my sore head. Loose strands of hair, tiny pieces of white scalp attached to the end, came off in my hand.

She slumped down against the opposite wall.

'You're imagining things,' she said.

'I'm not.'

'You're crazy and you're imagining you look like Eugene.'

'I'm not the crazy one.'

'You're the one on the pills,' she said. 'I've seen them in your drawer. I know what they are. Do they even

238

work?'

'I took a couple recently, but——. I've seen the photos, Sophie. Look at them, I'm just like him. You can't deny it.'

Sophie stood and picked up some of the photographs.

'So, what?' she said, flicking through them. 'I have a type. Lots of people have a type. Some men like blondes with big tits, I like mousy haired, average looking men.'

'You know it's more than that.'

She dropped the photos back onto the table.

'What do you mean?' she said.

'You're with me because you imagine I'm Eugene.'

'You're being ridiculous.' Sophie paused and thought. 'How are your headaches? Have you been imagining other things?'

'No,' I said, looking away.

Sophie's trainers crunched over the rubble as she came to kneel beside me.

'I'm worried about you,' she said, stroking my arm.

I shrugged her off. 'Worried about what?'

'You know.'

'No, I don't.'

She put her hand on my arm again, holding gently.

'You might be going mad.'

'I'm not.'

'All the best people go mad.'

'It's not funny, Sophie.'

'And even if you do look like him, that's not why I'm with you.' She smiled. 'It's because you're cool.'

I could never be described as cool. I'd done nothing cool, ever.

'I can't just pretend this is normal and forget about it,' I said. 'Not this time.'

I lifted her hand off me and got to my feet.

'Where are you going?' asked Sophie, as I stumbled over the mess on the floor and through the door to the garden.

'Admit it or I destroy your moss,' I said. 'Admit you're only with me because I look like Eugene. Admit that you don't love me.'

Trembling with anger, I stormed across the garden and grabbed the spade leaning against the shed. It was light in my hands as I swung it back and forth.

'Why are you being so aggressive?' she asked, following me. 'That's not you.'

The spade was the only way to break through her stubbornness.

I went to her special moss rising out of the ground, and stood, poised with the spade. The moss had risen so much it looked like a freshly turfed grave.

'You can't,' said Sophie. 'It's the most exciting moss discovery in decades.'

'Rubbish.'

'I'm applying to register the garden as a Site of Special Scientific Interest.'

I rested the spade on the moss and placed my foot on it, ready to press it down.

Sophie dropped to her knees and pleaded.

'Stop,' she said. 'You can't. It's Eugene!'

'Pardon?' The spade slipped from my grip and fell.

'I'm growing him back with the moss from his grave.'

I laughed with surprise.

'You're definitely the crazy one out of the two of us,' I said.

Her face was serious, her eyes sad.

I prodded the mound with my foot. It was bouncy, springing back under the pressure.

Was it a heartbeat I'd heard?

Sophie spoke as I stared at the mound.

'When I stroked the moss on Eugene's gravestone, I felt a warm tingle of energy and I knew that it was his energy, captured in the moss. And I thought, if I consumed moss, if I could somehow capture its goodness, then that energy would be inside me, and I could meet him half-way between the world of moss and this world. I would be part-moss. But I never dreamed I could grow him back until I heard his heart beating. All it needed was a spark from me, for me to lie down and give myself to the moss.'

'That's mad. Do you know what you're saying?'

'I know it sounds crazy, of course I do. But look. He's there, in the earth.'

'It's just moss. Special moss moving water around. That's what you said.'

I grabbed the spade and jabbed it into the moss where Eugene's stomach might have been.

Sophie cried, 'No!'

There was a groan as the spade bounced off the moss as if I'd hit rubber.

Sophie and I looked at each other.

I lifted the spade again—it couldn't be Eugene, could it?

'Stop it!' Sophie grabbed my legs from behind, sending me sprawling to the ground. The spade fell beside me, and she jumped on my back. 'He's not grown yet. He's not ready.'

'It's not Eugene!'

'It is.' She stood and grabbed the spade, and I tried to wrest it from her grip. We struggled back and forth until Sophie wrenched it away from me, causing her to stumble and fall backwards. With a thud, her head hit a jagged stone in the rockery, and she lay still with eyes closed.

'Are you okay?' I asked, edging towards her. 'Sophie?'

241

No part of her body stirred or twitched. She was motionless, her chest not rising and falling.

I knelt, rested my head on her chest, and listened. Silence. What had I done?

'I'm sorry,' I said, brushing her cold, pale cheek.

Suddenly, her eyelids shot open, and I gasped as Sophie coughed and spluttered back to life.

'I thought you were dead?' I said.

She sat and felt behind her head. Her hand came back smeared with blood.

'Oh shit, Sophie.'

She looked at her hand, groaned, shut her eyes, and rested her head back on the ground.

'Does it hurt?' I asked.

Another groan came from deep within her.

After a moment, her eyes opened again, and she glared at me, holding my gaze, not blinking. She stood shakily, turned her head left, then right, to remove the stiffness in her neck, and without a word walked into the house.

'I'm sorry,' I said.

I continued to apologise as I followed Sophie up the stairs. Blood dripped from her hair, spotting the floor in glossy red drops.

'You're bleeding everywhere,' I said.

Sophie entered the bedroom and shut the door. I heard the creaks of her getting into bed.

'Do you need a doctor?' I called through the door.

'I'm fine,' she said faintly. 'Leave me alone.'

'I'll get you a bandage.'

'No. Fuck off.'

I took my phone from my pocket and held it, trying to decide what to do. Should I call an ambulance?

The phone rang in my hand—my parents were calling. Why now? I went downstairs, took a deep breath, and answered the phone.

'Hello,' said Dad. 'It's Dad.'

'Hi.'

'I'm just calling to see how you are.'

Should I tell him what's happened?

A wave of nausea passed through my head.

'I'm fine.'

'You sound funny,' he said. 'Are you sure you're okay?'

My vision was becoming hazy, unfocused.

'I'm just busy.' I realised I was almost shouting. 'Can I call you later?'

Pain shot through my head. An earthquake tremored beneath my feet. My knees gave way, and I was on the floor, with the phone repeating, 'Ben? Ben? Ben?'

'I, I—'

Mum joined in the chorus. Both of them asking if I was there, what was wrong, did I need help?

Did I need help?

The phone slipped from my hand, and I seemed to float on a cushion of air as my body soundlessly jerked around. I tingled as my floppy limbs danced, then sharp pain as I bit my tongue, metallic blood tainting my saliva. A black mist drifted from the corners to the centre of my vision, inking over until blind.

'You shouldn't have hurt Sophie like that,' said the rasping voice of Eugene. 'Now you're in trouble.'

I tried to plead for his help but couldn't speak.

A bright light shone in my eyes, its whiteness dazzling. Through the glare, I saw a woman kneeling beside me—big shoulders, blonde fringe hanging low, dressed in the dark green overalls of a paramedic.

'Can you tell me your name?' she asked.

My mouth opened but I could only stutter, 'B—, B— B—.'

'Let's get him loaded quickly.'

She vanished.

Eugene was there in the darkness.

'It's worked, you know? She's grown me back. I'm almost fully formed. My heart is beating, blood is flowing through my veins, I'm filling out. I can bend my fingers, wiggle my toes. Another day, and I'll rise from the ground and start running around. I can't wait. First thing I'm going to do is fuck her, fuck her hard with my giant moss penis. She'll love that. Can you imagine how much she wants it from me after all this time?'

I woke briefly in the ambulance as it rattled along, rainwater rushing under the tyres, a cold wailing of the siren, the paramedic seated by my side. I tried to sit up but was firmly strapped to the trolley on which I lay. An oxygen mask covered my mouth and nose, releasing a gentle hiss of gas. Sticky pads stuck wires to my chest. It felt as though an axe was buried in my forehead.

'Keep still for me,' the paramedic said calmly, lightly touching my arm. 'It'll be all right.'

'Sophie?' I said, before everything went black again.

'She's mine now,' said Eugene. 'You'll never see her again.'

11

Waking, I fought to open my heavy eyelids. My head was groggy, neck stiff, and stomach queasy. Fluorescent strip lights shone above from the off-white ceiling. A breeze from my left stirred the hairs on my arms, and a chemically clean aroma filled the air.

'You're awake.' It was Dad's voice. 'Thank God. You had us worried.'

My mouth was too dry to speak. I propped myself up on my elbows. I was in a compact room with bare, eggshell blue walls, a sink in the corner, with Dad stood at the side of my bed, tired, and smiling. Clear liquid dripped down a tube into my body through a canula stuck in my arm. A plastic beaker of water sat on a side table, just out of reach. Dad realised what I was after and placed the beaker to my lips. The water was cool and delicious. I drank greedily until too much water went down at once and I spluttered over Dad's shirt sleeves. He removed the beaker and I lay back on the firm pillows.

'Thank you,' I said, wiping my mouth. 'I'm in hospital?'

'You had a fractured skull.'

'Really?'

'It got infected and they had to drain some fluid. They said you probably had it a while but you didn't notice.' Dad patted me on the arm. 'You're all fixed now, though.' He lent down to hug me and sobbed. 'Do you remember when you were a little boy, you used to go into some sort of shock whenever anybody told you off? You'd go stiff as a pole, stare straight ahead with big, wide eyes, and fall backwards. Any slight telling off, like telling you to tidy away a toy, or to quieten down when you got too excited, and it'd happen. The first time you did it I caught you, but you weren't always so lucky. You crashed into a table once, smacked against walls, fell into a puddle—you ruined a new coat with mud—your mum was furious. Nothing so serious we thought we should take you to hospital—but we were pretty naïve back then. Luckily you grew out of it.' He paused. 'Anyway, what I'm trying to say is that you have a tough head.'

We laughed, causing me to cough.

'I better tell a nurse you're awake.' He turned to go. 'Your mum was too distressed to see you like this, so she's at your aunt's. I'll call her as well.'

'How long have I been here?' I asked.

'Two days.'

'Has Sophie visited?'

Dad shook his head. 'I've not seen her.'

I'd left her in the bedroom, bleeding from the head.

'Who called me an ambulance?'

'I did,' he said.

She'd said she was okay.

'You've gone white,' he said. 'Everything all right?'

Was she dead?

'I'm just wondering why Sophie hasn't visited,' I lied.

Dad left, and soon after, a nurse with beehive hair and thick-rimmed glasses came to check on me, followed by a large, perspiring doctor, sweat beading on her upper lip. They explained what had happened. I'd been put in a coma and operated on. But I'd be fine. I was to rest in hospital for a few days.

'You've been lucky,' the Doctor said. 'Did you have any symptoms? Headaches? Concussion?'

'Sometimes.'

She frowned.

'And I think I've been imagining things, hallucinating—is that normal?' I asked.

'What sort of things?'

'Dead people.'

'It's possible.'

'How do I know what was real and what wasn't?'

'I can't really help with that. Your head might feel a bit jumbled for a while, but you'll figure it out.'

'I've been in hospital before. I experienced a bit of psychosis.'

She picked up a clipboard hanging on the end of my bed and flicked through some pages it held.

'Did you see dead people then?' she asked.

'No.'

'I think you'll be okay. The two things are unlikely to be connected. But if you ever get a knock on the head again, go to a doctor immediately, please.'

After she'd gone, a sickening feeling grew, a trembling panic that I'd murdered Sophie. I needed to call her, to hear she was still alive.

Dad returned.

'Your mum's so pleased. She wanted to come straight away, but I said you need to rest for a bit. She'll come tomorrow.'

He pulled a plastic chair close and sat down. He shuffled to get comfortable. 'You're looking very pale.'

I motioned for him to lean in close and whispered, 'Dad, I think I may have killed Sophie.'

His laugh reverberated off the walls.

'What makes you think that?'

'Before I came here, she fell and hit her head.'

'So, that's where that sticky mess came from.'

'You've been to the house?'

'How else would I have brought you your pyjamas and things?'

I looked at my stripy pyjama top.

'And Sophie wasn't there?'

'Sorry, it looked to me like she'd gone.'

'She's gone?'

'Only your clothes were in the bedroom. Only your toothbrush in the bathroom. The place is in an awful mess.'

Sophie had left me. Despite the shock of what I'd discovered about her, about Eugene and me, the thought she'd vanished forever sickened me almost as much as thinking I'd murdered her.

'So, what's happened with Sophie?' Dad asked. 'Have you had a falling out?'

He listened as I described the last few months. The story gushed out, like I was talking a million words a minute. He made no comment, nodding only to show his attention, as I told him about Eugene, how Sophie couldn't get over him, how I was his doppelgänger, how we'd argued. I didn't tell him about Eugene growing under the moss—could I have imagined the entire thing? It seemed so unlikely to be true. I told him about my worries for Sophie, how she'd gotten so thin from eating moss, how her obsession had got worse.

'It sounds like you've had a weird time of it,' said Dad. 'Why didn't you talk to us?'

I started crying. An incontrollable stream of tears and gasps for breath. Dad held my head to his chest, patting my back, as I shook and cried it all out. I realised how lonely I'd been, how isolated. I'd given so much of myself to Sophie, all my love, and it'd flowed off her like water in the shower. When I pulled away, Dad's shirt was damp, and he gave me a reassuring smile.

'I'm sorry, Dad. I'm so sorry.'

'Why don't you come home for a bit? Your Mum and I would love to have you stay. Just until you're yourself.'

I agreed.

The doctors kept me in the hospital under observation for a week. Each day I asked whether I could leave. And each day they persuaded me I needed to stay.

A moment didn't go by when I wasn't thinking about Sophie. Where was she? What was she doing? I called Sophie's phone again and again, but it went straight to voicemail. I left long, rambling voice messages pleading to her to visit me. We needed to talk.

They moved me from my private room to a shared bay. The bay was so stuffy patients fanned themselves with their glossy magazines, or so cold we asked for extra blankets. The nurses repeatedly opened and closed the windows according to our complaints. They were long, lazy days filled with chlorine-scented puzzle books Dad bought from the hospital shop, and novels he thought I'd enjoy, selected from the shelves of his local charity shop.

For the first time, I truly had a broken heart. When Maggie left me, it'd been painful. When Sophie had cheated on me with Martin, it was excruciating. But they'd felt nothing like this—I'd been numb in comparison. Sophie hadn't even said goodbye. I'd got to age thirty without experiencing this wrenching, sickening, hollow feeling. No-one had explained how bad it could feel. I'd seen heartbreak on TV and read about it in the pages of books, but nothing prepared me for this. I held it together during the day, embarrassed to be seen upset, but at night I cried into a pillow to quieten my sobs. Would this ever end? I was in a hospital, yet there were no drugs or surgery that could cure this.

Despite the impossibility of it, I couldn't shake the feeling Sophie had actually grown Eugene back to life. I imagined her with Eugene, holding his hand on the street, cuddling in bed, walking in the park—but in my thoughts he became me—even I couldn't tell us apart. Would she confuse things she'd done with me with things she'd done with Eugene? And how would Eugene cope with coming back to life? Would he be angry Sophie had been with me—that she'd taken up with someone so soon after his death—someone that looked like him? Perhaps she wouldn't mention me?

The two-hour drive didn't stop my parents visiting at three o'clock every afternoon and chatting with me for a few hours. I was glad to see them, and I tried to be as cheerful as possible. Mum always asked about the quality of the hospital food and brought me grapes and biscuits, covertly hiding them in my bedside cupboard when no nurses were in sight, despite me insisting they weren't considered contraband. She seemed really well. And Dad gave me updates on the news and the goings on of their neighbours—Ronald had bought a new car and accidentally driven it through his garage door, and Helen, two-doors-down, was menacing the pavements with her new mobility scooter—until I grew tired, and they left me to nap.

The nurses permitted me to walk around the ward, but not pass through its heavy swing doors to the rest of the hospital. There was a small room for patients to relax in away from our beds. I sat there for half an hour one morning, as a middle-aged man attached to an oxygen cylinder wheezed through the television news. I left and didn't return.

The three beds in the bay with mine contained elderly men, quiet, bed-bound, with the occasional visitor who looked at them with pitying smiles and cheered them with news of the grandchildren. They looked at me, a much younger man, thick bandages around his head, and whispered theories of why I was there.

The nights were filled with moaning, crying, and sudden, desperate shouts demanding the attention of the few tired nurses, who wearily dealt with the patients' needs.

One night, I woke when a rasping voice shouted something close by. Eugene! I sat up and pulled the bedsheets around me. But it was a throat cancer patient I'd seen earlier in the day, a voice box implanted in his throat, calling for a nurse.

As the grogginess in my head cleared, it was as if a mist hanging over my vision lifted, and now there were searing colours—the red plastic plates my dinner was served on, the blue of the nurses' uniforms—and the definition between the stripes on my pyjamas was sharp and crisp. I'd never noticed textures in such detail: the pores of my skin, the weave of cotton bedsheets, the ripples on my beaker of water. And my hearing was improved—I heard keys jangling in pockets, the distant munching of biscuits, and the turning of paperback pages in fine, clear detail. I couldn't remember whether I'd experienced the world like this before. Had the knock on my head dulled my senses? Or was this brilliance all new? Had I been cheated from living life in full technicolour?

My headaches didn't return. I was free.

One morning, two weeks later, a sleepy, junior doctor introduced herself as Miss Chapman, and flipped through my paperwork. I was desperate for her to let me go.

'I can't see any reason to keep you in longer,' she said. 'Let's get you out of here.'

A nurse removed my bandages, tossing them into the bin.

'All better,' she said.

I packed my things, and Dad arrived to pick me up after lunch.

'Your mum's got your room ready and we're having your favourite for dinner,' he said.

'Do you mind if I stretch my legs for a bit before the drive?' I asked him. 'I won't be long. You could get a coffee from the canteen.'

He shook his head.

'You've been very ill. You're not supposed to go out.'

'I'm fine, Dad,' I insisted.

'Well, how about I come with you? Just up the street.'

I pointed at his walking stick.

He relented. 'Okay, I'll only slow you down,' he said. 'But don't go far. Stay within the hospital grounds.'

As I left the boundary of the hospital, I looked over my shoulder to make sure Dad wasn't watching me and inhaled a deep lungful of fresh air scented with recent rainfall—autumn had arrived. My stiff legs loosened with each step, glad to be tested after such a long rest.

The hospital was near the town centre and I knew the area well. I turned left along a street of neat Victorian terraces with small front yards and iron railings and noticed a narrow footpath squeezed between two houses. I hadn't noticed the path before and couldn't imagine where the path led, so curious, I followed it.

The path passed down the side of the houses and soon became a muddy track. Thick hedges arched over the path, forming a shady tunnel. Leaves stirred above in a breeze, but otherwise it was eerily quiet. I imagined woodland creatures silently watching me from their nests and burrows. I looked over my shoulder to where I'd come from, thought about turning around, to not leave Dad waiting too long, but kept going, to explore where the path led.

The hedges grew denser, and I could barely see in the

darkness. When the path turned at a right-angle, the hedges opened up, and I found myself skirting the edge of a wheat field. The wheat was limp, brown, and surrounded by tall hedges and trees. The crop looked rotten. Where had this field been hiding? The track hadn't been that long and I should still have been near the town centre.

I followed the border of the wheat field, passed through an opening in a hedge, and arrived at a riverbank. On the opposite bank sat the town's theatre and a couple of restaurants. A wooden bench faced the water. I'd not been walking long, but my legs were tired. With my hand, I swept away splashes of water from recent rain and sat on the bench, the remaining water soaking into the seat of my trousers. The sun emerged from the clouds, and I took off my coat and placed it beside me.

Unpleasant memories of attacking swans came back to me, but there were no swans today, only a lonely and harmless brown duck cruising in the middle of the sluggish river.

'Mind if I sit here?' said an adolescent girl, startling me. She wore a black leather jacket, with long, blonde hair swept over one side of her head, revealing an ear adorned with studs and rings. She held a bundle of grease spotted paper.

'No,' I said. 'It's free.'

I used my coat to dry an area for her to sit.

'Aww, thank you,' she said.

She sat and opened her bundle, holding it out to me.

'Want a chip?' she asked.

Vinegar fumes rising from the chunky chips tingled my nose.

'Thanks,' I said, taking a large chip from the centre.

It was salty and crisp on the outside, hot and fluffy

inside—the best thing I'd eaten in a while.

'You're not thinking of ending it all, are you?' she said.

I looked at her, surprised.

'No.'

'It's a popular spot for that kind of thing—walk into the current and disappear.' She nodded towards the river. 'I've heard it been called a ghost bath. Have you heard it called that?'

I shook my head.

'It's a pretty cool name for something so horrible. I had a teacher at school who drowned himself. Not in this river—in the sea. A girl from school said she saw him do it. But she was a liar. You couldn't tell he felt sad, though. He was just a normal teacher. I didn't like him much—he gave me detention once for something I didn't do. But it was tragic. No one knows why he did it. Are you sure you're not here for that?'

'No.'

'It's just that you don't look thrilled to be here.'

I forced a smile. 'I've had a difficult time of it lately.'

'Work trouble? Girl trouble?'

She studied me for my reaction.

'Girl trouble, I reckon,' she said. 'She left you.'

'You're very perceptive.' I laughed.

She nodded and ate another chip.

'So, why did she leave you? You got another woman?' Before I could answer, she continued, 'No, you don't look the type. She left you for another man.' As she talked, chewed potato sprayed from her mouth.

'Sort of.'

'It happens. You'll get over it.'

She held out her chips for me and I took another.

'When I've finished my chips, I've got something that'll do you some good.' She patted her pocket.

As she finished eating, I stared into the river, watching leaves and twigs, plastic bags and drink bottles floating past. She crushed the chip paper into a ball, sat it beside her on the bench, and took a joint from her pocket. It was bent slightly, and she massaged it straight. Her lighter's flint wheel grated, but she couldn't get it to ignite in the breeze. She unzipped her jacket. Beneath, she wore a tightly fitted, bright red t-shirt with a large A on the front—something a superhero would wear. She caught me looking.

'It's a uniform,' she said. 'For the fast-food place where I work.'

She used her outstretched jacket to shield the joint from the wind and tried to light it again. It lit, and she inhaled deeply, releasing the smoke slowly from her nostrils. It was fragrant, like freshly mown grass. She held it out for me to take.

'No, thanks,' I said.

'Why not? I know you've had it before. You've got the look.'

'It doesn't agree with me.'

'What? Are you a politician or something?'

'I had a bad episode.'

'An episode?' She paused at that thought. 'Okay. More for me then.' She took another drag. She looked so peaceful, so chilled, as she held her breath, then let the smoke escape. 'You can stay at mine tonight, if you like?' she said.

My cheeks flushed warmly, surprised by her forwardness.

'It just looks like you don't want to go home. I live with a mate, but she's at her boyfriend's place for the night. No funny business, if you don't want it, but I don't know how you could resist.' She shook her chest at me and laughed.

'I'm probably ten years older than you.'

'Age is just a number. I'm your opportunity to forget about her, whoever she is.'

'No, thanks,' I said. 'It wouldn't feel right. Thanks for the offer, though.'

'Okay. Forget I asked. Sorry. I'll smoke this then I'll go.'

A group of swans glided by, necks arched, gentle, V-shaped ripples formed by their bodies sent to each river bank. The lead swan turned its tiny black eyes towards me and hissed.

'They're vicious,' said the girl, pointing at the swans. 'My mum said she saw a guy trying to fight one once. And lost.'

She stood up and stubbed the joint out under her trainer.

'It was nice meeting you,' she said. 'Are you sure you don't want some company this evening? I've never seen anyone look so lonely.'

'I'm fine, really.'

She zipped her jacket and walked off, turning and waving from a distance, as I stood and headed back to the hospital.

'I didn't expect you to take so long,' said Dad, when I arrived back at the hospital, finding him in the canteen with two coffee mugs and an empty packet of sandwiches on the table in front of him.

'Sorry, I was enjoying the fresh air.'

Dad led us to his car. His walking, slow and staggered, was getting worse.

'I need to get some things from home before I come to yours,' I said.

As we drove through the town, I was sad about leaving this place for a while, anticipating the home sickness.

Dad parked outside my house.

'Shall I wait outside?' he asked.

I nodded. 'I'll be quick.'

As I stepped into the house, I immediately noticed the aroma of Sophie and damp moss suffusing the stale air.

I called for Sophie. There was no answer.

I went to the living room. Sophie's books and journals weren't strewn across the coffee table. Her golden fish statue no longer gleamed from the bookshelf.

A trail of blood drops, dried brown, led upstairs to our bedroom. The green bedsheets had been replaced with my old white ones. I opened Sophie's side of the wardrobe and pulled open her drawers—her clothes were gone, just like Dad said. All that remained were two sun hats. Her toothbrush, shampoo, make-up, and razor were missing from the bathroom.

Sophie never had to return. There'd be no arguments about who owned the sofa or the fridge, the cheese grater, or the wok. No dividing of books, records or CDs. We'd bought nothing together. No visiting rights to agree for children or cats. No reason for us to stay in touch at all. She was really gone—a separation too sudden, like a guillotine had fallen, and my head was still twitching and blinking, detached from my body.

Downstairs, I gasped at the mess in the kitchen. The clear up would take ages—lots of things to replace. Sophie had taken her box and all its contents, her microscope, her moss sieves, and blender. I'd never have to complain about the smell of stewed moss again.

I stepped over the debris and opened the door to the garden. In the centre of the lawn, the moss was peeled back, folded in a heap, revealing bare earth. It was impossible she'd grown him back, I knew that.

Impossible she'd run off with him.

When I returned to the house, Dad was in the kitchen.

'Did she do this?' he asked.

'Yes,' I lied.

He shook his head.

'There's a lot of tidying to do.'

'You're right, Dad. Sophie's gone. She's taken all her things.'

'I'm sorry to hear that.'

'It's for the best, I think.'

Dad knew when to say things and when not to. He just continued to look at the mess.

'Dad, I'm sorry. I want to stay here.'

'That's not sensible, Benny.'

'I want to tidy up.'

'But you need to rest.'

'I promise I'll take it easy. The hospital wouldn't have let me go if I wasn't okay. I'm signed off work for another week.'

'Your mum will be disappointed.'

'I'll come visit next weekend.'

'Promise?'

I waved Dad off in his car.

Tired, I lay on the sofa and stared at the ceiling. I'd imagined a whole life with Sophie and now there was no-one, just my parents. No-one to share my highs, my lows, my thoughts, my dreams. I'd been so scared of having another breakdown I'd kept everybody away, shied away from all relationships, until I'd met Sophie, and dropped my defences.

The sun set, and I pulled a blanket over me. Alone in the house, the creaks and noises of an empty home, the noise of the wind, of cars passing in the street, haunted me. I stretched my arm to switch on the radio and fell asleep to the soothing tones of the Shipping Forecast.

That night, I dreamt I was trapped under the moss in the garden. The earth was damp and sour. I lay on my back, pushing at the moss to lift it and escape. The moss stretched thin, daylight shining through, but it was elastic, and sprang back. No matter how hard I tried, I couldn't break through. And then, at its thinnest part, I saw the dark figure of a person standing over me.

'You're not ready yet,' the figure said. A booming, echoing voice, like a crowd shouting in a cave.

I pushed and pushed, panic rising, trying different spots, but the moss would not break. Until, suddenly, my index finger poked through, feeling the cold of the outside. I pulled it back, and a ray of sun blinded my eyes. The whole blanket of moss loosened, and as I escaped, I woke.

I went to the kitchen, and with a thick, black bin bag in hand, carefully avoiding cuts from sharp edges and splinters, I began picking up the mess. The bag soon grew heavy and I replaced it with another. And then another.

Standing back, happy with the progress I'd made, I stopped to make tea. In the tea bag container, I found a folded piece of paper, torn from a notebook. I unfolded it and written in Sophie's handwriting was:

> *You were there for me*
> *In the darkest, strangest place.*
> *My thanks, forever.*

The paper was translucent where droplets, possibly tears, had fallen.

I didn't want these to be the last words I heard from Sophie. I needed to know why she'd left—and if she'd left with Eugene.

I ran upstairs. In my jeans pocket, I found the bank statement I'd taken from Sophie's box, her old address in Luton. If this was her parents' address, maybe she'd gone back to live with them.

The sun was rising as my car tyres squealed leaving the driveway. I drove erratically, pulling out on to the main road in the path of an on-coming car, receiving the blast of a horn, and later, almost missing the junction off the motorway, cutting across two lanes of busy traffic.

As I neared Sophie's parent's house, I slowed, searching the numbers for the correct address. I saw it: a small, pebble-dashed semi-detached, with a neat garden, and red front door. An old car, polished paintwork and gleaming chrome, sat in the driveway.

I parked a little way down on the opposite side of the road, the house still in view, to gather my composure. It was still very early. I'd wait until later to call on them.

Would they let me in the house? If Sophie was there, what would I say to her?

In my rear-view mirror, an elderly man, leaning heavily on a walking stick, shuffled along the pavement carrying a newspaper. He reminded me of Dad. I watched him get closer. When he was level with my window, he peered in, and I smiled at him.

'Eugene?' he said. His jaw hung open with shock. He banged on the roof with the end of his stick. 'Is that you? What have you done with Sophie?' His hazel eyes and full mouth were just like Sophie's.

He brought the stick down, knocking on my window. 'Where's Sophie?' he shouted.

I turned the ignition key and he jumped back a little.

'Don't drive away!' His stick hit my wing mirror with a crack.

The tyres screeched and the car lurched forward. I watched him wave his stick in the air as I turned the corner.

It was a long shot, but the only person who might have a clue where Sophie had gone was Emily.

That morning, I parked in the town centre, and as I walked down the main road towards the stationery shop, I passed Alan. Now in his red raincoat, he was bent low, looking at the pavement, and didn't see me among the other people on the street. His legs shook, stumbling like he'd topple forward any moment, head swaying from side-to-side. The tall man I'd seen him with outside the hospital walked a short distance behind him, attention focused solely on Alan, obviously there to care for him. Alan was a sad sight—poor guy. Rather than the anxious young man I'd seen before, it looked as though a degenerative illness was ravaging him. Losing his mother must have hit him hard.

I stopped and watched as his carer steered Alan into a fast-food restaurant.

The stationery shop was across the street. As I entered, the bell on the door tinkled my arrival. I half expected Sophie to be there behind the counter, but instead there was Emily. She'd lost weight and straightened her messy curls into waves.

'It's been a while,' she said coldly. 'Sophie not with you?'

'I was hoping you'd know where she was?'

'Have you lost her?'

'She's gone,' I said. 'She's left me.'

Emily looked shocked.

'Really? And you don't know where she's gone?'

'She left without a word—moved out all her stuff.'

Her eyes narrowed.

'What did you do to hurt her?'

'Nothing.'

'Well, I'm not surprised she left. She was too good for you. She's too good for anybody.'

'Maybe,' I said.

With all my options for finding Sophie gone, I turned and left the shop, Emily laughing cruelly behind me.

'Bye, Ben.'

Across the road, in the restaurant, Alan sat at a table by the window with a book, furiously colouring-in something, his brow furrowed in concentration, pressing hard enough to snap the crayon he was using. I put my face to the window. Alan was so absorbed, he didn't see me. He was crayoning a black and white outline of a horse—the same one as the note through the door. It had already been coloured blue, yellow, and green, and Alan was over-layering with red wax, going outside the lines, colours bleeding into a brown mess. The page was deeply contoured and creased. He needed a fresh book.

I ran back across the road, clanging through the stationery shop door.

'I just saw Alan,' I said to Emily, who'd come out from behind the counter to tidy the display of pens.

'Alan? Sophie's friend?'

'He's over the road in the restaurant.'

'And?'

'Do you know what Alan used to always buy in the shop? Was it colouring books?'

'Yes,' she said. 'Always the same one. He would complete one book then get another.'

'Do you remember which one?'

'We've got a whole stack of them. Sophie ordered a bulk lot, figuring Alan would keep buying them.'

'Can I buy them? For Alan?'

Emily disappeared to the back room of the shop and brought back eight colouring books.

'Forty Pounds,' she said.

262

I took the money from my wallet and passed it to her.

'This is a nice thing you're doing,' she said. 'Maybe I had you wrong. If you ever see Sophie again, tell her to come and say hi. I miss her.'

I crossed the road again and entered the restaurant. Alan was still colouring his book with one hand and eating an egg muffin with the other. I stayed out of Alan's eye-line, half-hidden by a column surrounded by rubbish bins, and gestured at Alan's carer to come near me.

'Me?' he mouthed, looking behind him then back, wondering whether it was really him I wanted to talk to. I held up the colouring books. He walked over to me without Alan looking up.

'These are for Alan,' I said, passing him the books.

He looked at me with suspicion and took them. He flicked through a few pages and smiled.

'When these run out, you can buy more from the stationery shop over the road. Just tell them you want colouring books for Alan. They'll know the ones you mean.'

'Thank you,' he said.

'Tell him they're a gift from Sophie.'

On my way home, I stopped to buy paint and brushes, and spent the day covering the walls Sophie had painted green. I was giving up hope of ever seeing Sophie again, and with each rapid white brushstroke, I erased her from the house. Afterwards, with my clothes, hands, and face speckled white, the aroma of paint slowly drifting out of open windows, the house seemed lighter, brighter, and purer.

I considered tearing up all the moss in the garden, all of Sophie's hard work, but the moss was so beautiful I couldn't do it—I couldn't kill something so alive. I unfolded the moss blanket under which Eugene may have grown, and as I flattened it down by walking across it, I admired the *Zygodon viridissimus* growing up the trunk of the oak tree, the *Schistidium crassipilum* covering the shed roof, and the *Didymodon sinuosus* lining the crevasses of the rockery, looking as though it'd lain there for millennia. Sophie's moss knowledge had absorbed into me by osmosis. I'd become a moss geek without trying. I would enjoy the moss garden.

12

'You're looking well,' they said, when I started back at work. 'Take it easy,' 'My friend had the exact same thing happen to him,' 'Make sure you don't work too hard.'

I felt like a fraud when they looked at me with pity, like I'd survived a terminal illness. To me it'd only been a persistent headache, cured with painkillers, before a brief scare, and waking completely fixed.

When I saw Elise head for the coffee machine, I went over for a chat.

'Glad to have you back,' she said. 'Are you okay?' She looked at my head, but I had no visible injuries.

'Sort of,' I said.

Nervously fumbling with my coffee cup, I told her I'd broken up with Sophie.

'Oh, no. That's sad.'

She put a hand on my shoulder and stuck out her bottom lip to make a sad face.

'She's moved out and doesn't want to see me again.'

'What did you do?'

'Nothing.'

'It's usually the man's fault.' She laughed.

'It's complicated.'

'I'm sorry to hear that,' she said, taking her coffee and going back to her desk.

I moped around the office for the rest of the day. If there was a glimmer of opportunity for me with Elise, I couldn't see it. And when my boss said I could leave early, I couldn't leave quick enough.

When I got home, I packed a backpack with jeans, t-shirts, socks, and pants; toothbrush, toothpaste, deodorant. I pulled on my walking boots and waterproof coat. Patting my jeans pocket to check I had my wallet, I locked the house, threw my bag in the car boot, and drove north. I'd do some walking, see some different scenery, go where I fancied, stopping at B&Bs I'd find along the way.

I'd eat pies, and fish & chips, and sausages. Lunch on cheese, soft white rolls, and crisps. Stop at cafés for tea from a teapot and homemade cakes.

I drove out of town onto the motorway, planning to drive until I felt hungry. Tomorrow, I'd call the boss, tell her someone had died, and I'd be away for a week. If she was too mean to grant a holiday at short notice and decided to discipline me, I didn't much care.

The speedometer needle kept pleasingly high as I turned up the radio, tapping the steering wheel out of time to the music, shouting along to choruses I only knew a few words to, until in triumph, and much quicker than I imagined, I reached the coast.

In a tired resort of decaying hotels with neon vacancy signs and gutters weeping down weathered paint, I bought fish & chips from a shop on the promenade, and walked beneath dark grey clouds to the deserted beach. The sea roared as it washed pebbles along the shore. The wind tossed my hair and scoured my face with salt water as I crunched across the shingle, sliding on loose stones, and stood with foam washing over my boots before heading higher and sitting down. I ate staring into the churning brown waves, fat sea gulls clamouring around me, waiting for a chip to be thrown in their direction. My fish batter was soggy, the chips too salty, hard, and cold.

'What are you doing?' I asked myself.

Why did I think I could just get in the car and drive away from my sadness? I hoped a change of scene would be a distraction from thoughts of Sophie. But she was here. Her face was in the gleaming pebbles, the way she moved in the powerful waves, her voice in the wind. This escape wouldn't help me get over Sophie. This was lonely.

I looked down at the stones on the beach. There was no life among them, no plants, no moss—a dead place.

I stood as I saw someone approaching from further up the beach, and scattered my remaining chips to the gulls, who fought over them, screeching like winged monsters. It was time to go home.

I arrived home just before midnight. I'd just closed the front door behind me when the doorbell rang. Opening the door, I was surprised to see Emily, her arms wrapped around her shivering body.

'I'm here because I'm lonely,' she said abruptly, pushing past me. 'I thought you might be lonely too?'

She wore a tight white vest, skinny jeans, rouged cheeks, and thick mascara. Goosebumps covered her arms and she bit her lip nervously.

We stood in silence, looking at each other, before Emily opened her arms and I collapsed into them. She pulled me tight to her cold body. I cried, and she patted me on the back as she would a crying child, telling me everything would be all right. We held the embrace for several minutes until Emily suggested we make a cup of tea. When we released, I was embarrassed to find I had an erection pushing against my zip. How long had it been there? Had she felt it? It relaxed slowly.

'Sophie was the best friend I've ever had,' said Emily as we waited for the kettle to boil. 'We didn't see each other outside of work, but that was fine. We spent more time together than most couples do.'

She looked at me for agreement.

'Working in the shop is so boring now. It wasn't like a proper job when Sophie was there—it was too much fun. When I was little, I had a playhouse in the garden which I called my shop. I'd sell my parents things made from mud, leaves I thought were pretty, or serve them empty, plastic cups which they pretended to sip. I had a toy till full of pennies with an annoying bell whenever the drawer opened and closed. Bing, bing, bing, bing. It must have driven my parents mad. I was an only child, and when Sophie started at the stationery shop, it was like she was the sister I should have had all those years ago, to play shop in my garden. Sometimes you meet people and you just click.'

'That's how I felt when I first met her.'

'She's a pretty girl.'

'No, not that. There was something about her. I wasn't looking for a girlfriend, but when I saw her, it was love at first sight. Before I met her, I didn't have a life. I didn't love anyone or anything. I didn't laugh or cry—I didn't live. But now I know she was only interested in me because I looked like her dead boyfriend.'

'What are you talking about?'

'I look like Eugene. Exactly like him.'

She considered this for a moment.

'I had no idea. I never met him,' she said.

The kettle finished boiling. I only had one mug left intact, and Emily raised an eyebrow as I made my tea in a chipped glass.

'She loved you,' she said, as I passed her the mug.

'I don't think so. She didn't love me, she loved Eugene.'

'You're a good guy. She wanted someone safe.'

'Boring, more like.'

'You're not boring.'

'I lost the woman of my dreams to a dead man made of moss,' I mumbled.

'What did you say?'

'Nothing.'

Emily put down her mug and held me again. She planted her chin on my shoulder, and her nose touched my neck.

'Don't beat yourself up,' she said, her moist breath warm against my neck. She kissed me and my body tensed.

'It's okay,' she said. 'Relax.'

Her hand stroked my back, and she kissed me again, further around my neck towards my face, and again, until she placed her lips on mine. Her warm, moist mouth smelt of sponge cake fresh out of the oven. We gripped each other, pressing our bodies hard together. Emily was feverish, pushing her tongue deeper into my mouth. Her hands slid their way down to my bottom, and she pulled my groin into hers. I imagined Sophie watching us at the window, and Emily suddenly pulled away.

'Perhaps we shouldn't,' she said. 'What if Sophie comes back?'

'She won't.' And it was true. Sophie wouldn't be back. I could start again. I could let this happen.

'I loved her you know,' said Emily, as I led her upstairs. 'Really loved her, like lesbian loved her.'

We kissed as we undressed each other, then laid upon the bed. Emily sat astride me and guided me into her.

'You can pretend I'm Sophie if you like,' said Emily.

'I'd like that.'

I shut my eyes tight and imagined Sophie there. But it felt different: warmer, closer, more sensuous. It was passionate and free.

'Let yourself go,' said Emily.

I opened my eyes and looked into Emily's as we reached orgasm together.

We fell asleep in each other's arms. And as the sun rose, and I woke, body loose and relaxed, muscles melting into the mattress, experiencing happiness for the first time in a long time, Emily dressed, kissed me on the cheek, and left, leaving me to drift back to sleep.

My mobile woke me as it rang on the bedside table. It was probably Dad—he sometimes called first thing in the morning if he'd seen something on the news he thought I should know about—like extreme weather or that it was National Bring Your Dog to Work Day. The phone rang out, then started again. Reluctantly, I answered it.

A harsh hiss, like someone blowing into the mobile's microphone, perhaps the wind, blasted from the speaker.

'Ben?' said a faint female voice amongst the noise.

'Yes,' I said sleepily.

'It's Sophie.'

'Sophie!' I gripped my phone tight and pressed it to my ear. 'I can't hear you well.'

'Wait,' she said.

There were the sounds of a busy road, cars driving past sloshing water in their tyre treads, before the noise died down.

'Is that better?' she said.

'Yes. Where are you?' My heart was thumping.

'I can't tell you. Listen, I don't have long, but I wanted to talk to you before I go. Once I go, I don't want us to talk again.'

'Go where?'

'You need to listen. Don't ask questions.'

'But we can't leave it like this. We need to talk.'

'That's why I'm calling. But a phone call is all we can

do.'

'Okay,' I said.

'You need to know that I love you. I love you so much. But that love is confused. The past and future are woven into one and I can't separate them—I don't know how. I never wanted to hurt you; you have to believe that.' She paused and sniffed. The boom of a horn sounded in the background. Perhaps a ship? 'You need to forget me,' she continued. 'You need to move on with your life and forget you ever met me. You're a good guy, Ben.'

The background noise ceased, like she was covering the microphone.

'Are you there?' I asked.

The noise returned.

'I have to go now,' she said. 'Promise me you'll look after yourself.'

'Don't go. Not yet. We need to talk.'

'Sorry.'

'I just want to know one thing: are you with him now?'

'Who?'

'Eugene.'

'Bye, Ben.'

The phone went silent. I looked at it, stunned.

'Call back,' I said to the phone. 'Please call back.'

I got out of bed, naked, and paced around the house, staring at the phone, climbing up and down the stairs, in and out of each room, unable to rest, willing the phone to ring. The walls seemed to get closer, hemming me in. The air became suffocating. I pulled on clothes and left the house, escaping my phone, leaving it on the kitchen table.

A bitter wind bit my earlobes and flung my hair about as I meandered through the quiet streets. There was no-one around as I entered the park and followed a dirt track between dense trees, stepping over rotting logs, skirting, and jumping muddy puddles. To warm up, I rubbed my hands together, and jogged, twigs snapping under my feet, stumbling over exposed roots, dodging brambles, leaping from one side of the track to the other to avoid sinking in its thick mud. A shiver of energy shot up my spine and I ran—breathing rapidly, beads of sweat forming on my brow, feeling alive and wild. I pulled my jumper and t-shirt over my head, held them scrunched in my hand, and sprinted, raising my arms high to cool my armpits, the air hitting the perspiration on my bare body, deliciously cold.

In a spacious clearing, I staggered to a stop and rested, bent over, hands on knees, taking deep breaths. This place was familiar—the sturdy trees, the strange circular mounds of earth, the fallen trunk so wide I could climb inside, the damp fragrance of leaf mould, and decaying wood. Sophie had darted around the clearing as she'd harvested moss from the trees and mounds, stuffing it into little bags. I should have stopped her, stopped the destruction.

'I'm sorry,' I told the clearing.

I snatched up a handful of leaves, dried like brown paper on the surface, damp and fragile where they'd sat upon the earth. I inhaled their heady scent, then threw them high. They drifted down, falling on my head. Some caught the wind and floated away. I picked up another bunch and did the same. I kept going, diving my hands into the leaves, until it seemed every leaf had been overturned, and I was filthy from their fragments. Spinning around in circles, I said, 'Sorry,' again, and again, to each and every tree, until dizzy, collapsing to the ground. I lay on my side, panting, breath forming vapour clouds, sweating freely. And among the trees, leaves, and earth, covered in early morning dew, shining like green diamonds as the sun burst through the clouds, was moss, more moss than I'd realised, its tiny leaves clinging to the bark and earth. I shut my eyes and opened them again—the moss was still there, thriving. It had survived.

I brushed leaves off my head, put on my t-shirt, and ran out of the park into the streets. And there was moss—moss everywhere—on roof tiles, chimneys, and climbing up lampposts. Between my feet, moss flourished in the cracks in the tarmac, the gaps between paving slabs, and among the slick, decaying leaves of gutters. Walls of brick, limestone, and concrete thrived with all sorts and shades of incredible moss, absorbing nutrients, water, and carbon dioxide, exhaling fresh, beautiful oxygen. Moss was returning to the neighbourhood, bringing life to the tiniest, barren places—growing thicker, softer, brighter, greener.

ACKNOWLEDGEMENTS

Thank you to all those who have set eyes on Under the Moss and given me their valuable feedback. You've helped shaped a jumble of thoughts and ideas into something resembling a novel.

And thanks to Verulam Writers, the nicest and most talented group of writers you're ever likely to meet, for providing inspiration and motivation, and for making me a better writer.

ABOUT THE AUTHOR

Steven Mitchell grew up in Peterborough and now lives in St Albans, UK. He has an MA in Creative Writing, and is a member of the writing group, Verulam Writers. His short stories have been published in journals and magazines and have won several prizes. Under the Moss is his first novel.

To discover more of Steven's writing, visit his website at www.stevenmitchellwriter.com

SRL Publishing don't just publish books, we also do our best in keeping this world sustainable. In the UK alone, over 77 million books are destroyed each year, unsold and unread, due to overproduction and bigger profit margins.

Our business model is inherently sustainable by only printing what we sell. While this means our cost price is much higher, it means we have minimum waste and zero returns. We made a public promise in 2020 to never overprint our books just for the sake of profit.

We give back to our planet by calculating the number of trees used for our products so we can then replace. We also calculate our carbon emissions and support projects which reduce CO_2. These same projects also support the United Nations Sustainable Development Goals.

The way we operate means we knowingly waive our profit margins for the sake of the environment. Every book sold via the SRL website plants at least one tree.

To find out more, please visit
www.srlpublishing.co.uk/responsibility